SHADOWS OF DOUBT

SHADOWS OF DOUBT

A Novel

Palma Harcourt

BEAUFORT BOOKS
Publishers · New York

C.2
M

Copyright © 1983 by Palma Harcourt

Library of Congress Cataloging in Publication Data

Harcourt, Palma.
Shadows of doubt.

I. Title.
PR6058.A62S5   1985   823'.914   84-24467
ISBN 0-8253-0264-1

Published in the United States by Beaufort Books Publishers, New York.

Printed in the U.S.A.   First American Edition

10 9 8 7 6 5 4 3 2 1

For June and George

'The wiles of men cast shadows of doubt.'

ONE

The once-beautiful wife of Colonel Alexei Bonalov lay neatly in her narrow, high, hospital bed. On her back, her arms at her sides, her toes pointing upwards, she made only a small mound beneath the bedclothes. Most of the time she was heavily sedated, but in her increasingly rare intervals of painful consciousness, she could see through the window of her private room the cupola that surmounted the main building of the Kremlin Clinic, one of the medical complexes in and around Moscow reserved for the treatment of the Party élite and their families. In these moments of lucidity she knew – though she had never been told – that the part of the Clinic she occupied housed only terminal cases.

Periodically her nurse wiped away a thin film of sweat that formed on her grey, pallid skin. There was nothing to be done with her hair, though it also was dank with sweat. Or about her smell. She wasn't unclean – she was given a daily blanket bath – but nothing could disguise for long the faint odour she exuded, a warning that death was imminent.

The nurse stood up quickly when the two doctors came into the room. They stood at the bottom of the bed and studied the patient's records. They made no attempt to examine her, for they knew it would serve no purpose. She was beyond their aid. All they could do was ease the pain – and make sure her husband had no cause for complaint.

'Will she last till morning?' one doctor asked.

'*Nyet.*' The specialist shook his head decisively. 'She'll go before dawn, most likely well before.'

'Then I should phone him at once. You agree, Comrade? He gave me an emergency number. He said it would always be answered and he would be informed, whatever the hour.'

The two doctors avoided catching each other's eyes. They could imagine the telephone message being received, and

7

passed on through KGB channels until it reached the Colonel. In the circumstances it was important to be absolutely correct, to make no error of judgement.

The specialist gave a thin smile. 'Yes, I agree. Contact him immediately. He should come as soon as possible if he's to be sure of seeing her alive.'

Alexei Bonalov was at the British Embassy, at a reception in honour of the Royal Ballet Company which was making one of its periodic visits to Moscow and Leningrad, and he was not enjoying himself. Normally he rather liked this kind of gathering, for both professional and social reasons, but tonight he was tired and on edge. His thoughts constantly reverted to his dying wife, and he found it hard to concentrate on the trivia of the conversations taking place around him. Suddenly he realized that Lady Gatling, the wife of the British Ambassador, had asked him a direct question that he had not heard. Forced to repeat it, she was acid.

'I enquired if you had enjoyed the curtain-raiser, Mr Bonalov.'

Though his English was excellent, Bonalov took a moment to understand her meaning. She was, in fact, referring to the short modern ballet that had preceded *Giselle*.

'Delightful,' he said, and he didn't care a damn if the word sounded like the lie it was. He had no patience with all that squirming around on the ground. You couldn't call it ballet. And there had been no story-line. The whole thing had been an insult to the intelligence of an audience, especially so when that audience was mainly Russian. 'However,' he added, 'I am old-fashioned. I prefer the great classical ballets.'

'Of course.'

Stroking his neat pointed beard, Bonalov hid a smile as he saw Lady Gatling make an almost imperceptible gesture that brought a young man to her side.

'Mr Bonalov, you've met Neil Tarrent, our Cultural Attaché, haven't you? It's largely due to him that we've had the pleasure of seeing the Royal Ballet Company tonight.'

8

'Really?' Bonalov offered a well-manicured hand as Lady Gatling made her way to other guests. 'I'm most grateful to you, Mr Tarrent. You're to be congratulated.' He sipped his champagne and looked over the rim of the glass at the bright blue eyes meeting his. An interesting face, Bonalov thought, its intelligence only partly disguised by the over-long red hair, the dust of freckles on the pale skin and the wide velvet bow tie.

'Thank you. That's very kind of you,' Tarrent said. He had a light voice with a faint Scots accent. 'I must admit it's been a lot of work bringing such a large company to the Soviet Union. But it's been done before, and your authorities have been most helpful.'

Tarrent continued to chat, and Bonalov continued to study him. It was not the first time he had met Tarrent, but he had not before had an opportunity for prolonged conversation. Tarrent's official title was irrelevant, for Bonalov was fully aware that his cultural activities were merely a cover. The dossier on Tarrent in the KGB central files made it quite clear that he was one of the SIS 'legals' in the British Embassy. Undoubtedly, Bonalov thought wryly, Tarrent's files made his own position as a KGB officer equally clear. Nevertheless, and in spite of its unreality, this social fencing had a purpose. 'Know your enemy' was an international maxim.

'Comrade!'

There was a light touch on Bonalov's elbow. His aide, Oleg Kerensky, had managed to push through the crowd, and stood beside him. Kerensky's face was expressionless, but Bonalov knew what he was about to say.

'Comrade, a phone call from the Clinic. It's urgent.'

For a moment Bonalov let his shoulders droop. The babble of voices round him seemed to grow very loud, the lights to become very bright, the people shadowy. Then he became aware of Kerensky's hand on his arm and, drawing a deep breath, he straightened himself. He gave his champagne glass to a passing waiter.

'If you'll excuse me, Mr Tarrent, perhaps you'd be kind enough to make my apologies to His Excellency and Lady

Gatling. I have some most pressing business.'

'Of course.'

Neil Tarrent bowed. Kerensky had spoken to Bonalov softly and very fast and, though Tarrent's Russian was fluent, he had caught only the word 'urgent'. Watching Bonalov stride purposefully from the room with the tall, gangling Kerensky hard behind, he wondered what was so important that the KGB men didn't bother to disguise their haste.

A little later Bonalov was sitting beside his wife, his face mirroring her suffering as the effects of the last injection wore off, and pain began to reassert itself. She had become very restless. She no longer lay neatly in the neat bed, but tossed from side to side, groaning and plucking ineffectually at the sheet that covered her.

To quiet the nervous fingers Bonalov took her hand in his. It felt like a small bird, frail, palpitating. He had a sudden wild desire to crush it, to destroy it, as if by so doing he could put an end to her agony. Olga, his dear, beautiful wife. He had loved her passionately and deeply. He still loved her. But it was difficult to equate the lovely, sparkling girl he had married with this small, grey, wasted figure.

He sat, holding her hand and letting thoughts of their life together wander through his mind. Time passed. She grew more restless. Once she cried out, and the nurse on duty outside the room came in, thinking he had called. But Bonalov sent her away again. He wanted to be alone with Olga for the short time remaining to them.

Yet it wasn't his own name, Alexei, that his dying wife had cried, he thought sadly and a little bitterly. She had called for Pavel, their son and only child. Olga was already ill when the news came that Pavel, a Captain in the Soviet Army, had been killed fighting in Afghanistan, but the cancer had been caught early and the doctors were at first very hopeful. Their hopes had proved unjustified. Once Pavel was dead, Olga had no longer shown any desire to live. She had seemed almost to welcome what had turned into a long and painful illness. And now it was nearly ended.

Bonalov sighed. Much as he loved his wife, he would be thankful when the ordeal was over. He didn't mind admitting this. People thought him cold, ruthless, calculating, and he knew he was all these things. But he also knew that with his ruthlessness went a hard core of integrity that forced him to be honest with himself and made him face sometimes unpalatable facts. The vacuum in which he had lived for so many months – automatically coping with his duties, visiting the Clinic and watching Olga suffer – had been a kind of hell. Why should he reproach himself for wanting to escape from it?

Suddenly he was aware of a change in the atmosphere of the quiet, antiseptic room, and he glanced quickly at his wife. Her eyes were open, her lips curled in a half smile. He felt the pressure of her fingers, then she withdrew her hand from his and, with what appeared a stupendous effort, made the sign of the cross in the air above her breast.

Bonalov caught his breath. Olga had never shown signs of religious tendencies. With his position it would of course have been impossible for her to take any part in formal observances, but even in the privacy of their own home she had never expressed any such desires. Yet now, at the moment of death . . .

Bonalov had seen death often enough to know its face, but it was minutes before he pushed back his chair and stood up. Bending over the bed he kissed his wife on the brow and the lips before drawing up the sheet. He left the room without a backward glance.

'She's dead,' he said to the nurse, his voice level, controlled.

'You wouldn't have guessed he was talking about his wife,' the nurse said later as she lay beside her lover. 'It might have been a – a – favourite cow. He visited her regularly enough, but he can't really have cared a kopek for her.'

'Probably gone straight off to his mistress,' the man agreed.

*   *   *

11

They were quite wrong. Sitting beside Bonalov as their chauffeur-driven Zil pulled away from the Kremlin Clinic, Oleg Kerensky cast anxious glances at the man who had been his superior for the last six years. In the iridescent bluish glare of the street lamps Bonalov looked pale and haggard, as if all his spirit had been drained from him. Even his clothes, normally immaculate, no longer seemed to fit him; it was as if he had physically shrunk. Leaning back in the corner of the car, he appeared totally spent.

Kerensky drew the blinds across the car windows. Winter had lingered late in Moscow this year, and the icy-cold and snow-covered streets were deserted. Nevertheless, he didn't want Bonalov to be exposed to some chance observer. He was attached to the man who, whatever his professional reputation, had invariably treated him fairly and with kindness. He wished he could think of something to say that would not sound utterly banal.

'Comrade Colonel, tomorrow – that is, today—'

'I shall be in the office in the morning.'

'But there's no need. Everyone will understand. You—'

'I'll be there.' Then, as if repenting of his harshness, Bonalov smiled wryly. 'A little late, perhaps. But I'll be at home if I'm needed.'

'Of course, Comrade Colonel, but—'

Kerensky gave up. They relapsed into silence. Kerensky thought of Pavel Bonalov, who had been his friend, and of his own wife, Mariska, no doubt anxiously awaiting his return, though he had warned her he might be very late or might not come at all. He couldn't leave the Colonel alone tonight.

The Zil crunched to a stop in front of an imposing block of apartments, the home of the more important members of Moscow's establishment. The driver leapt from his seat to open the car door. Kerensky hastily followed him to the pavement. It had begun to snow yet again and they shivered in the cold as they waited for Bonalov to climb out. He took his time about it, like an old man, but he shook off Kerensky's helping hand.

'Good night to you both.'

'But, Comrade Colonel—' Kerensky's voice showed his surprise.

12

'What do you want?'

'To – to come in with you. It's not right you should—'

'No. No need. It's late. Go home to your wife. I'll see you in the morning.'

It was an order, and Kerensky swallowed the protests he yearned to make. He waited till Bonalov had disappeared into the building, then got back in the car. He hoped he hadn't made a bad mistake. Perhaps he should have insisted. But how could he, in the face of the Colonel's blunt refusal? Nevertheless, he was worried.

Bonalov tore off his fur coat as he kicked the door of the apartment shut behind him, and made straight for the dining-room. He seized a bottle of vodka from the sideboard and, without bothering to get a glass, blew out his breath and took a long swig. Then, as the fire burnt his throat, making his eyes water, and he felt the punch of the liquor in his stomach, he gave a great shuddering sigh of relief. He was going to get drunk, beautifully, stinkingly drunk.

Two hours later he was slouched over the kitchen table. In front of him was the bottle of vodka, together with the heel of a brown loaf and some pickled cucumber. He had been drinking steadily and the bottle was almost empty. Upending it over a tumbler, he spilt most of what remained, and swore.

Olga would be angry if she could see him now, he thought. But there was no Olga, no Pavel, no one, not any more. He didn't count his sister; she lived in the Ukraine and he only corresponded with her once or twice a year. Effectively he was alone, with a long, empty, purposeless life still stretching ahead of him. Involuntarily he began to weep maudlin tears.

And it was at this point, or so he decided afterwards, that the idea first came to him. At the time he didn't take it seriously, though it did have one immediate effect. Instead of fetching more vodka, as he had intended, he staggered into the bedroom, kicked off his shoes, struggled out of his jacket and trousers and fell on to the bed. He was asleep as soon as his head touched the pillow. He was still wearing his fur hat.

*   *   *

13

It was after ten the next morning when Alexei Bonalov woke. Even so it had been a short night, and for a moment he lay, wondering why he had gone to bed in his underclothes. Then memory flooded back. He sat up, too fast. The room rocked. He shut his eyes, but that made things worse.

Gingerly he got out of bed and went into the kitchen. He ground the beans for his coffee, Brazilian beans, nothing but the best, like everything else in the apartment. He looked around him. Because of his position in the KGB, Olga had been able to enjoy the special passes that allowed her to buy goods in the shops reserved for members of the Party élite. As a result the apartment – large by Russian standards, with its four rooms plus kitchen and bathroom – was excellently furnished and equipped, mainly with Western products.

Not that he cared particularly, but it had given Olga a lot of pleasure. Now . . . He drank the coffee, black and scalding hot. His head ached and his stomach felt uncertain, but the after-effects of the vodka were beginning to wear off.

Pouring himself another cup of coffee, he took it into the living-room and put it down beside the telephone. He called his office and asked for Captain Kerensky.

'Comrade Colonel!' The relief in Kerensky's voice was enormous. He had been sweating blood, genuinely worried about his superior. 'Comrade Colonel,' he repeated thankfully.

'My car, in half an hour,' Bonalov ordered.

'Yes Comrade Colonel.'

'And, Oleg.' There was a silence on the line as Kerensky waited. 'Requisition the file on Neil Tarrent, will you?'

'Neil—?'

'Tarrent. He's nominally an attaché at the British Embassy. I talked to him last night, and he intrigues me,' Bonalov said smoothly. 'And make sure the file's fully up to date. But be tactful with Central Registry. I don't want to cause any comment on our interest, at this stage. You understand?'

'Perfectly, Comrade Colonel.' Kerensky was only too eager to please.

It had been an impulse that had made him ask for the

14

dossier, Bonalov decided as he went along to the bathroom. But if the idea that had come to him last night was to bear any fruit, some very careful planning would be required, and someone like Tarrent would be essential.

But it was still no more than an idea, he reminded himself, though already it was serving a useful purpose. He smiled wanly at his reflection in the mirror. At least for a few brief minutes he had been able to forget his loss, the loneliness . . .

By the evening of that day Bonalov knew he was hooked. The idea had taken on shape and substance. What had started as a wisp of drunken imagination had become a possibility, if only as a planning exercise with which to amuse himself, to give him an interest in the dreary months that lay ahead. He couldn't see himself dropping the idea now.

Already, in pursuit of the idea, Bonalov had committed an almost unforgivable offence. He had brought home with him Neil Tarrent's dossier. It was a risk, but only a small one; senior officers' briefcases were rarely searched. And Bonalov was sure that the intense study the dossier required would be better done at home, free from interruptions.

Settling himself in a comfortable chair, Bonalov opened the grey folder with the lengthy reference number so typical of Soviet bureaucracy. From its inside front cover Tarrent's face confronted him; one of the many photographs demanded by the Soviet authorities for a diplomatic visa had been affixed to it. The personal details that followed were surprisingly complete, the results of information from a multitude of sources in a variety of places.

Neil Le Gros Tarrent was thirty-two years old. His father, a Scot, now deceased, had been a doctor, as was his elder sister. His mother was French, from Caen in Normandy. He had been educated in the United Kingdom and had a degree from Edinburgh University, but he had spent most of his holidays in Europe. He spoke fluent French, German and Russian, and had a good working knowledge of Polish. He was said to take a keen interest in the arts, and at school and university had been known as a promising amateur actor.

One source suggested that he had considered becoming a professional, but this was probably not a serious ambition, as on leaving university he had gone straight into the Foreign and Commonwealth Office. There followed a list of Tarrent's postings – available to anyone with the money to buy a copy of *The Diplomatic Service List*, issued by Her Majesty's Stationery Office. It was a long list – London, Bonn, Warsaw, London again, Washington, East Berlin and lastly Moscow, where he had been for some six months. Neil Tarrent never seemed to stay in any one post for the normal length of time, and to anyone who could read between the lines, it was quite clear that this was no ordinary foreign service officer.

Bonalov skimmed the section headed 'Sexual Activity'. It was much as he had expected. Tarrent was cheerfully heterosexual. He was unmarried, and no single one of his succession of girl-friends had lasted very long, though as far as was known, they all continued to regard him with affection. If the object had been to compromise Tarrent and turn him in some way, such reports would have been disappointing. As it was, they merely served to round out the general character portrait of the man.

The file concluded with the series of direct observation reports on Tarrent since his arrival in Moscow. Bonalov read these with care, and almost at once he found a nugget. Tarrent, it seemed, had made the acquaintance of one Sergei Dronsky, a teacher at Moscow University. Nothing was known against Dronsky. Married, with a small daughter, his wife was typical of a young member of the Moscow intelligentsia, and his relationship with Tarrent appeared to be due solely to a mutual interest in the theatre. After a good deal of discussion, the KGB had decided not to interfere in this relationship, but to let it run; some use might be made of it at a later date. But, thought Bonalov, they weren't thinking of the use he had in mind. Here, in Dronsky, might be the perfect go-between.

Well content with his evening's work, Alexei Bonalov closed the dossier and locked it carefully in his briefcase. Tomorrow he would return it to his office safe, and, in a few

16

days, to the Registry. Now he would have a nightcap, and go to bed. He was, he realized, happier than he would have believed possible twenty-four hours earlier.

TWO

'Sergei?'

'Yes. Who is that?'

'Neil Tarrent here. Listen, I've had a bit of luck. I've managed to get hold of a couple of extra tickets for the summer visit of our National Theatre next week. It's *Romeo*. I thought you and Tamara would like them. Shall I drop them in?'

'No! No, it's not possible. Thank you, but no.'

'What? You mean you don't want them?' Tarrent sounded surprised. 'Why on earth not?'

'I have said, it's not possible. We cannot go. Thank you for asking. It was kind – but – but now I must go. Goodbye.' The line went dead.

Slowly Tarrent replaced his receiver and shook his head. There was no doubt that Sergei would have wanted to see *Romeo*, and no way he could have got tickets for himself. For any big cultural event, such as a performance by a foreign touring company, so many seats were allocated to the privileged members of Moscow society, including the embassies, that just a token few were available for the general public.

There could only be one explanation for Dronsky's refusal. He was afraid. He had probably been warned about his relationship with a Westerner, and a suspect Westerner at that. Neil Tarrent had no illusions about his cover; he knew perfectly well that his SIS connection was known to the KGB, and had recently become aware that their routine surveillance of his movements had intensified. Maybe they were thinking of setting him up for something, and therefore had told Dronsky to keep away. You never could tell in this damned country.

Tarrent threw the two unwanted tickets on to his desk. He

18

had offered them as a gesture of good will, with no ulterior motive, and their somewhat curt refusal, though understandable, left a sour taste in the mouth.

For his part, Sergei Dronsky was far too worried to regret either his rudeness, or the fact that he would not see *Romeo*. Much more important things were at stake. He also knew that he was under strict surveillance, a surveillance that extended to his family. Tamara was sure that quite often recently she had been followed. On several occasions when she had gone to fetch Maya from the day-care centre, she had been aware of a woman watching her. The woman, who looked like a *babushka*, had made no effort to hide her interest. She had even smiled several times at little Maya. But Tamara was afraid.

'Sergei, why did you ever talk to that Englishman? It must be because of him that we're under suspicion. There's nothing else, is there? You've not been saying anything at the University? Complaining, or anything?'

Sergei's worry made him irritable. 'No, of course not,' he said shortly. 'Why should I complain?'

'You do sometimes. That the apartment's too small, or will be when Maya gets older. That we don't have a car to get to the country. That you can't get tickets for the ballet or the theatre when you want to. You must be careful.'

'I only complain to you,' Sergei said. 'Surely that's allowed. Everyone grumbles a little. And I am careful – always. I know the hotheads at the University and I avoid them. You know I'm not political.'

It was true, Tamara thought. On the whole, Sergei was a contented man, who appreciated that they had a lot going for them. They both had good jobs, he as a teacher and she as a laboratory assistant at a hospital. Their apartment wasn't large enough, but in Moscow many a bigger family lived in one room. Maya had a place in Kindergarten-Nursery No. 104, where she was very happy, and it was no one's fault that both her grandmothers were dead, so that she had no *babushka* to take some of the load of caring for her from Tamara's shoulders. The only trouble was his relationship with the Englishman from the British Embassy. Everyone knew that such friendships were dangerous.

'It's Tarrent,' she repeated. 'You should never have talked to him. And you should certainly never have brought him here, to our home.'

'It was only once. The other time he came uninvited, to bring us a book. He's been very kind to us, Tamara. Without him we'd never have seen the English dance *Giselle*. You know what it's like about tickets.'

'Oh, you and your tickets,' she said in exasperation, though she had enjoyed the ballet as much as Sergei. 'There are more important things than tickets – our lives together, for one. Sergei, we can't have any more to do with him – or any other foreigner – ever again.'

'I know,' he agreed sadly. 'That's why I refused those seats for *Romeo*. If Neil Tarrent tries to get in touch with me again, I'll hang up or refuse to talk.'

It was Alexei Bonalov who had instigated increased surveillance on Tarrent and the Dronskys for the past six weeks. He wanted Tarrent to be aware of it, to ask himself why, and he wanted Sergei and Tamara Dronsky to be thoroughly fearful. It hadn't been difficult to arrange.

Now he was ready to act. Summer had finally arrived in Moscow, and by now the snow had gone from the ground and there were long queues at the ice-cream stalls in Red Square. The city was full of foreign tourists. By next winter . . . Curiously, as the decisive moment drew near, Alexei Bonalov felt no regret, but only excitement.

The day on which he initiated the first positive action was fine and warm. Maya Dronsky was at school. She was a happy, contented child, not particularly pretty, but appealing, with dark curly hair and wide eyes. On such a day she would have preferred to be in the country, wandering through the forest where in autumn they went to pick mushrooms, but she had learnt to be obedient, to do what was expected of her.

20

She was working hard, carefully painting a daisy. Painting was not her best subject and, glancing to each side of her, she saw with some dismay that her daisy was different from Sasha's and Misha's. She had given hers an extra leaf, and that was quite wrong. Already, at five, she knew it was best to conform, in small things as well as large. But what could she do about it now? It was a surprise when the Director came into the room.

'Good afternoon, children.'

They all leapt to their feet, abandoning their paintings. 'Good afternoon, Comrade Director,' they chorused.

The Director smiled at them and murmured something they couldn't hear to the supervisor. Maya hoped the Director hadn't come to look at their daisies. She swallowed hard. If they thought she'd added that extra leaf on purpose, she might be excluded from the games that were to follow.

The Director said, 'Sit down, all of you, and get on with your work. I've just come to fetch Maya Dronsky. She has a visitor.'

The Director held out her hand and Maya went forward willingly to take it. She didn't understand about the visitor, but she was glad there would be no trouble about the daisy. And standing outside the door was the nice, friendly *babushka* she had seen quite often recently when her mother came to collect her from school.

'Maya!'

The elderly, grey-haired woman bent down and enveloped the child in her arms. Maya was used to being embraced, both at home and at kindergarten. She accepted it as natural. She had never had any reason to be distrustful of adults. It didn't occur to her to wonder how the kind grandma knew her name or why she was being fetched from school in the middle of the afternoon.

Clutching the woman's hand, she said goodbye politely to the Director, who hugged her, and kissed her on both cheeks, then watched a little anxiously as the child was led out of the building and helped into the black chauffeur-driven Zil.

*   *   *

21

Less than an hour later Tamara Dronsky was called to the telephone. There was an instrument in her laboratory for official use, but private calls had to be taken in the box in the corridor, and Tamara was not pleased at the interruption. She was very busy, checking blood tests. Dr Popov expected the results to be available before she left for the day, and she didn't want to be late collecting Maya. She hurried down the passage.

'Tamara Dronsky?'

'Yes. Who's that?'

'It doesn't matter who I am. Just listen to what I have to say. We have your little daughter, Maya, and if you hope to see her again you must do exactly as you are told.'

'What – what do you mean?' Tamara leant against the glass. She was so frightened she could scarcely breathe. What had happened to Maya? What had they done to her? Where was she? She should still be at the nursery, but – A sob rose in Tamara's throat, nearly choking her. She couldn't speak.

'Are you there?' The voice demanded. It was a man's voice. It didn't sound too unkind, and somehow she managed to murmur a response. 'Good. Then listen, Comrade. This is what you are to do. You will tell your colleagues that you feel unwell. You will go straight home to your apartment and remain there until your husband joins you. You will tell no one of this phone call. You and your husband will wait in your apartment till you receive further instructions. Do you understand?'

'Yes. Yes. But what about Maya? Don't hurt her! Please don't hurt her,' Tamara pleaded desperately. 'She's only a child. We'll do anything you want, anything, but—' She began to cry.

'Control yourself!' the man said sharply. 'Remember you are in a public place. Someone might see you.' Then he seemed to relent. 'If you obey your instructions, no harm will come to your daughter and she will be returned to you. But if you fail—' The threat was left unstated.

'We won't fail. I promise you. We'll do exactly as you say, whatever you want—'

'Right. So go home quickly now, and wait.'

The line went dead and Tamara replaced the receiver. She couldn't believe it. Little Maya kidnapped! She forced herself to think. Why? For ransom? Such crimes were almost unheard of in the Soviet Union. And who would be stupid enough to think that a young university teacher could afford to pay ransom? No! The man had spoken with authority, and this was Moscow. There was only one answer. It was all tied up with the watch on Sergei and herself. For some reason Maya had been taken by the authorities –by the KGB even! At the idea, nausea overcame her and she ran to the cloakroom and vomited into the lavatory pan.

'Are you all right, Tamara?' It was one of the girls she worked with, and a close friend. 'You're not pregnant again, are you?'

'No.' For a moment Tamara was tempted to confide in her friend, but the man's warning had been explicit. 'It must be something I ate. I feel ghastly. I must go home. Will you tell Dr Popov. I'm sorry, but I can't help it.'

The doctor would be annoyed, Tamara thought. He might report her. But what did that matter? Nothing mattered but obeying the instructions. She must get back to the apartment and wait for Sergei. She had already wasted too much time. The man had told her to be quick.

She hurried from the building. She saw a tram in the distance and started to run, but she had no hope of catching it. Then she spotted a taxi. Its green light was on, and she waved furiously. Almost to her surprise it drew up beside her. She wasn't used to taxis. They were much too expensive for normal transport, but today . . . She had directed the driver and was slamming the car door behind her before she realized that she was still wearing her white lab coat. As she collapsed into the seat she felt anxiously for her purse in the pocket of her skirt. She wasn't sure of the fare. She could only hope she had enough money.

Living in a nightmare, Tamara Dronsky reached her home. Sergei had not yet arrived. She paced up and down, yearning for him to come, and he was scarcely inside the door of the apartment before she had flung herself into his arms. Not that her husband had any consolation to offer. His experience had been similar to her own – a phone call summoning him from a lecture he was giving, the order to go home and wait, the threat to Maya if he failed to obey.

'Surely there's something we can do,' Tamara said for the umpteenth time as the minutes crept by.

'We must wait.'

'Supposing we hear nothing. Supposing—'

Sergei shut her mouth with a kiss. 'We'll hear. These people don't play games. They must have a reason.'

'But what? Oh, Sergei, if only you'd never had anything to do with that foreigner—'

Instantly he was angry – or guilty, perhaps. He knew his conscience was clear, but he still felt responsible for whatever might be happening to little Maya.

'Make us some tea,' he said, 'and perhaps we should try to eat. At least it will help us pass the time.'

In the event, the telephone rang as Tamara went to the kitchen. She turned back, her face white, as Sergei answered it. It was the same voice, but now the man sounded quite pleasant, hardly menacing at all.

'You are both at home,' he said without preamble.

'Yes.'

'Then listen. First, your daughter. She's been taken to the country, where she'll stay for a few weeks, until our business is completed. She'll be well treated. You've no need to be anxious about her – as long as you and your wife are sensible. You understand what I'm saying?'

'Yes. Yes, of course. We told you before, we'll do anything you say.'

'Good. Now, if anyone asks, you will tell them that Maya has not been too well lately, and has gone to spend a holiday with your wife's family. And you must behave as if you are happy with this arrangement. No long, worried faces. You and Tamara must behave normally. Can you do that?'

'Yes, but –but that's not all, is it?'

'Not quite. I'll explain the rest when I see you. In ten minutes leave your building, turn left, walk to the end of the street. A black Zil will overtake you. The door will be open as

24

it stops beside you. Get in quickly, and we can talk. Tell your wife you won't be away more than half an hour. She can prepare your supper while she is waiting.'

And ten minutes later Sergei Dronsky, leaving behind him a distraught Tamara, took the lift to the ground floor. He managed a cheerful greeting to the *dezhurnaya*, the old woman who sat in the hall noting all comings and goings, and walked down the street. He had to resist a temptation to look furtively behind him.

The Zil was on time. Dronsky sensed rather than saw it draw up. His arm was seized and he was half pulled, half helped into the car. As he collapsed into his corner someone leant over him and slammed the door. The Zil was already moving away from the kerb.

'Don't look at me. We won't bother with blindfolds or nonsense of that kind, but keep your eyes down.' The voice was that of the man on the phone. 'Just sit back and relax.'

Dronsky did his best to obey. He couldn't prevent himself from being tense, but he arranged his limbs in seeming comfort and fixed his gaze on the floor of the vehicle. With the curtains drawn it was like being in a dark, gloomy box – a hearse, perhaps. He could feel the man studying him.

'Tell me about Mr Neil Tarrent,' Oleg Kerensky said.

Sergei Dronsky cleared his throat nervously. The mention of Tarrent's name hadn't surprised him, but that didn't make it any easier to reply. He knew there would be no point in attempting to deny his acquaintance with the foreigner. 'What – what do you want to know?' he said.

'Everything.'

'I know very little.'

'Tell me what you do know.'

The information that Dronsky produced was scrappy in the extreme, and added nothing to the dossier in Colonel Bonalov's office. Kerensky smiled to himself, but let Dronsky talk. When Dronsky finally stammered to an end, Kerensky allowed the silence to lengthen between them.

'Please!' Unthinking, Dronsky turned to him.

'Eyes down!' The interview was following a routine pattern, Kerensky thought. Once the initial nervous monologue had come to an end, the real questioning could start. 'Tell me, when you want to get in touch with Neil Tarrent, what do you do?'

'But I don't. Get in touch with him, I mean.'

Kerensky laughed. 'You expect me to believe that?'

'It's the truth. I wouldn't lie to you, not when – when Maya . . .'

'I see. Well, it seems I've been mistaken.' Kerensky simulated annoyance. 'That's too bad, especially for your Maya, poor child.'

'What? I don't understand.'

Kerensky leant forward and knocked twice on the glass panel that separated them from the driver. Immediately the car slowed, drew in to the kerb and stopped. Kerensky opened the door on Dronsky's side.

'Goodbye, Comrade.'

'No.' Dronsky pushed himself back into his corner, refusing to get out. 'What about Maya? What about Maya? What will happen to her?'

Kerensky shrugged. 'Since you can't get in touch with Neil Tarrent, that won't be your concern.'

'I didn't say I couldn't get in touch with him.' Dronsky was desperate. He gritted his teeth. 'I said I don't make a habit of it, as you implied. Actually I never have got in touch with him. He's always got in touch with me. But if that's what you want, of course I'll contact him.'

'Ah, good. You may shut the car door then.'

Dronsky slammed the door. Kerensky tut-tutted his disapproval at the use of such unnecessary force, but he signalled to the driver, and at once they accelerated. Relieved, Dronsky swallowed his frustration.

'I'm not asking much of you, Comrade. All I require is that you should be an – intermediary. As must be obvious to you, I'm in no position to have direct dealings with Mr Tarrent myself. So you will help me – be my stand-in, as it were.' Kerensky paused, but Dronsky made no response. 'There are just two things,' Kerensky continued. 'First, you must take care over your meetings with Tarrent. It would never do for our security people to accuse you of consorting

26

with a foreigner, would it?' He laughed as if this was a big joke. 'And secondly, you may tell your wife what's going on, but neither of you must give so much as a hint to anyone else. Do I make myself clear?'

Dronsky nodded. It was hot in the car, and he was sweating heavily. 'Yes, crystal clear, Comrade. But what of Maya?'

'The child is merely an insurance policy, shall we say – a guarantee that you'll not try to play any tricks. As I said, she'll be returned to you, safe and sound, in a few weeks. Then you'll be able to forget this little incident.'

'I'll never forget it. Never!' Dronsky was vehement. 'Not as long as I live.'

Kerensky felt a quick shaft of sympathy. He knew that he himself was unlikely ever to forget it. It could alter his whole life. He had tried to dissuade the Colonel, but Alexei Bonalov had been adamant, and somehow he couldn't let him down. If that was what the Colonel really wanted, he, Oleg Kerensky, wasn't prepared to stand in his way. But it was going to be a dicey business.

'Listen to what I have to say,' he said, suddenly menacing. 'Listen carefully, and remember there must be no mistakes.'

'It must be a trap,' Tamara whispered, as late that night she lay beside her husband in the darkness of their bedroom. Conscious as they both were of Maya's empty cot, sleep was eluding them.

'Don't be foolish,' Sergei said miserably. 'Of course we're trapped. He has Maya.'

'I didn't mean for us. I meant, for Tarrent. Oh, Sergei . . .' Tamara's voice broke. 'Do you truly believe we can trust this KGB man?'

Sergei put his arms around her and held her close. 'I don't know and I don't care. We've got to go along with him, for Maya's sake. As for Tarrent, he'll have to look after himself.'

'What exactly will you do? Have you decided?'

'Phone the British Embassy tomorrow morning and try to arrange to meet Tarrent at the *banya*, as the man suggested.

27

There couldn't be a more casual meeting place than a bath house, and luckily I've no classes in the late afternoon.'

'What if Tarrent's busy – or refuses to come?'

'I don't think he'll refuse,' said Sergei slowly. 'And if he's busy tomorrow afternoon we'll have to fix another time. But it must be soon. The man said it was essential to deliver the message in the next day or two.'

'And the message?' said Tamara. 'That an important KGB officer wants to defect to the West, and are the British interested in helping him. That's all?'

Sergei Dronsky heaved a sigh. 'That's all – for now. But we can bet it's only a beginning.'

THREE

Alexei Bonalov's thoughts paralleled Sergei Dronsky's words. They had made a beginning, but there was still a long way to go. Nevertheless, he could feel the excitement rising in him. It made him feel young again.

'I wish I could be there,' he said. 'I'd like to watch Tarrent when Dronsky breaks the happy news.'

'At the *banya*?' Kerensky pretended to be horrified, but he was grinning. 'You wouldn't learn much, Comrade Colonel. Tarrent won't give anything away.'

'No, I'm sure he won't, but . . .' Bonalov shrugged. He wasn't prepared to explain. 'This man Dronsky?'

'As I said, Comrade Colonel, he's an intellectual – long on brains, but short on common sense. However, he's devoted to the child, and so's his wife. While we hold this child Maya, they'll both do what they're told. Afterwards, who cares? Neither Dronsky nor his family are of any account.'

'Afterwards, they must be rewarded.' Alexei Bonalov spoke decisively. Oleg, he thought, didn't understand; the Kerenskys were childless. But when he himself remembered Pavel – and Olga – he could appreciate what the young Dronskys were going through. It was necessary to use them. He didn't regret that – there was too much at stake to consider individuals' feelings – but they had committed no crime and they were paying dearly for their stupidity in associating with a foreigner. 'They must be rewarded,' he repeated, 'whatever happens to the project. I leave it to you, Oleg. You will arrange it when the time comes.'

Kerensky bowed his head. 'If it's your wish, Comrade Colonel,' he said; and if I'm in a position to arrange anything by then, he added to himself. In spite of Bonalov's enthusiasm he was still beset by doubts. So much could go wrong and, fond though he was of the Colonel, he had no wish to be the one left holding the can.

'Telephone me this evening. I'm dining with my old friend, Mikhail Borostovich. You can call me there.'

'He's not in the picture, is he, Comrade Colonel?' Borostovich was a senior official in the Central Committee, and Kerensky was surprised.

'No, of course not,' Bonalov replied. 'But we play chess together regularly, and I've no intention of changing any of my habits at this stage. Just be careful what you say, and tell me if things progress as we expect.' He smiled grimly. 'I suspect they will. Tarrent may be cautious, but he can't fail to take the bait.'

After Dronsky's curt refusal of the tickets for the performance of *Romeo*, Tarrent had assumed that their friendship, casual as it had been, was at an end. He accepted the fact with regret but, in the circumstances of life in the Soviet Union, no great surprise. Dronsky's phone call, therefore, intrigued him.

'I couldn't possibly refuse,' he said to Kenneth Palfrey, the other SIS officer in the British Embassy, with whom he was lunching later that day. 'An invitation to meet him at a *banya*! It fills me with curiosity. I know they're a kind of equivalent of a British pub for the Muscovite male, but I've never been to one. Have you?'

'Once,' said Palfrey, 'and that was enough. It's a cross between a Finnish sauna and a steamy Turkish bath. I couldn't swear it made me feel any healthier, but it surely sweated off a few pounds, and I've had a certain affinity with boiled lobsters ever since.'

Tarrent laughed. 'It sounds a dangerous place.'

His companion shot him a quick glance. 'I wouldn't have thought so, not really. Everything's open and communal. People are ready to talk to each other, even to strangers. It's a bit like a club. And as a meeting place it's got advantages – for both sides. It's hard to carry a recorder if you've only got a towel round your waist.'

'I see. Maybe I'll enjoy it. I'll let you know.'

'Okay, but – Neil, if you'd care for some company, to cover your back, I'd be glad to come along. We needn't know each other there, and you wouldn't have to introduce me to this Russian chap.'

Tarrent shook his head. 'Thanks a lot, Ken, but I won't take you up on the offer. I'm sure there's no need, though I do catch a very faint smell of something cooking. Let's wait and see if anything comes out of the oven.'

Had he wished to continue with the metaphor, Tarrent might well have said that the smell of cooking became much more apparent as soon as he met Dronsky outside the bath house in the early evening. Dronsky was clearly highly nervous; though Tarrent was there at his invitation, he behaved as if they had met entirely by chance. He waited while the Englishman paid his own admission charge – no more than a few kopeks – and then, as a couple of other Russians arrived, hurried in ahead of him.

Accepting the situation, Neil Tarrent followed, clutching the large square of thin coarse towelling and the bundle of twigs that had been handed to him by an attendant. It occurred to him that Dronsky might have been unwilling to bring him to this cavernous place – a cross between the indoor swimming pool he had known as a child in Edinburgh and an elaborate Roman bath and, by his present odd behaviour, was trying to warn him. But of what remained a mystery.

There were no lockers in the changing-room, but Dronsky had saved a hook for Tarrent next to his own. They undressed side by side, in silence, and hung up their belongings. Dronsky tipped the attendant.

'To keep an eye on our gear,' he murmured.

Tarrent, who had been careful to wear casual clothes and an old pair of shoes, nodded. 'Thanks.'

'Don't forget your *venik*.'

'My what?'

Dronsky pointed to the bundle of twigs that reminded Tarrent of one thing only – the birch that a sadistic schoolmaster had once, years ago, applied to his bottom until it drew blood. The Russians could do what they liked, he thought. He didn't propose to thrash himself. But, not wishing to appear different from the other bathers, he picked up the birch bundle.

Once again Dronsky strode off, as if he and Tarrent were strangers, and once again Neil Tarrent meekly followed. He entered the steam room on Dronsky's heels at the precise moment that fresh tubfuls of water were being thrown on to the fire-bricks. Without warning a wave of hot, heavy air hit him in the face. He had not expected such a violent onslaught and gasped for breath. The steam engulfed him, blinding him, but somehow he managed to climb after the Russian, up half a dozen stone steps to the hottest balcony.

Here he sat, while time ceased to be. After the preliminary shock, the heat had become a prolonged agony, which grew gradually less and less bearable. The air was burning the inside of his nostrils and he tried to keep his breathing shallow. The steam hurt his eyes, even through closed lids. He shifted his weight from one buttock to the other, but nothing eased the torment. His heart was pounding. He began to feel ill. And when someone shouted to a newcomer to bring more water for the fire-bricks, a groan escaped him.

'You are not used to this?'

The question came from the man on Tarrent's left, a mountain of rosy pink flesh, who was belabouring his thighs with his *venik*.

'No. It's my first time.' Tarrent could scarcely speak.

'Then you must leave at once. Ten minutes is too much for the first time. Come along.'

The big man seized Neil Tarrent by the arm and led him down the steps and out of the steam room. The relief was overwhelming. Tarrent felt the sweat that trickled from his hair line and armpits and between his pectorals suddenly grow chill. He opened his mouth and took in great gulps of cool air. He was aware of the big man supporting him on one side, and Sergei Dronsky on the other. Momentarily he felt a flick of fear.

But the room was full of bathers, some naked, some in their sheets. They were talking and joking. One or two were reading. Others were playing dominoes. The atmosphere was relaxed and jovial.

'Thanks,' Tarrent said, including both Dronsky and his new acquaintance in his smile. 'I'm afraid that was a bit much for me.'

'Well, it'll do you no lasting damage. You look in pretty good shape.'

The big man was regarding Tarrent's body with interest. It was strong and supple, well-muscled and with no surplus fat. It was also hairless, except for a straggle of dark red growth around the genitals. But the man's gaze was focused on a scar that ran from just below the heart to the right shoulder, bisecting the nipple. It was an old scar, hardly visible normally, but now showing white and puckered against Tarrent's skin. To a professional, it was unmistakably the result of a knife wound.

'How did you get that?' the big man asked, pointing.

'A car hit me,' lied Tarrent.

He saw the instant and revealing disbelief in the man's eyes, and was glad to turn away and take the sheet that Dronsky was holding out to him. He wound it round his body, toga-fashion. The stuff was rough against his skin, but he felt less vulnerable with his nakedness covered.

'Thanks again for your help,' he said.

The big man nodded affably, and wandered off to watch the domino players. Tarrent followed Dronsky to a couple of seats in a corner, where they were reasonably secluded. Dronsky seemed more nervous than ever.

'Who was that man?' Dronsky murmured.

'I haven't the faintest idea, but if he hadn't noticed my agony in the steam room, I might have been boiled alive,' Tarrent said irritably. It was a gross exaggeration, but he was getting a little tired of Dronsky's behaviour. 'Why in hell's name did you have to meet me here?'

'I – I'm sorry.' Dronsky was still staring after the big man, whose back was now turned to them. He signalled to the attendant. 'Let's have some beer. It'll make you feel better. And some *vobla*. It's a great delicacy of ours.'

The beer was watery, but anything to drink was welcome. The *vobla*, dried, salted fish to be chewed and sucked, was

33

indeed delicious. Tarrent's flash of ill-temper faded. He was suddenly sorry for the unhappy-looking Russian sitting beside him.

He said more gently, 'Something's wrong, Sergei. Is there anything I can do to help?'

'No! No, nothing's wrong.' The Russian was over-vehement. 'All is well with us. My work at the university is progressing well. I'm hoping for a promotion next term. And Tamara's happy at the hospital. Maya – Maya has gone into the country for a while, to stay with some relations, so Tamara doesn't have so much to do.' His words tailed away, as if he realized he was talking too much.

'Splendid!' Neil Tarrent said, letting the one word speak volumes.

Dronsky ran his fingers agitatedly through his hair. He had been so preoccupied worrying about Maya and what might happen to her if he displeased the KGB, that he had given no consideration as to how best to approach Tarrent. Now it seemed impossibly difficult. To give himself time to think he ordered more beer.

'I'll have to be going soon,' Tarrent prompted.

'Oh no. Not yet. You can't. It's usual to sit around for ages here, after the steam. Besides, I – I – There's something I need to discuss with you.' Dronsky lowered his voice until it was a conspiratorial whisper. 'Mr Tarrent – Neil, please listen. It's a very confidential matter.'

'Okay. Go ahead. I'm listening.'

'A – a certain person wishes to leave the Soviet Union – to go over to the West, to the British – and to do this, he needs help.'

'You?'

'Me? *Nyet*! I wouldn't – He's a most important person in the – the KGB.'

'Really?'

Neil Tarrent had swivelled round so that he could watch Dronsky's thin, bony face, and his hands clasped between his knees like a small boy's. Dronsky could be telling the truth, he decided, at least as far as he knew it.

'Yes. Me – I'm only an intermediary, a go-between.'

34

'And the VIP? Who's he?'

'I can't tell you. It might be someone I met, but it might not. Anyway, I don't know.'

'You expect me to believe that?' Tarrent laughed aloud, as if Dronsky had just produced the punch-line of a joke. 'Come on, Sergei! What's happened. What's this all about?'

'A man telephoned me. He told me where to meet him. He said he'd pick me up in a Zil with a chauffeur . . .'

Sergei Dronsky told his story straight, which gave it a ring of authenticity. He even produced a vague description of his contact, though he seemed to have caught only a glimpse of the man. But, as he had been instructed, he did not mention Maya's abduction. He merely said the man had threatened him, had sworn that, unless he did as he was told, he'd be accused of plotting with a foreigner. Then he'd lose everything – his job, his apartment, probably his wife – and suffer exile from the city to a remote area.

'If you didn't end up in the *Lubyanka*,' Tarrent murmured, tugging at the rough sheet chafing his skin. The big man, he saw, had abandoned the domino game, and was chatting to a friend. Catching his eye, Tarrent waved a casual hand, and the man waved back. 'I understand,' he said to Dronsky.

'You don't!' Suddenly Dronsky was so tense that Tarrent could almost feel the kind of electricity he exuded. 'You think you understand, but you don't. You can't. I'm a Russian, a Muscovite. I love my country. I don't want to help some KGB guy go over to the West and betray our secrets. But – there's no alternative. Can you imagine yourself in that position – having to choose between being a traitor and losing all you loved?'

Tarrent didn't try to answer that one. He said softly, 'What do you want of me, Sergei – that I agree to help some unknown character get out of the Soviet Union? I'm sorry, but that's simply not on. He could be a criminal, a murderer or worse. I've only your word he's a KGB bigwig and, from what you tell me, you can't be sure of that yourself. Even if he is what you say, and it were possible for me to help, which I very much doubt, I wouldn't consider it. Not until I knew a great deal more about the affair. It wouldn't be worth the risk to go into something like this blind.'

'You must! You must!' Dronsky seized Tarrent by the arm. 'Please! I beseech you!'

'No. I'm sorry, but no.' Releasing his arm, Tarrent noticed that Dronsky's nails had bitten into the skin; clearly the Russian was desperate. He stood up. 'I have to go now.'

'But what am I to do? What am I to say to him?'

'You can contact him? You have a phone number?'

'No.' Miserably Dronsky shook his head. 'He said he'd get in touch with me.'

Tarrent hesitated, then gave a half smile. 'When he does, you can tell him that no one in his senses would touch an unknown defector – not unless he produced some proof that he was genuine and could pay his way. Tell him that, Sergei. If it's really a KGB man you're in touch with, he'll understand. Sorry I can't be more help. Goodbye.'

Sergei Dronsky made no effort to keep him, or to go with him. But as Tarrent ran to catch a taxi, he saw the big man hurry from the *banya*, climb into a *Volga* illegally parked right outside, and drive off. It was a very thoughtful Neil Tarrent who directed the taxi-driver to the British Embassy.

Dronsky stayed in the *banya* for another hour. He sat gloomily by himself, ignoring the babble of talk and gossip going on around him. He drank a lot more beer. He didn't want to go home. He hated the prospect of telling an anxious Tamara that he had achieved nothing, that the Englishman had only laughed at him.

He was pretty drunk by the time he reached his apartment block. The *dezhurnaya*, sitting beside the lift, spat her disapproval at him as he stumbled into the cage, and he had difficulty fitting his latchkey into the lock. Tamara flung open the door while he was still fumbling with it.

'The phone! Quick, Sergei. He's on the phone. He wants to speak to you.'

He didn't need to ask her who it was. He staggered across the room and picked up the receiver. 'D – Dronsky here.'

Oleg Kerensky didn't bother with niceties. 'What have you to report?'

'N – nothing, Comrade.'

'Nothing? You sound intoxicated. What were the two of you talking about after you came out of the steam?'

Dronsky wasn't surprised the KGB man knew that his meeting with Tarrent had taken place. He was too fuddled with beer and misery to think clearly. He grasped the receiver until his knuckles shone white, and tried to force his brain to work.

'What did we talk about? I told him what you wanted. I did my best. But he refused. He laughed in my face. He said no one in his senses would consider such a pro – proposition. It was too one-sided. He said that the person – whoever it is – would have to prove he was worth it. He said you'd understand.'

'I see. Interesting.'

'I'm sorry. Desperately sorry. I did my best. I can't do any more.'

'Oh, but you can. You will, Comrade. I'll get you all the proof he wants, and you'll deliver it to him. I'll let you know when. Meanwhile, be careful how you behave.'

'Wait!'

'Why? Have you thought of something else?'

'No. I mean, yes. What – what about Maya?'

'Maya? Of course. If you bring me good news after the next meeting with your friend, perhaps it could be arranged for you to speak to her on the telephone. Goodbye.'

Smiling to himself, Kerensky put down the receiver. He was not, as Alexei Bonalov was well aware, an imaginative man. He didn't feel even a momentary pang of conscience for the anguish he was causing the Dronskys. His mind was already centred on what he would say to the Colonel.

He looked at his watch, then shrugged. It was impossible to tell whether Bonalov and Borostovich were still eating, or had started their chess. Either way he would be interrupting them. But Bonalov had given orders.

A woman answered the phone, presumably Borostovich's wife. Her voice was discouraging but she agreed to get the Colonel and, after a long pause, Alexei Bonalov came on the line.

37

'Comrade Colonel, you told me to call you.'

'I've not forgotten, Oleg. What's the news?'

'They met, Comrade Colonel, and the reaction was exactly as you foresaw.'

'Splendid. Now you can go into action again. Good night, Oleg.'

'Good night, Comrade Colonel.'

The Dronskys once more. At this rate he would never get home tonight, Kerensky thought, as he waited for the phone to be answered. Why were they so slow? What were they doing now? They couldn't have gone out. At last, when his patience was almost exhausted, Tamara Dronsky lifted her receiver.

'I must speak to Comrade Dronsky.'

'You can't. It's not possible.' She sounded breathless.

'Why not?'

Tamara hesitated. She didn't know what to say. Sergei couldn't come to the phone because he was in a drunken stupor. He had found the remains of a bottle of vodka and that, on top of all the beer, had been too much for him. He had no head for liquor. She'd only got him to bed with great difficulty.

'He's asleep.'

'Then wake him.'

'I can't. He's – unwell.'

'Drunk, you mean? The fool's dead drunk?'

Kerensky swore. This was a complication he hadn't foreseen. He wondered if he could use the woman instead. It seemed the only answer. It might even turn out to be an advantage, if he could get her to understand what he wanted.

'All right, Tamara,' he said quietly and persuasively, using her first name. 'If Sergei's incapacitated, you'll have to take his place, won't you. Now listen carefully. This is what you have to do.'

It was over an hour before the Embassy Duty Officer managed to trace Neil Tarrent. Tarrent was having supper with some American friends and was not pleased at the interruption. Grudgingly he agreed to telephone Tamara Dronsky at once.

'May I?' he asked his host.

'Be my guest. But don't blame me if the line's bugged.'

Tarrent grinned. 'I'm not about to tell them any secrets.' He would have liked somewhere more private for the call, but the Duty Officer had stressed its seeming urgency. And when Tamara picked up the phone on its first ring, he was glad he hadn't delayed.

'Hello,' he said. 'Neil Tarrent here. What can I do for you?'

'Mr Tarrent, I'm speaking for Sergei. There's something he forgot to tell you when you were at the *banya*. Perhaps it's of no consequence. But it might be important. You understand?'

'Not really. Why are you phoning, and not Sergei himself?'

'Because – I – I'm ashamed to have to say it – but he's drunk, very drunk. So am I, a little.' She giggled, but it could have been nervousness. 'We've been drinking vodka, and Sergei had a lot of beer before. We were just chatting and drinking. And suddenly he remembered what he'd forgotten to say to you, and when he'd gone off to bed I thought I ought to let you know about it. It might be important,' she repeated.

'Maybe it is. Tamara, what was it Sergei remembered?'

'The person you were talking about at the *banya*—'

'Yes?'

'There are international meetings in Paris next month. Sergei says you'll know of them; they're concerned with arms limitations in Europe. Well, the person you were talking about will be there as a member of the Soviet delegation. That's all. It's not much, but I hope it interests you.'

'Yes, it does. Thank you, Tamara, and good night. I hope Sergei won't have too bad a hangover in the morning.'

Step two, Tarrent thought as he went to rejoin his friends, and what am I supposed to make of it? Tamara had been lying. Sergei certainly hadn't known anything about a Paris conference at the *banya*; he wasn't drunk then, and it wasn't the kind of thing he'd have forgotten. That probably didn't matter. What was important, or could be, was the actual information. If this were the prelude to a genuine attempt at defection by a senior KGB officer – an operation that should have the utmost encouragement and support – the fact that the man would be in the West would make it infinitely simpler. But the conference was, he knew, scheduled for early in the month, which gave a new urgency to the project.

FOUR

It was five days before Neil Tarrent heard any more about the potential defector, which was long enough to let self-doubts seed themselves. He began to wonder if he had blown everything, if a genuine appeal for help was even now being repeated elsewhere, perhaps to his opposite number in the United States Embassy; the Americans might well be more forthcoming, and thus gain all the advantages to be derived from the operation. He considered getting in touch with Sergei Dronsky in an effort to find out what was happening, but decided it would be a waste of time; if an approach was being made to someone else, it was highly unlikely that Dronsky would again be used as a channel. Knowing it was possible he might hear no more of the affair, Tarrent resigned himself to waiting. In any case, when he and his colleague, Ken Palfrey, had reported the sequence of events to their London headquarters, the reply had instructed them to await any developments passively.

But on the morning of the fifth day a phone call was put through to Tarrent's office. It was Dronsky, urgent and tense. Tarrent, glad as he was to hear from him, was nevertheless irritated by the Russian's agitation. He was not to know that, if he had found the last few days irksome, for the Dronskys they had been almost unbearable.

'I'm phoning from the University, so I must be quick,' began Dronsky. 'I've got something for you, something you'll think very interesting. I've shopping to do this afternoon, and I'll be at GUM about four o'clock, by the fountain. You be there too, but don't acknowledge me.'

Tarrent, stifling his annoyance at the Russian's bland assumption that he would drop everything to meet him, hesitated a moment. Why, he asked himself, could't he and Dronsky see each other casually, as they used to? He

41

appreciated the need for secrecy – a KGB defector would naturally be ultra-cautious in his approach -- but childish meeting games could easily defeat their own ends. And Dronsky wasn't in any sense a professional. Still, it wasn't Dronsky's fault, for it was a fair assumption that he was merely obeying orders, and it was unreasonable to take it out on him.

'Okay, I'll be there,' he said.

'Thanks.'

Instantly the line went dead. Tarrent sighed. It was typical of the Russian mind – especially the establishment mind – to prefer obfuscation and conspiracy to simplicity, but it did tend to cloud the issues. And the Arms Limitation Conference in Paris was not far away now. Time was getting short, and no genuine potential defector could afford to miss such an opportunity.

For the rest of the day Tarrent found concentration difficult, and eventually, abandoning his desk, he set off, far too early, for his appointment. Though he rarely shopped at GUM, the great Government Department Store, he had been in it often enough. It held no mystery for him, as the *banya* had done. He made his way first to the fountain in the middle of the building, but Dronsky hadn't arrived yet, so he wandered among the throng of shoppers, keeping a wary eye open for possible tails.

On the whole he found the GUM depressing. The actual construction was impressive, light and airy, rather like an aircraft hangar, and full of lively bustle. But the imported goods displayed in the window were only available in a special section tucked away on the third floor, where only the privileged were allowed For the multitude of would-be purchasers, the goods were shoddy, of poor quality and in limited supply. Nevertheless, at that time of day the main floor of the place was packed.

As four o'clock approached, Tarrent began to push his way through the crowds towards his appointed rendezvous. Almost at once he spotted Dronsky coming from the opposite direction. It was simple to make their arrival at the fountain coincide. And here luck was with them. Moments ago the benches around the centrepiece had all been occupied, but as if on cue a couple got up and left. It was the most natural thing in the world for Tarrent to sit down beside Dronsky, who ignored him and immediately opened a copy of *Pravda*.

From behind the shelter of the newspaper, which fluttered with his agitation, Dronsky said, 'I've been followed. A fellow in a blue shirt and slacks. With a camera. He looks like an American tourist, but I'd swear he's not. I tried to shake him off, but I couldn't. I – I'm not used to this sort of thing.'

In other circumstances Neil Tarrent might have been amused by the Russian's naïveté. But here and now Dronsky's appearance shocked him. In the last few days he had visibly lost weight. Never fat, he had become gaunt. His clothes no longer fitted, and a tiny nerve plucked at the corner of his eye.

Tarrent glanced around. 'I don't see any sign of him,' he said.

Dronsky was breathing hard. 'All right,' he said, 'but listen carefully. I must be quick. I've got an envelope inside this *Pravda*, and I'm going to leave the paper between us on the bench. Pick it up when you go. Everything you want to know is inside – at least I hope so. Phone me tonight. And please, please, help if you can.'

There was an unmistakable note of agonized entreaty in his voice, and Tarrent glanced up sharply at him. Dronsky folded the newspaper, put it on the seat and leapt to his feet. He moved off rapidly, without a backward glance, thrusting his way through the crowd. Tarrent watched him go, but it was impossible to tell whether or not he was being followed.

Then, casually, as if a headline had caught his eye, Tarrent picked up Dronsky's *Pravda*. He could feel the bulk of the envelope inside the newsprint. He pretended to read the folded paper for a moment, and when he looked up he saw that the supposed American tourist, blue shirt, blue slacks, expensive camera slung round his neck, had sat down opposite and was staring straight at him. It seemed that he had transferred his attentions from Dronsky to Tarrent.

Tarrent didn't like it. He realized the extreme vulnerability of his position. God knew what was in the envelope. Arrest with it in his possession was an obvious KGB ploy. He wished he'd got his own cover and back-up – an arrangement to pass the envelope to a colleague, perhaps. Somehow he had interpreted Dronsky's remarks on the phone as indicating that he merely wanted further conversation. He cursed Dronsky for not making it clear that he intended to pass documents. As it was, he was left literally holding the bag.

He considered his options, but could see no way out of the dilemma. He could, he supposed, abandon the newspaper and its contents – it was probably the sensible course – but he was reluctant to abort a possibly significant operation. In the end, he decided there was nothing for it but audacity.

Taking a firm grip on the newspaper, he got up and began to make his way through the store to the exit. Once he stopped, feigning an interest in some amber necklaces, and glanced behind him. Blue shirt was close, but he too had stopped, and he was making no apparent effort to narrow the gap between them. Nevertheless, Tarrent didn't hurry, and didn't try to shake the tail. There was no point; if the KGB were involved, there would almost certainly be other men watching the proceedings.

But nothing happened. There was no attempt to detain him. No one tried to snatch the envelope from him. No one bumped against him as if by accident, while someone else tried to steal it surreptitiously. Outside GUM, in his car with its diplomatic plates, Tarrent relaxed slightly. If they'd intended any action, it would surely have taken place by now.

And in the event, though he was fairly sure he was followed by a boxy little Zhiguli, Tarrent reached the British Embassy without incident. Once there, he went immediately to his office and, as he threw the copy of *Pravda* into the wastepaper basket and inspected the large brown envelope that had been inside it, it occurred to him that the purpose of the tails, first on Dronsky, then on himself, might have been to ensure and report its safe delivery. Or perhaps, he

44

thought, the intent had been to impress him with the importance of the envelope's contents.

In either case, the precautions had been successful. Here he was, safe in his office and acutely curious. He took a knife and slit open the big, heavy envelope.

Inside was a folded piece of paper and another envelope, sealed and marked 'Top Secret'. Tarrent grinned. Evidently the would-be defector had a sense of humour, something not usually associated with members of the KGB. Tarrent turned first to the paper, and skimmed through it.

Typed, and in excellent English, it amounted to a list of demands. The British would undertake to get the officer safely out of continental Europe and into the United Kingdom. The officer would not be required to make himself known to the British before the conference in Paris. Once in the United Kingdom and after debriefing, the officer would receive for the rest of his life the salary of a British brigadier, together with free accommodation suitable to that rank. In return the officer would make his expertise available to the British Government. Naturally, the British Government would at all times be responsible for the security of the officer and for his well-being.

Tarrent drew a deep breath, and blew it out slowly. The demands, though not totally unexpected – defectors were apt to have an exaggerated idea of their importance to the other side – were in this case exorbitant. The man must be either slightly mad, or very high-powered indeed. But how to decide which, in the face of this insistence on anonymity until the last possible moment? How to form a judgement of his potential worth if they were not to know who or what he was? Apart from the usual propaganda effect – and that was becoming old hat – he might be of little value, his vaunted expertise useless. On the other hand, he could be the catch of the century.

Tarrent was thankful the final decision would not be his, but London's. But he and Ken Palfrey would be expected to analyse, to give opinions, to make recommendations. He didn't mind admitting to himself that he was hopelessly unsure about the whole affair. If there hadn't been the pressure of the Paris deadline, he would have suggested playing for time, insisting on more information, but that alternative was not really open. It was an immediate question of thumbs up or thumbs down, and the wrong answer could be pricey, in more ways than one.

Deep in thought, Tarrent had opened the second envelope almost without conscious effort. But one quick glance at its contents, and his attention was riveted. 'Christ!' he murmured under his breath as he began to read. 'Christ!' He shook his head in disbelief.

What he was reading were photocopied extracts from a United Kingdom Joint Intelligence Committee report to the British Chiefs of Staff. The extracts were in fact whole pages, and looked totally authentic. The report was concerned with French military nuclear policy, their apparent progress with the development of an enhanced radiation weapon – the so-called 'neutron bomb' – and the possibility of the whole French nuclear force being placed under NATO command and control. There were some highly technical sections, that Tarrent didn't really understand, but there was absolutely no doubt that the document, if genuine – and London could readily establish that – was of the greatest significance and sensitivity. Yet it was seemingly in the possession of a KGB officer who wanted to defect to Britain. He could not have chosen a better bait.

Tarrent let out a long, slow whistle. The situation had altered drastically – and not for the better.

For the next few hours Neil Tarrent and Ken Palfrey were frantically busy. Obviously, the security implications of the affair had now assumed paramount importance. At the very least they must ensure that no agent-in-place in London or elsewhere became aware of the activity of the potential defector, or of the dramatic information he seemed able to acquire. This meant that, in spite of the need for haste, phone calls to London were impossible, even with the newly-installed speech encryption equipment. Instead, they had to activate their rarely-used 'Eyes Only' teleprinter link to their Director.

46

It was nine o'clock before Tarrent phoned Dronsky, and by then the Russian was frantic. The KGB man had already telephoned him once, and he had been forced to admit that so far there had been no response from the British. Dronsky couldn't bear to think what might happen if Tarrent didn't contact him at all. He sat beside his phone, waiting, but when it rang he could scarcely bring himself to lift the receiver, in case it was the KGB man again.

'Dronsky speaking.'

'Ah, good. I've just had a couple of wrong numbers.'

Sergei signalled wildly to Tamara. 'Tarrent,' he said, as she came to listen beside him.

'About that proposition we've been discussing,' Tarrent continued.

'Yes – yes,' said Dronsky eagerly, then hesitated as he felt Tamara touch his arm. She was frowning, pointing to her lips and to the mouthpiece. She was quite right; he had forgotten the probability that the line was tapped. Wrong numbers were frequent enough in Moscow, but perhaps Tarrent had been trying to warn him.

'Most interesting,' Tarrent was saying. 'As a matter of fact, I'm flying home tomorrow and I'll put it up to my boss. I'm sure you appreciate I can't make a decision myself.'

'No, but – but – you're hopeful?' Dronsky was almost pleading.

'Oh yes. I think you can say that. I'll let you know as soon as I get back. I realize we don't have too much time in hand. But I shouldn't be away more than two or three days.'

'Splendid! Splendid! That's wonderful!'

Dronsky's relief was so obvious and so intense that Tarrent was tempted to warn him not to count his chickens in advance. There was always the possibility that London would decide it was a trap or too hot to handle, though it was hard to see how they could take such views if the document proved authentic. In any case, it seemed a pity to spoil Dronsky's little happiness.

Tarrent said carefully, 'I'm glad you're pleased, Sergei. I hope all goes well.'

'Yes. Thank you. Thank you very much.'

Sergei put down the phone and turned to Tamara. His haggard face was alight with joy. He picked her up and whirled her round until they both collapsed in a laughing heap on the floor. He began to make love to her. Then, suddenly, they were sober, jerked back to reality. The telephone was ringing again.

'Answer it! Quick!' Tamara said, pulling herself free.

Sergei, his trousers round his ankles, staggered to the instrument. This time he was glad to hear the hated but familiar voice. He repeated what Tarrent had said. He didn't exaggerate. He remembered that his conversation with the Englishman could have been recorded. He waited, hopefully.

'Right,' Kerensky said. 'I'll know when he returns, and I'll be in touch.'

'But – but—' Dronsky stammered. 'What about Maya? You said we might speak to her, if – if I could persuade . . . You promised!'

'*Nyet*. You must wait. After all, I doubt if it was just your persuasion that brought about your – friend's interest.'

There was the sound of a laugh, then a jumble of words, background noises and a lot of loud clicks. Sergei held the receiver away from his ear.

'Dronsky, are you there? Dronsky?'

It was a different voice, one Sergei Dronsky had never heard before. An older man, he decided, not unkind, but authoritative, and somehow even more frightening. Dronsky cleared his throat.

'Yes, I'm here, Comrade.'

'Good. Now, listen. It's too late today. Maya will be asleep. But tomorrow, at six o'clock, you and your wife will be able to speak to her on the phone. Just remember, she's on holiday and happy. Take care what you say to her.'

Alexei Bonalov cut short Dronsky's incoherent flood of thanks, and grinned at Kerensky. 'Things are going well for us, Oleg. We can afford to be generous.'

'If you say so, Comrade Colonel.'

'I do say so. I say so, indeed. Why are you so dubious, Oleg? What more do you expect? Tarrent will be back in

Moscow within a week, and all our terms will be agreed. You mark my words.' Bonalov stroked his neat beard to cover his emotion. 'And then, my dear boy, we can look forward to Paris.'

'Yes, Comrade Colonel.'

Kerensky suppressed a sigh. He was not looking forward to Paris – or to what might happen afterwards. If it had been anyone but Alexei Bonalov, Pavel's father . . .

FIVE

Fortunately there was a British Airways flight from Moscow to London the next day; Tarrent would have been unwilling to travel by Aeroflot. He arrived at Sheremetyevo airport in a staff car, having allowed himself what he hoped would be nice time before the flight was called. He had no wish to hang around, but no desire to appear to rush, either. He was accompanied to the airport by Ken Palfrey, and they had thought it wise to bring with them the Embassy Security Officer. In the circumstances an escort of some kind was essential, though there was very little that Palfrey or the Security Officer could do in the event of any trouble, except report. However, the company was welcome, if only as moral support. Tarrent was very conscious of the package in the inside pocket of his jacket.

He checked in and went through the usual formalities, though he noticed that as soon as he left the counter the Aeroflot desk clerk was on the telephone – Aeroflot were the handling agents for British Airways in Moscow. Tarrent hoped his bag wouldn't be searched too thoroughly. There was nothing in it except toilet articles, a couple of shirts and a change of underclothes, but it was new, and he didn't want the lining ripped to pieces.

The flight was called and he said goodbye to his colleagues. 'You understand. As soon as I get the papers to London, I'll give you a call.'

Palfrey nodded. 'I understand. When I hear from you, I'll shred the copies we made. Good luck, Neil.'

'Thanks.'

Tarrent went through passport control. Again he had no difficulty. His passport was stamped and handed back to him without question, but a pair of hard brown eyes regarded him with curiosity, and Tarrent didn't miss the quick nod exchanged with the man in plain clothes standing behind the desk. Yet none of this was in any way unusual. The comings and goings of all members of the diplomatic community were subject to the same close scrutiny. Tarrent had no way of telling whether any particular interest was being taken in his movements today.

He sat in the airside departure lounge, and waited. The flight was delayed, of course – 'late arrival of incoming aircraft' was becoming almost a routine announcement, he thought. But the plane was half empty and boarding was quick. In the end they took off only forty minutes late. Tarrent relaxed. Like so many people leaving Russia in a non-Soviet aircraft, he breathed an involuntary sigh of relief as the wheels left the ground.

The flight was uneventful, and Tarrent was met at Heathrow. To his surprise, the driver had instructions to deliver him, not to his headquarters in the new tower block south of the river, but to the Foreign and Commonwealth Office main building in Whitehall, where the Director kept a small suite of offices for occasional use.

'Go straight in,' the secretary said. 'He's expecting you.'

Tarrent smiled his thanks. It was hot in central London, even in the early evening, the air stale with over use, and he was feeling sticky and dirty after the flight, his suit too thick for the unusual heat-wave. What he would have liked would have been a long, cold shower and a long, chilled beer. But Sir Patrick Cordar couldn't be kept waiting. There was one thing he must do, however.

'Look,' he said. 'I must speak to Mr Palfrey – Kenneth Palfrey – in the Embassy in Moscow. Get him on the line, and put him through to me in Sir Patrick's office.'

'Sir Patrick has given strict orders that you're not to be interrupted,' the secretary said doubtfully.

'I assure you it's essential. I'll fix it with the Director,' Tarrent said as he knocked on the door of the inner office.

'Hello, Neil. Come along in. We're just having a glass of sherry. Help yourself.' Like many of Sir Patrick's casual

51

remarks, it sounded like a command.

'Thank you, sir.'

Tarrent had imagined that Sir Patrick would be alone, but Simon Mont was with him. Tarrent liked Mont. They were good friends outside the office, and he sincerely hoped that, when the old man retired a couple of years hence, Mont, brilliant, intuitive and utterly unmilitary in appearance, would succeed to the directorship. It was rumoured, however, that Sir Patrick, a retired Major-General, personally favoured John Kenmare, whose father had been both a famous soldier and a family friend. Sir Patrick's recommendation would probably carry a lot of weight. Tarrent suspected that Mont's chances were not good.

Tarrent poured himself a sherry, and sat down in the chair indicated. Sir Patrick said, 'Our exchange of signals yesterday gave me a bad night, Neil. This morning I decided to put Simon here in the picture – but no one else for the moment. That's why we're seeing you here, rather than at the office. We want to keep your visit home as quiet as possible. Now, show us these papers.'

Tarrent sipped his sherry, and slowly took the package of documents from his inside pocket. 'Here they are, sir. You'll probably know at once if they're genuine.'

Sir Patrick looked through the pages in silence. He glanced up sharply as the phone rang.

'What the hell's that? I told—'

'I think it's Moscow, for me, Sir Patrick. I took the liberty of asking your secretary— It's important, sir.'

Sir Patrick held out the receiver. 'Go ahead.'

Tarrent listened for a moment, and then said, 'Ken, I'm here, with the Director.' He paused, and added, 'Good. Any developments? No. Fine. I'll be in touch.' He hung up.

'We took a copy of each of those pages in Moscow, sir,' he explained. 'Ken Palfrey will shred them now he knows I'm here. No one else at the Embassy knows anything about the affair.'

'That's one good thing,' said Sir Patrick. 'I can tell you at once that these documents are dynamite.' He passed the photocopies to Mont. 'They're authentic, all right – we took the report in the Joint Intelligence Committee only a month ago. It's appalling to think the Russians have got their hands on this information – and who knows what else they've had from the same source? And the political repercussions if they decided to print the text in *Pravda* or *Izvestiya*, or release it through one of their anti-nuclear fronts in the West! You know how sensitive this neutron bomb business is . . .'

He relapsed into silence for a moment, staring at the papers in Mont's hands as if they themselves had been explosive. As, in a sense, they were. He hated to contemplate the Prime Minister's reaction to another spy scandal. The consequences could be catastrophic, nationally and internationally. Everyone would blame everyone else, and the repercussions and enquiries would go on for months or years. It was a job for the Security Service, but he would inevitably be involved. God, he'd be thankful when it was time for him to retire, and forget the whole messy intelligence scene . . .

Tarrent had waited till the Director's eyes returned to him. 'I realize the security implications are horrendous, sir,' he said, 'but I don't think Soviet publicity will be a problem. Or at least we can avoid it—'

'Let's hope you're right.' Sir Patrick interrupted him. 'Suppose you tell us the whole story in detail, as if we knew nothing.'

Tarrent collected his thoughts, and did just that, clearly and fully. 'So,' he concluded, 'it looks as if this KGB man who wants to come over has produced these papers as a kind of surety for his good faith, and proof of his worth to the West. And, what's more, with an implied threat of publicity on this sensitive subject if his demands aren't met.'

'That would only apply if no one else on their side knew about the documents,' Mont pointed out quickly.

Tarrent looked at the Director, who nodded to him to continue. 'I've been thinking about that point,' he said, 'and it must be so. Look, if the Russians made the papers public after we'd accepted our chum, it wouldn't exactly make him popular with us, would it? And he must realize that.'

'So it's a kind of blackmail, as you say,' added Mont. 'If we don't accept his terms, he gives the papers to his political bosses, and the fat's in the fire. Either we're being over-subtle, or your Comrade X is a very clever man.'

'I think I agree with all that,' said Sir Patrick, 'but I'm not clear where this man Dronsky comes in. Why couldn't Comrade X just walk into our Embassy in Paris and ask for asylum in the usual fashion?'

'I suspect he's being very careful, sir,' replied Tarrent. 'If he's as important as he thinks he is, it might not be too easy for him to make the move in Paris without any preparation. Don't forget he puts the onus on us – he demands that we should spirit him out of France and protect him.'

'And there's also the point that all this build-up adds to his importance and credibility in our eyes,' said Mont.

'And Dronsky?' asked Sir Patrick again. 'He's apparently acting under duress?'

'I think so,' replied Tarrent. 'He certainly has been looking like it. He tells me he resents the would-be defector, but he's too terrified not to help him, because of threats to his family. I really believe that if he knew the identity of the man he'd report him, but I could be wrong about that.'

'Do you think it's occurred to him that the whole thing might be some kind of KGB trap or conspiracy for us – that there might not be a real defector at all?' Mont asked.

'No. I'm sure it hasn't. For what it's worth, he thinks the man's genuine, which is why he's equally afraid of the KGB. His problem is to know which bit of the KGB is which. Part could be being used by Comrade X to further his own ends, and part might be after him – Dronsky, I mean.' Tarrent gave a sudden grin. 'He's probably as confused as I am. It's a problem for me too, after all.'

'The big man at the *banya* you mentioned, and the pseudo-American at GUM,' said Sir Patrick. 'You don't know which side they're on either. Surely they must be working for our friend, if he really is a friend.'

'I wouldn't like to swear to it.' Tarrent shook his head doubtfully. 'But it's evident he's got some help. There's the chap Dronsky seems to be in contact with, for instance.'

'Who could be Comrade X himself,' Mont said.

'I somehow doubt it. Judging from an admittedly inadequate description, he seems much too young. And I don't think our man would expose himself so near to the scene of action, if you see what I mean. But Dronsky's contact certainly knows what's going on, so he must be very close to our man.'

'Our man, you call him,' Sir Patrick said. 'Do you really feel he's our man? Would you accept him, on his terms?'

Tarrent hesitated for some seconds. Then, 'Yes,' he said. 'I'd accept him, yes. After those photocopies he's produced, I don't think we've any choice. But I'd be very slow to trust him once we've got him.'

Mont nodded his agreement. He'd reached the same conclusion. But somehow he didn't like it. He could see a lot of possibilities for error and embarrassment – danger even, if an operation was eventually mounted.

Both the SIS officers turned to the Director, but Sir Patrick took his time. Finally he gave his opinion. 'Personally, I'm inclined to agree with Tarrent,' he said slowly, 'but the decision won't be mine alone. We shall have to bring in the Head of the Security Service, and consult the Prime Minister.'

'But, sir, you'll advise them that—'

Sir Patrick continued as if Mont hadn't spoken. 'Also, I propose to get John Kenmare over from Paris. I want to hear his views on all this. And he'll be involved if we agree to accept this character.' He pushed back his chair and stood up, a smallish, very upright figure, now in command. 'I'll see you both again tomorrow. Sorry to have to break into your weekends. Good night to you.'

Tarrent avoided catching Mont's eye as, thus dismissed, they left the Director's office. Sir Patrick was already telling his secretary to get hold of Kenmare. 'I don't care where he is. Find him. I must speak to him tonight.'

Curbing his resentment at the abrupt way in which Sir Patrick had curtailed their discussion, Mont managed to grin as they walked along the wide FCO corridors. 'If you've not made any plans, Neil, why not come and stay with us? You won't be in the UK more than two or three days – we've

obviously got to decide about Comrade X pretty quickly –
and Betty would love to have you.'

'If you're sure, thanks a lot. I'd thought of calling a friend,
but—'

'Just as you like. But you're welcome in Wimbledon.'

Tarrent was grateful. It would be much less bother for him
to stay with the Monts, and he would enjoy it. They lived in a
big, dilapidated house, full of shabby furniture and a variety
of animals. Meals were wonderful. Betty, Simon's wife, was
an excellent cook, and all their fruit and vegetables came
from the garden. It was a relaxing home, which sometimes
made Neil Tarrent regret he was a bachelor.

'How are the family?' Tarrent asked, as he climbed into
Mont's five-year-old Ford.

'Well, the kids are flourishing but, as you know, Betty's
health is none too good. That last operation took the stuffing
out of her. She has her off days when she stays in bed, though
mostly she's all right. But she's not going to be a hundred per
cent for a long time, if ever. And she worries about money,
like all of us.'

'But, surely—'

'I know what you're going to say, Neil. I get a good screw,
and it ought to be enough. But you lose a lot of allowances
when you're posted home – and it's not like diplomatic life
abroad. And you're not married – you wouldn't know about
kids and their education. We've got two boys at
Westminster, and Simone's just won a place at Cheltenham.
Expenses mount up. There's a big mortgage on the house,
and you know I help to support my parents. Medical insurance doesn't pay all Betty's bills, either. Money's hell, Neil,
or rather the lack of it.'

'I'm sorry, Simon.'

'Oh, it's not as bad as it sounds. And anyway, I shouldn't
be boring you with my troubles.'

They were silent while Mont negotiated a tricky turn
across the stream of late evening traffic and, when they
began to talk again, it was of other things – their work,
politics, the state of the country. It wasn't until they had
reached Wimbledon and were approaching the house that

Mont referred once more to his personal affairs.

There was a brand new station wagon beside the garage and, when Tarrent commented on it, Mont said, 'I had to buy it. The old one wasn't roadworthy. But the damn thing took the last of my savings, such as they were. We don't have even a small cushion now.' He sounded grim.

'Let's hope you'll get the Directorship when the old man retires,' Tarrent said. 'That would make a difference, wouldn't it?'

'A hell of a difference! Unfortunately the odds are all on John Kenmare, as you probably know – not that he needs the money. God, how I wish I'd had a rich father!'

'And a famous one, Simon? Kenmare may not need the money, but he'd love the knighthood that goes with the job. It'd be proof he'd achieved something himself.'

'Yes. You're right. I suppose it's not much fun having had a great man for a father. Sorry I sounded so bitter. To be honest, it's just plain envy.' Mont gave a regretful smile. 'We all have our problems.'

'Even John Kenmare?' Tarrent said, and they were laughing together as Betty Mont came out of the front door to welcome them.

The man of whom Mont and Tarrent had been speaking – John Kenmare – held the nominal rank of Counsellor at the British Embassy in Paris. He was an attractive character, tall, good-looking, with brown hair and blue eyes and a certain arrogance of manner. It was this arrogance that made some people dislike him, though basically he was not an arrogant man.

He was, however, ambitious. Neil Tarrent was right about that. Kenmare wanted very much to succeed Sir Patrick Cordar as Director and at the moment he was pretty confident that, in due course, he would. He knew that Simon Mont was his main rival – the only serious one unless an outsider were brought in – but he didn't believe that Mont had much of a chance against him.

Life, in fact, was going well for John Kenmare. He was, he

57

thought, as happy as any man of forty-odd had a right to be, and the reason was Helen. He was in no doubt about that. How glad he was that he had married her, in spite of his mother's opposition. How lucky that she had agreed to marry him.

Going up in the lift from the basement garage where he had parked his Jaguar, Kenmare patted his breast pocket, just to assure himself that the package was still there. Tomorrow was the first anniversary of their marriage, and he had bought Helen a diamond necklace. She had always refused to wear any of the rather heavy jewellery that had belonged to Rhoda, his first wife, but this was different. It was a beautiful piece, light and delicate, and he had every hope it would please her.

He let himself into the apartment. He could hear Helen and his mother talking in the salon and would have joined them, but he was interrupted by Anna, his mother's devoted companion. She came stomping out of the kitchen, a thickset, dour woman, wiping her hands on her apron.

'You're to phone your London office, Mr John.'

'Right. Thanks, Anna. I'll just say hello to Helen and—'

'At once. They said it was very urgent.'

'Okay.'

John Kenmare resigned himself to acquiescence. It was no use arguing with Anna. He had been brought up to obey her and, though she now called him 'Mister' John, he knew it was only a courtesy title. Their relationship hadn't really changed from the time he was a small boy.

He went along to his study and dialled his call to London. After all, his pleasure at seeing Helen was merely postponed. He thought of the next, very special day. Thank God, it was a Saturday and he didn't have to work. They would have a lazy morning, perhaps a short walk in the Bois. Lunch in the apartment; his mother would expect that attention. In the afternoon, Longchamp and the races. Later, dinner for two at Maxim's. And even later . . .

'Hello! Hello! John, are you there?' The switchboard had put him straight through to the Director, and Sir Patrick's irate voice interrupted his musings.

58

'Hello. Yes. Kenmare here, sir. I'm sorry I've been so long returning your call. I'm afraid the Ambassador . . .' He left the rest of the sentence to Sir Patrick's imagination.

'Quite. But what matters is I've got hold of you now. John, I want you in London, as soon as you can tomorrow morning.'

'Tomorrow?'

'Yes. Sorry if it interferes with your plans for the weekend, but it's absolutely essential. Something important has come up, and I need you.' Sir Patrick paused. The line was crackling angrily. 'I can't discuss it on the phone. Just let's say that someone coming to Paris for those meetings would like to extend his holiday – or so I'm told. You follow?'

'Yes, sir.' Momentarily Helen was forgotten. The Director had all his attention. Kenmare said, 'And there are problems, I assume. Right. I'll be on the first available plane in the morning. If there's any trouble, I'll get an air taxi.'

'Splendid. Let us know, and I'll send a car to Heathrow or wherever for you.'

'Thank you, sir.'

'Good night then, John. Regards to your dear mother.'

John Kenmare put down the receiver and immediately picked it up again. He had no difficulty getting a seat on the eight-thirty Air France flight from Charles de Gaulle, and he phoned London to leave the appropriate message. His mind still on what Sir Patrick had said, he turned to find his wife standing in the doorway.

'Helen, darling!'

'Hi, John. I thought I heard you come in.' She was attractive rather than beautiful, in her mid-twenties, with black curly hair and big black eyes, the heritage of her Spanish-American grandmother. 'And I couldn't help hearing—' She glanced at the telephone.

'Darling, I'm sorry. I couldn't be more sorry.' John Kenmare took her in his arms, kissed her, then held her away from him. 'It's the worst bloody luck. I'd arranged a perfect day for our anniversary, but now we'll have to postpone it. I've got to go to London first thing tomorrow.'

'Hell! Well – if you must, you must, honey.' Suddenly her

face lit up. 'John, why don't I come with you? I could amuse myself while you're working during the day, then we could have dinner together, perhaps do a show.'

Kenmare hesitated. There was nothing he would have liked more than to take Helen with him. But it wasn't practical. He wouldn't necessarily be keeping office hours. Sir Patrick would expect him to be completely free of commitments, and they might easily work late into the night. He just couldn't let himself be tied.

'Darling, it's not possible. I'm sorry. I promise I'll make it up to you when I get back.'

Helen didn't argue. In their year of marriage she had learnt to accept the vagaries of her husband's job and the demands it put upon her. She was used to him going away unexpectedly, working late and at weekends, and sometimes being elusive about his movements. Once she had met him accidentally at the Musée d'Art Moderne, when she believed him to be at his office in the Embassy. On another occasion she was positive she saw him standing on the platform at the Place d'Italie Métro station as her train drew out, though on his return home that evening he had denied it and treated the matter as a joke.

As for the demands upon herself, they were mostly slight and pleasurable. Helen enjoyed the diplomatic round, the parties and social functions. She found it easy to meet people and her French, with the help of private lessons, was improving daily. She would have been happy to entertain for her husband, but regretfully she had learnt that this was not expected of her. Clara, her mother-in-law, who, together with Anna, had always lived with John in the various cities to which he had been posted, continued to act as his hostess. And Helen, to whom so much was new – husband, Europe, money in abundance, leisure to follow her own inclinations, a way of life undreamed of while she had been earning her living as an assistant in a New York art gallery – had so far acquiesced.

'Come on, darling.' John Kenmare put his arm around her waist. 'Mother will be wondering what's happened to us. Besides, I need a drink.'

Together they went into the salon, where Clara Kenmare sat listening to a tape of Tchaikovsky's *Swan Lake*. John bent over the wheelchair, to which his mother had been confined since her accident more than forty years ago, and kissed her.

'You're looking especially beautiful tonight,' he said. 'Are we expecting important guests?'

Clara laughed. She liked compliments. 'No, it's all for your benefit, John – and Helen's.' She smoothed the long brocaded dress which covered her wasted legs. 'Were you talking to London? To Patrick Cordar? What did he have to say?'

'Oh, there's a panic on. I have to go over there in the morning.'

'Tomorrow, on your anniversary? What a shame!'

'Incidentally, he sent you his regards. I suspect he'd have liked to make it his love, but he didn't dare,' Kenmare teased.

'He's a good friend,' Clara said, and then added to Helen. 'I expect John's told you the story. It's rather amusing. Though Patrick and I are of an age, his father and my late husband were at Eton together. Of course, people today pretend to despise these sort of links, but I assure you they can be useful sometimes.'

'Very useful!' John Kenmare agreed, and smiled fondly at his mother.

They met the next morning, again in the FCO building in Whitehall – Kenmare, Mont and Tarrent. The former had been briefed by Sir Patrick earlier, before the Director went to his hastily-arranged conference with the Prime Minister and the Head of the Security Service. But Kenmare's flight had been late, and there had been little time for private discussion.

As they met, Kenmare was still assimilating the implications of his briefing, but again things moved rapidly. The three of them had merely greeted each other before Sir Patrick arrived.

He said at once, 'It's on. Subject to any operational

objections or problems, we go ahead. We get him out. It could be a great coup for us.'

'Or a great disaster,' Mont said. 'And on French soil.'

'Of course we recognize that,' Sir Patrick said, with an edge to his voice. 'That's what the PM means by operational problems. The main point is that we can't appear to be kidnapping him. For one thing, as the PM pointed out, it would give the Russians an excuse to withdraw from the talks – which may be what it's all about anyway. But we've got to take the risk.' Suddenly the Director was impatient. 'On the evidence we've got, he's too important to lose, from both the intelligence and security points of view. What's more, if we refuse him, he could probably do us untold harm.'

Sir Patrick paused, and looked round the table. 'What we've got to do is plan carefully – and securely. We're going to hold this very tight – very tight indeed. The Security Service is going to start some enquiries into the distribution of that Joint Intelligence Committee paper, but they'll be very low key till we've got our hands on this chap. Apart from that, our team in Paris will consist of you three, and you three alone. Here in London everything will be in my hands. All communications will be on an "Eyes Only" basis. And we'll make the reception arrangements without giving anything away. Now let's get down to details.'

'There's just one point, sir.'

'Yes, John, what is it?'

'I really think we ought to make some effort to discover who this Comrade X is, before the Paris meetings. We say, "Yes. Right. We'll get you to the UK. We accept your terms – only we would like to know who you are."'

'And he says, "No. Stop fooling around. Either you want me or you don't."' Mont looked disgusted.

'He just might say "Yes". What's your opinion, Neil?'

Coming from Kenmare, the question startled Neil Tarrent. He thought of Sergei Dronsky. The man was an unwilling intermediary, forced into a situation he feared and didn't understand. What he wanted was a clear-cut affirmative answer, to get him off some kind of hook. Then he might hope to forget the whole episode. Almost certainly he would conveniently forget to pass on an unwanted question that might cause added complications.

He said carefully, 'You've got to remember that our only contact is through this man Dronsky. I'll ask the question, if you like, but I believe it would be a waste of time. Knowing Dronsky's position, I doubt if the message would be delivered. Even if it were, I guess Comrade X would refuse to answer. He'd gain nothing by agreeing, and it might mean that Dronsky would get to know his name. I'm not sure we'd want that ourselves. As I said yesterday, Dronsky doesn't love him, or his intentions. He might well try to shop him.'

There was a pause, and Sir Patrick said, 'Very well. I accept your assessment, Neil.' He looked at Kenmare for confirmation, and Kenmare nodded. 'We'll play it absolutely straight, then. Now, as I said, let's tackle the mechanics.'

For the next hour or so they talked and argued, debated options, decided on tactics. It was useless to make hard and fast plans; there were too many inponderables. The best they could do was cover possible contingencies. Eventually they reached agreement.

As they rose and stretched themselves, Simon Mont said, 'There is another thing, sir. Who's to head the team? The operation's going to need someone in command on the spot.'

Without answering Sir Patrick continued on his way towards the cabinet where he kept the sherry. Mont's question was one he had hoped to avoid until he had a chance to discuss the point with John Kenmare. Now he would have to use all his tact. Mont might be the most brilliant member of his staff, but he was extremely prickly these days, heaven knew why.

Sir Patrick was a practised hand at this kind of diplomacy. He smiled from Mont to Kenmare, and waited.

John Kenmare responded quickly. 'Surely there's no problem. I shall only be involved as far as the aircraft. Simon's bringing him back. He's got to be in charge.'

'That seems reasonable.' Thinking what an excellent Director Kenmare would make when he himself had retired,

Sir Patrick was benign. 'What about it, Simon?'

'If it makes everyone happy, sir,' Mont said. He caught Neil Tarrent's eye and grinned.

SIX

The main conference had been planned to last for the inside of a week, after which detailed negotiations would be left to a series of working parties and committees, with instructions to report to a second plenary session in some months' time. By the Thursday evening, only one more day was left of the week, and the more important delegates, those whose time was said to be most precious, had already departed. So far no one had approached Neil Tarrent, and intimated that he was the would-be defector.

'What do we do if nothing happens?' Tarrent asked Mont. They were staying in a small hotel on the Avenue Kléber, and Tarrent, who had already bathed and changed for the evening, had come to Mont's room. They were due at an informal *vin d'honneur* that the French were giving at the Cercle Militaire for the more senior delegation members who were still in the city.

Simon Mont came out of his bathroom, naked except for a towel around his waist. He was a gaunt, slightly stooping figure and his hair, newly washed under the shower, was streaked with grey. He looked at least five years older than he was.

'What do we do, Neil? We go home and say we're sorry, but it was all "Much Ado About Nothing".'

'Don't use that damned expression. Please!'

Tarrent groaned, and grinned. On the first day of the conference he had bumped into one of the interpreters, who had slipped on the polished floor and fallen. Apologizing profusely, he had picked her up. She had told him not to worry, she was all right, it was all 'much ado about nothing'.

At the mention of the agreed recognition signal by which the unknown Russian was to identify himself, Tarrent had reacted automatically. 'I'm sorry. It was my fault. I was

65

dreaming – "A Midsummer Night's Dream".' The girl had looked at him oddly, nodded and hurried away.

Tarrent said, 'It's a pity that wretched girl wasn't Comrade X.'

'Not a chance, Neil. I told you. I did make a few tactful enquiries, and she's a Czech, not a Russian. It was just chance she used the phrase.'

'Well, she's the only one who has.' Tarrent was bitter. 'And if no one else volunteers, we're left with the question of those photocopies.'

'Which, hellish as it is, isn't our problem. Not at the moment, at any rate,' Mont said firmly. 'But cheer up, Neil, the meeting's not over yet. Let's get along to the *Cercle* and soak up some free champagne.'

It was a fine summer evening as they strolled gently up the Avenue towards the Etoile, looking for a taxi. Paris was at its best and the pleasant city life around them contrasted sharply with their private thoughts.

The Cercle Militaire is in the Place St Augustin. From the outside the building is not impressive. Inside, however, is a different matter. The club is a gilded haven. With its fine marble staircase, crimson carpets and draperies, statuary and splendid chandeliers, it speaks of opulence, privilege, security. The finest reception room is on the first floor.

Mont and Tarrent walked up the wide, shallow stairs side by side, and passed along the receiving line. However informal, no French official party was complete without one. Because they had had difficulty getting a taxi they were not among the first arrivals. About fifty guests were already present and stood in small groups, glasses in hand, pecking at smoked salmon and caviare amid a buzz of multi-lingual conversation.

They each took a glass of champagne from the tray offered to them, and moved further into the room. 'Good luck,' Mont murmured as they separated.'

Neil Tarrent wandered over to the buffet and helped himself to a savoury tartlet. Casually he glanced around him, noting the people who were there. No Russians were among them. It was usual on such occasions for the Russians to arrive together, and stay in pairs. Even the most senior always had an aide at his shoulder.

Kenmare, Mont and Tarrent had made it their business to know the entire Soviet delegation by name and by sight. What was more, they had pooled their impressions, and sent a short list of six candidates to London for comment. None of them, however, seemed particularly likely starters, and they had no favourite.

A French Army Commandant drifted towards Tarrent, and they chatted amiably about the quality of the champagne. Afterwards Tarrent circulated, making himself as obvious as possible to anyone who might be seeking him. By chance, as more guests arrived and groups formed and reformed, he found himself standing alone, but near a dark-haired, dark-eyed girl, whom he regarded with approval. When she gave him a small half-smile, he said, 'Forgive me staring. I was admiring your beautiful necklace.'

Because earlier he had been speaking French, Tarrent had continued in that language. Helen Kenmare sensed that his admiration was as much for herself as for her necklace, and stammered badly as she attempted a suitable reply.

'You're not French,' Tarrent said at once. 'You're American.'

'Yes, I'm a New Yorker.' Her smile was friendly. She was intrigued by his slight accent. 'Are you in the Embassy here? You sound a little American yourself when you're speaking English.'

'Oh no. That's my Scots blood. I'm at the British Embassy in Moscow. I'm just in Paris for the conference.'

'Moscow,' she said with interest. 'I'd love to go to Russia. But there are lots of places I'd like to go to, and I must admit that presently I'm very happy in Paris.'

They laughed together, and Tarrent looked at her appraisingly. He noticed her wedding-ring. The diamond necklace apart, her dress had that elegant simplicity that is always expensive. Which meant she was rich. But she wasn't at all blasé. There was an eagerness, an enthusiasm about her that wasn't often found among diplomats' wives – if that was what she was. It wasn't naïveté, but a sort of infectious verve that he remembered in the American girls he had known in Washington.

'Yes, Paris is a wonderful city,' he said. 'The most beautiful in the world, I think. Incidentally, my name's Neil Tarrent.'

'And mine's—'

'Helen Kenmare,' an amused voice said behind Tarrent. 'How nice you two have met. I should have introduced you earlier, Neil. Remiss of me.'

John Kenmare put his arm around his wife in a casual, possessive gesture and, for a split second, Neil Tarrent hated him. Not because of the girl. She meant nothing to him. He'd only just met her, and she was Mrs Kenmare. It was, he told himself, Kenmare's air of conscious superiority that riled.

He said, 'As so often, John, you're to be congratulated.'

'Thanks.' Kenmare grinned. 'Come along, darling. If you'll excuse us, Neil, there's someone Helen must meet.'

Neil Tarrent bowed. The Russian contingent, he saw, had arrived. They had passed along the receiving line and were mostly standing in a solid group, though some couples were moving through the room. He stayed where he was. He was luckily in a good position, easy to approach and not too conspicuous. He watched Helen Kenmare being introduced to an eminent nuclear physicist, and wondered why her husband had thought the introduction so essential.

'Good evening, Mr Tarrent. I've seen you in the distance in the last few days, and I told myself I must have the pleasure of meeting you again. This is hardly your line of country, is it? Or are you arranging another artistic triumph for us here in Paris?'

Neil Tarrent turned slowly towards Alexei Bonalov. He had been aware that Bonalov and his aide, Kerensky, were approaching, but he had expected them to ignore him or, at most, give him a casual greeting as they passed. Bonalov, however, was offering his hand.

'Good evening,' Tarrent said politely. He didn't bother to answer Bonalov's question or explain his presence. He could hardly tell the truth, and he saw no reason to lie. 'I hope you're enjoying Paris.'

'Very much, Mr Tarrent. I'll let you into a secret. French champagne is better than Russian.' Bonalov chuckled as if he considered this a great joke. Then he drained his glass and handed it to Kerensky, who stood somewhat nervously beside him. 'Go and get me some more, Oleg, there's a good fellow.'

As soon as Kerensky was out of earshot, Bonalov continued, 'As for the meetings, I find it difficult to take them very seriously. To me, they seem a lot of much ado about nothing. Don't you agree, Mr Tarrent?'

For a moment the words didn't register. Then Tarrent was suddenly alert. Christ! Bonalov! It couldn't be Bonalov – not a KGB Colonel of his seniority and position. It had to be another mistake. But this time the use of the phrase was no accident, for Bonalov, his brown eyes bright with amusement or malice, was repeating it.

'I said, Mr Tarrent, that to me these meetings seem like much ado about nothing.'

'I heard you, Mr Bonalov,' Tarrent was thankful he sounded so composed. His brain raced. Either Bonalov was the man, or the KGB had penetrated the operation and were planning to take advantage of it in some way. Instead of giving the agreed response immediately, he temporized. 'I was wondering what answer you expected from me,' he said.

'Oh, you mean you weren't really listening,' said Bonalov at once. 'You were dreaming – a midsummer night's dream, perhaps?'

'You – you surprise me, Mr Bonalov.'

'Do I indeed?' Bonalov gave him a long, hard stare. 'Mr Tarrent, if your people have been playing with me, I swear I'll use the documents you know I've got – and others you don't know of yet. You must know I can do it – and you must have considered the effects, for Britain, for France, for NATO.'

Tarrent nodded. He had made up his mind. Rather, he had no choice. Bonalov must be accepted at his face value – for the moment. 'You'll be welcomed, as we agreed, sir,' he said.

Alexei Bonalov smiled broadly at the 'sir'. 'That's better! I'm glad–'

'Comrade, your champagne—'

Bonalov swung round and, with a sweeping gesture of his hand, knocked aside the glass the unfortunate Kerensky was offering him, spilling its contents. 'Oleg, how clumsy of me!' he said. 'You'll have to get me another.'

Kerensky made no protest, but the look he gave his Colonel was neither respectful nor affectionate. Nevertheless, he went off obediently, and Bonalov turned again to Tarrent.

'We haven't much time,' he said urgently. 'Kerensky has been a big help to me, but I don't want him to know the final details. Luckily he flies back to Moscow in the morning, so he won't be involved. Now listen carefully—'

'Yes—'

'Tomorrow evening. Nine o'clock. I shall come out of my Embassy, turn right and walk along the rue de Grenelle. Your car will be a few yards round the corner in the rue du Bac, and you will be standing on the corner where I can see you. And once I reach you, Mr Tarrent, I am your responsibility. Please make sure there are no mistakes.'

With a casual nod, as if they had been discussing trivialities, Alexei Bonalov moved away. Despite his excitement Tarrent drained his glass with equal casualness, and picked another from a passing waiter's tray. His glance searched through the crowd for Mont and Kenmare. He saw Mont first, and made for him.

'Simon.'

'Hello, Neil.'

'Contact. He's made contact.'

Mont gave no sign that he had heard the half-breathed words, but introduced Tarrent to the group he was with, and continued chatting idly. In a few minutes he made an excuse, and strolled with Tarrent towards the main entrance to the room. When he heard the identity of the defector, his eyes merely widened.

'Aren't you astounded?' Tarrent asked.

'Yes. It had to be someone pretty senior, but Bonalov

70

would have been my last guess.' Mont seemed lost in thought. 'And the rendezvous is tomorrow. 'We'll have to get cracking. Neil, get hold of Kenmare and find out where his car's parked. Tell him to meet us there in ten minutes. We must let London know at once and activate the arrangements.' Abruptly he turned away towards the party's hosts.

Tarrent went in search of Kenmare, whom he found standing with Helen. He went up to them, and drew Kenmare aside, saying quietly but urgently, 'Simon and I need a lift to the Embassy, John. Can we meet at your car in ten minutes? Contact!' he added in a whisper.

'Who?' asked Kenmare at once.

'Bonalov.'

Kenmare's immediate reaction was quite different from Mont's. He drew a deep breath and swallowed hard. Tarrent was surprised.

It was Helen Kenmare who spoke first. She had caught only the first words of an apparently rather curt request for a lift, and she said, with a certain amount of tartness. 'You and your friend may have to wait a few minutes, Mr Tarrent. I'm not sure we're ready to leave yet.'

Tarrent's glance went to Kenmare, who by now had regained his composure. 'All right,' he said. 'The Jag's parked at the end of César-Caire, beside the church.'

'Thanks.'

'But, John, why—'

'Sorry, darling, I'll have to leave you.'

'Leave me? Now, you mean? Right here?'

'Yes. You can get a taxi back to the apartment.'

'But where are you going – the Embassy? Then why can't I come with you? We could drop off Mr Tarrent and Mr Mont, and go on home.'

'For God's sake, Helen, this is no time to start being difficult.' Kenmare spoke through his teeth, keeping his voice very low. 'Please. Do as I ask.'

Neil Tarrent didn't wait to hear the end of the argument. One glimpse of Helen's startled face had made it clear she wasn't used to being treated in such a cavalier fashion. But there was no doubt of the outcome. Whatever his wife want-

71

ed to do, Kenmare would be by his car in ten minutes. Tarrent went to report to Mont.

Fifteen minutes later, Mont said, 'Are you sure he understood, Neil?'

'Quite sure.'

'Then where the hell is he?'

Tarrent thought of saying, 'Finding his wife a taxi, probably,' but decided that such an answer would hardly be fair. In fact, he was as puzzled as Mont.

The two of them had found the Jaguar without difficulty, opposite the Church of St Augustin in Avenue César-Caire, just as Kenmare had described. But Kenmare was not there. They waited, Mont growing more and more annoyed.

'If he's not here in two minutes, we'll find a taxi and forget him, though I suppose we'll have to get hold of him later. What a bloody waste of time! Damn the man!'

From where he stood Tarrent couldn't see the entrance to the Cercle Militaire, and he let his gaze wander round the Place St Augustin. Suddenly he frowned and half-uttered an exclamation. He had seen someone crossing to one side of the statue of Jeanne d'Arc, someone whom he had instinctively taken to be John Kenmare, but— Anyway, whoever it was had disappeared behind a car.

'Here he comes. At last,' Mont said.

John Kenmare was approaching at a loping run on the near pavement. Either he had moved very quickly, Tarrent thought, or he himself had been mistaken.

'Terribly sorry,' Kenmare said, breathing hard. 'I got caught by that Soviet attaché – what's his name? Igor Gregorov – and I couldn't get away from him. He practically reproduced the speech his boss made at the meeting yesterday. I can't imagine—'

'Forget it,' Mont was abrupt. 'You're here now. Let's go. We can talk on the way.'

SEVEN

'The men are arriving at six-thirty, in about half an hour. We shall eat at seven,' Clara Kenmare was decisive. 'There'll be just the five of us, naturally.'

'Naturally,' Helen said.

She was still angry, partly with John, partly with herself. She had found no difficulty in getting a taxi the previous evening. Indeed, as she came out of the Cercle Militaire, one was drawing up in front of the entrance. But the driver, on purpose or otherwise, had misunderstood the address she gave him, and took her half way to Vincennes before she realized he was going in the wrong direction. During the altercation that followed, the black and white mongrel who sat in the front seat beside his master had growled fiercely and bared his teeth at her. Helen, none too fond of dogs, had been frankly scared.

Nor, on her eventual return to the apartment, had Clara shown much sympathy. According to her mother-in-law, Helen, after a year in Paris, should have been able to make herself understood by a taxi-driver. And, as for John leaving her at the party, John's work must always come first. If Helen didn't understand that, she had better ask her husband to explain.

But Helen had been given no chance to ask John anything. He had come home very late. She was in bed, though not asleep. She heard him go to say good night to his mother, as was usual, and waited expectantly. He was a long time with Clara, however, and when he finally did leave her and come to bed, his replies to her questions were monosyllabic, and he made it quite clear that all he wanted to do was sleep. In the morning, when Helen awoke, he had already left for his office.

'We'll leave them to have coffee at the table. Then they

73

can talk and we won't be in their way.' Clara Kenmare manoeuvred her chair across the room. 'I must go and consult with Anna. I said we'd have strawberries and cream, but I'm not sure the men don't need something more substantial.'

'You make it sound as if they were setting off on an expedition,' Helen said lightly.

Clara didn't answer, but turned her chair away. Helen looked hopelessly after her mother-in-law. John had warned her before they married that Clara was an autocratic old lady, used to getting her own way, used to being spoilt. What he hadn't mentioned was her possessiveness, which Helen resented because so often it made her feel cut off from her husband, as if she and not Clara were the odd one out.

She wandered over to the window and gazed across the road to the chestnut trees bordering the Bois de Boulogne. It was a lovely summer evening, typical of Paris at this time of year. It was wonderful being here – as she had told Neil Tarrent last night. He was an intriguing man, Tarrent, she thought, and attractive. She had warmed to him at once, and found it easy to laugh with him. It was a pity so many of the Kenmares' friends were such stuffed shirts.

Her reverie was disturbed by voices in the hall. John had arrived with his guests. She heard him introducing them to his mother, then he was in the room, ahead of the others. He held her tight, kissed her on the mouth, murmured, 'I've missed you, darling.' Moments later he was presenting Simon Mont and saying, 'You've already met Neil Tarrent.' The previous night might never have been.

They seated themselves and, when everyone had a drink, the conversation became general – the latest French scandal, Ascot, Wimbledon, Longchamp, what life in Russia was really like – but it was nervous and a little sporadic. Outwardly everyone seemed reasonably relaxed, but Helen sensed a curious tension. She didn't understand it, and it made her uneasy. Even Clara appeared to be affected. It was a relief when Anna announced that dinner was served.

As always in the Kenmare household, the food was excellent – a cold soup, poached salmon, green vegetables, cheese, chocolate soufflé or strawberries. The men ate well. To her surprise, Helen, who normally had a healthy appetite, did not feel hungry. She drank rather more than usual. Everyone else, she noticed, was very abstemious, apparently content with only one glass of wine each.

'That was a superb meal, Lady Kenmare,' Simon Mont said. 'Thank you.' His smile included Helen.

'It's Anna you should thank,' Clara corrected him. 'I choose the menus, but she does all the shopping and cooking. Helen doesn't speak French,' she added gratuitously, 'so she can't really help a great deal.'

It was a most annoying remark, and quite untrue – in fact, she was never given a chance to help – but normally Helen would not have allowed herself to be provoked by it. Tonight, however, either because of the amount of wine she had drunk or because of the general air of tension that surrounded the dinner-party, she refused to let it pass.

She said sharply, 'As a matter of fact, I'm an excellent cook. If you were at all interested in what I can or cannot do, Clara, you might have discovered that.'

A brief but embarrassed silence followed. It was broken by Simon Mont. 'My wife's an excellent cook,' he said, 'but she always complains I'm a poor advertisement for her. However much I eat I never get any fatter. The children are the same.'

'It's a question of genes, isn't it? Nothing one can do about it.' John Kenmare dismissed the subject. 'Mother, if we might have coffee? In here, I think. There are a few things we have to discuss.'

'Of course, dear. I'll tell Anna.' Clara moved back her chair and everyone rose. 'Perhaps I'd better wish our guests good night now.' She smiled at Mont and Tarrent and, ignoring Helen, wheeled herself off to the kitchen. Helen, her anger subsiding as quickly as it had flamed, also smiled round the table, and went along to her bedroom. Though she regretted her outburst, she had no intention of apologizing for it, but she felt on edge and in need of reassurance.

It was not very long before she heard the men come out of the dining-room. She gave them a minute or two, then went

75

into the corridor, rather tentatively. She wanted to see John, but alone, without his mother. Instead, she found herself confronting Neil Tarrent.

'Goodbye,' he said. He took the hand which without thinking she had offered to him, and held it. His eyes met hers. 'Don't worry,' he added gently. 'It's not a bit necessary. John'll be home tonight.

Helen stared at him. She had no idea what he was talking about. Why should she worry about John? And of course he would be at home. Here he was, right now. She would ask him. She retrieved her hand from Neil Tarrent's grip.

'Darling,' John Kenmare said. 'I shall probably be late. Don't wait up for me.'

'You're going out?'

'Yes, we have a meeting.'

'But you'll be back tonight?'

'Yes. Why ever not? But late, as I said.' He kissed her. 'I won't disturb you.'

'It doesn't matter. However late, I'll be waiting.'

'All right. That's a promise.'

He kissed her again, and was gone, with his two colleagues. Thoughtfully, Helen returned to their room. She could still feel the pressure of his fingers on her bare shoulders and, when she looked in the glass, she could see the marks they had left. He had gripped her hard, and somehow she knew then that it wasn't all her imagination. Something out of the way had happened, or was about to happen – something to be feared. And she made up her mind that when John got home that night, however late he might be, she would make him tell her about it. She had an unhappy feeling that Clara already knew.

It was still light at a few minutes to nine, when John Kenmare parked his grey Jaguar in the rue du Bac, around the corner from the Soviet Embassy. Sitting in the back of the car, Tarrent was outwardly calm, but he was aware of his quickened pulse. He only half listened to Kenmare and Mont chatting in front of him. He knew their conversation was irrelevant, that they were only talking to ease their nerves.

'. . . beautiful,' he heard Mont say. 'The high cheekbones and those great sunken eyes. She can afford to wear her hair in that severe ballerina style.' Tarrent realized they were speaking of Clara Kenmare. 'You know,' went on Mont, 'my mother once saw her dance with Anton Dolin in *Spectre de la Rose.*'

'Really? At Covent Garden?'

'Yes, in 1939, shortly before she went to the States. John, what really happened? How was she hurt?'

'It was a freak accident. Her partner dropped her during a performance of *Sylphides*, and she injured her spine. The dreadful thing was it could have been avoided. The boy wasn't up to the part. He nearly dropped her in rehearsal and she complained, but no one paid any attention.'

'Tragic! Tragic. And then she married General Sir Peter Kenmare, VC, DSO, etc. That must have been some compensation.'

'Oh yes. She shared in my father's military and political career as much as she was able, and she was a great help to him. But of course it's years since he died.'

Simon Mont thought of his own parents and their dull, uneventful lives. Then he turned round in his seat. 'One minute to go, Neil.'

Neil Tarrent's hand was already on the door handle. He got out of the Jaguar and walked back to the corner. There was a fair amount of traffic, but few pedestrians. Tarrent waited, and suddenly he felt very vulnerable.

His eyes went to his watch. Three minutes past nine. When he glanced up again Alexei Bonalov was striding towards him. Bonalov walked fast, but without great hurry. He carried a small black attaché case. Immediately Tarrent glanced around, but everything in the vicinity seemed normal. The French police guarding the entrance to the Embassy were paying no attention, and there was no sign of any danger. He grinned. The prize was within their grasp. Unbelievably, Colonel Alexei Bonalov of the KGB was coming over to the West, to the British. Though they had been suspecting every kind of trap, everything seemed simple and straightforward.

Too simple?

Bonalov was no more tha ten yards from the corner when two men, one big, the other of medium build, dashed out of the Embassy. Tarrent had a vague impression that the big man was familiar, but there was no time to think about it. As if alerted by some sixth sense, Bonalov started to run. Simultaneously, Tarrent signalled urgently to the car, which backed up across the corner.

At first it looked as if it was going to be a very near thing. Tarrent grabbed the car door that Mont had opened, and held it ready. His object was to bundle Bonalov safely inside, even if he himself were left on the pavement. But Bonalov's attaché case hampered him, and the situation was only saved by the behaviour of the other two Russians. They seemed to take no advantage of the delay, but to hesitate as if at a loss, not quite knowing what to do. As he followed Bonalov into the Jaguar, Tarrent saw them both stop dead. Then the big man hurried back to his Embassy, while the other just stood, watching.

Tarrent heaved a sigh of relief as the Jaguar accelerated into the traffic. They'd made it. Bonalov was theirs. It was a moment of triumph.

Simon Mont was not so sanguine. As soon as their car had backed to the corner, he and Kenmare had been able to see what was happening in the rue de Grenelle. Now he turned in his seat and regarded Bonalov coldly.

But it was Bonalov who spoke first. 'So these are your colleagues, are they, Mr Tarrent?'

'Yes,' said Tarrent. 'I expect you know them from the conference – Simon Mont and John Kenmare.'

Kenmare was concentrating on the one-way streets in order to reach the Boulevard Raspail as soon as possible, and Mont made no direct response. Instead he said, 'What happened, Colonel?' It was a short, sharp question.

'I don't know. Someone must have become suspicious. They were watching me very closely. But it was my only chance. I knew that if I didn't come now, I would have no other opportunity.'

Mont said, 'If your people had been more efficient . . .'

'I know.' Bonalov looked at Tarrent regretfully. 'I'm sorry,' he said. 'It seems to me that you may have been in some danger. This is not a good beginning, but it is not my fault.'

Tarrent nodded. Scrambling into the car he had bruised his knee, and there was a triangular tear in his right trouser leg. But that was all. It was unimportant against the prize of Alexei Bonalov. He stared at the black attaché case that lay between them on the car floor.

There was no more talk for some time. Kenmare drove steadily and as fast as was possible in the city. They crossed the Seine by the Pont Royal and headed generally north-west. They had been driving for more than half an hour and were well beyond the Périphérique when Mont started looking anxiously in the rear-view mirror.

'What the hell's the matter?' said Kenmare irritably.

'I'm not sure, but I think we've got a tail.'

Tarrent twisted in his seat and gazed out of the window. There was a thin stream of traffic behind them, mostly cars, with the occasional van and motor-bike. He watched it carefully for a minute. The volume was small, but it wasn't easy to tell if they were being followed.

'Which one, Simon?'

'A big Renault, Neil, light blue. We picked it up on the Boulevard Malesherbes, and it's been with us ever since.'

'The police?' asked Kenmare.

Mont said, 'I don't see why. One thing's for certain – the Russians won't have made a complaint – not yet, anyway. It's a pity we couldn't have picked up the Colonel round the corner out of sight of his Embassy, but anyway the whole thing happened so fast the police on duty didn't seem to react. It could be an unmarked DST car, I suppose, but I doubt it.' He looked at Bonalov. 'No. If it's anyone, it's your friends, Colonel.'

Kenmare grunted. 'What do you want me to do?'

'Nothing. There's nothing to be done at the moment.'

'Then for God's sake stop playing with my driving mirror. You'll make me have an accident.'·

Mont muttered something that Tarrent didn't catch, but he didn't touch the mirror again. Kenmare's nerves were obviously raw, and there was no point in exacerbating them further. Tarrent continued to keep watch from the rear window and, from time to time, he reported on the blue Renault, which kept a steady distance behind them.

Alexei Bonalov had reacted anxiously to the possibility of a tail, and he too kept peering back at the road unwinding beneath the Jaguar's wheels. Tarrent felt a certain sympathy for him.

'We turn off in a couple of kilometres,' he said. 'We'll know better then. If he turns too, he's probably a tail.'

'Where are you taking me?' Bonalov demanded. 'To an airport?'

'Not exactly. We've laid on a private—'

Mont cut Tarrent short. 'Colonel Bonalov, there's no need for you to worry, or concern yourself with details. You're in our hands, and we're responsible for your safety, as you requested. Everything's been carefully planned, and I assure you you'll be in the UK tonight.'

'Good. I'm delighted to hear it.' Bonalov glared at the back of Mont's head. 'I hope your plans include the present situation. As you say, I'm your responsibility.'

Mont said, 'As we understood it, Colonel, you were to leave the Embassy unobserved. You made no mention of the possibility of such immediate action on your countryman's part.'

'I agree, Mr Mont. It was unfortunate my Embassy were so suspicious of me, but it seeme to me surprising that they have managed to follow us so quickly and so efficiently.'

'We're not sure it is a tail, not yet.'

They were slowing for the turn, and Tarrent said, 'I think we are. Yes,' he added, 'they're turning too. They're still with us.'

Mont swore, and turned to Kenmare. 'Okay,' he said 'Remember our dry runs? You know what to do.'

John Kenmare didn't answer immediately. There was a certain amount of local traffic on the road, and it wasn't easy to maintain a reasonable speed. Even a minor traffic accident would be a disaster.

A moment later, as the silence lengthened, Mont turned sharply to Kenmare. 'Did you hear me?' he asked. 'We've got to get off this road, as we planned. You remember the turning?'

'All right, all right. Keep your hair on,' Kenmare said finally. 'It's not yet. They can't make a move here; it's too populated. And you know the problem, Simon. The track's not far from our rendezvous with Peterson.'

Mont said, 'I know, but there's no alternative. We'll go ahead.'

Bonalov had been listening intently to this exchange. Suddenly he intervened. 'What do you intend? To turn off on some farm track? What if the Renault's too close? What if they see? We'll be worse off on some isolated lane. We should have—'

'Colonel Bonalov, I told you before. You've no need to worry.'

'And I don't believe you, Mr Mont. I think I've every reason to worry.' Bonalov was getting angry. 'Mr Mont, if you allow me to be recaptured, all that will happen to you is that you'll – you'll – What is the expression you use, when you do badly?'

'Put up a black,' Tarrent murmured.

'Yes. Thank you. As Mr Tarrent says, all that will happen to you, Mr Mont, is that you will put up a black. But what do you think will happen to me? I am the one who will be taken back to Moscow and thrown into the Lubyanka. If I survive that, which is quite unlikely, I am the one who will be consigned to a mental hospital for the rest of my days! Not you, Mr Mont! Nor any of your comrades! You'll be having your eggs and bacon every morning as usual.'

Alexei Bonalov ended his tirade with a snort of disgust and, except for the purr of the Jag's engine and the swish of its tyres, there was silence. No one attempted to refute his comments. How could they? Bonalov wound down his side window as if in need of air and the rush of wind was added to the other sounds, but no one objected. They were six or seven

81

kilometres further along the road before anyone spoke again.

'We're getting near,' John Kenmare said.

'So is the Renault,' Bonalov said quickly. 'They're gaining on us.'

'That's the idea, Colonel. We don't want to lose them till the right moment. As soon as we reach a straight stretch through the forest ahead I'll accelerate.' Kenmare hooted as he passed a small car. 'Around the next corner, and you'll see.'

With a roar, the Jaguar leapt forward. The needle on the speedometer crept higher and higher. Seventy. Eighty. Ninety. They were doing well over the ton when Kenmare began to brake. As they burst from the shadow of the pines into the last of the daylight and faced a series of S-bends, Bonalov shut his eyes tightly. What a damned stupid way to die, he thought.

But they had achieved their purpose. The Renault, taken by surprise at the sudden change of pace, had dwindled to a dot behind them before, screaming into the first curve, they lost it completely. Five hundred metres beyond the S-bends Kenmare suddenly shouted, 'Hang on!', and swung the Jaguar in a tight right-hand turn into a narrow lane.

The lane was gloomy between high banks, but it was still just possible to drive without lights. It climbed steeply until it became little more than a rutted track. Progress was inevitably and agonizingly slow. Finally, in the shelter of some trees, they halted.

'Why have we stopped?' Bonalov asked immediately.

'Because it's open country further on,' Kenmare said. 'This track winds around the side of a hill, but the hill's bare and it's not so dark that someone looking up wouldn't spot us from below. We must wait.'

'But not too long, John,' Mont was gazing anxiously behind them. 'They'll soon realize they've lost us, and they might come back. If they do, this track's unmistakable. Neil, get out and have a quick look.'

Obediently Neil Tarrent got out of the car and glanced about him in the gathering dusk. He needed something to give himself height. He didn't propose to climb a tree, but some fifteen yards off to the left was an outcrop of rock. As he picked his way across to it, he thought he heard a car revving its engine, somewhere along the road below. He broke into a run and hauled himself up to the top of the outcrop. He could see nothing. There was no sign of the Renault. He was turning away in relief when a shaft of brightness, a reflection on chrome perhaps, caught his eye. At the same moment he heard a car engine straining.

Christ! The Renault was climbing the hill almost directly beneath him. No wonder he hadn't seen it. The Russians hadn't been deceived. They had followed the Jaguar up the lane, and were scarcely more than two hundred yards behind, the high banks deadening the sound of their approach.

As the thoughts tumbled through his head, Tarrent was sliding down the rock and racing back to the Jaguar. He flung himself into the car.

'For God's sake get going! They're right behind!'

Kenmare's reactions were quick, but somehow luck was against them. He stalled the engine, and by the time the Jaguar spurted away, the Renault was already in sight. Bonalov groaned aloud.

There was no question but that John Kenmare did his best. His driving was superb as they snaked up the hill on the corniche-like track with a sharp drop to the right. But the driver of the Renault was equally good, and by now the distance between the two cars was diminishing. Yet the Russians were frustrated; there was very little they could do. The track was too narrow for them to overtake the Jaguar and try to force it off the road and over the edge. Ramming from the rear was a possibility, Tarrent thought, but if Kenmare could only keep ahead until they joined the upper road, they might somehow regain the advantage they had at present lost.

The Russians in the Renault had other ideas, however. There was a loud crack as a bullet ricocheted off the Jaguar.

'Get down,' Mont shouted. Rashly he poked his head out of the window. 'They're probably aiming for the tyres.'

The next few minutes were confused and shocking.

Almost before Mont shouted, Tarrent had wrestled Bonalov to the comparative safety of the car floor. But crouching beside him he could see nothing and, more curious than afraid, he raised himself carefully to look out of the rear window.

The Renault was so close that he could see quite clearly there were two men in it. Behind the tinted windscreen the driver was merely a blur but, as the cars swayed in opposite directions, each fighting to hold the road, the big man firing at the Jaguar was plainly visible. Seen clearly, even in the gathering dusk, that square face and those massive shoulders were unmistakable. The last time Neil had seen him – and spoken to him – had been in the steam room of the *banya* in Moscow.

Slithering back to the floor as Mont again shouted to him to get down, Tarrent was aware that Bonalov was taking a hand in the game. For once, Tarrent was slow to react. It was something he was later to regret bitterly. Before anyone was able to stop him, Alexei Bonalov had leant out of his window, taken aim at the Renault's driver and fired.

Everything happened at once. Either the driver had been hit or his shattered windscreen had momentarily blinded him, for he drove the Renault straight off the road. But, as the car went over the edge in a kind of slow-motion dive, the big man continued to shoot wildly at the Jaguar. There was a sound of rending metal and breaking glass. Lying half on top of Bonalov, Tarrent felt splinters raining down on them. Then the Jaguar slewed sideways and rammed the hillside.

For a moment no one in the Jaguar moved, though the engine died as Kenmare switched off the ignition. What filled the air was the horrendous noise of the Renault being torn apart as it bounced down among the rocks below. Quickly this receded and ceased. In the dead silence that followed Kenmare got out on to the road. Cautiously he opened the rear door nearest to him.

'Careful,' he said. 'We've got a wheel over the edge. We're quite stable, but we don't want to follow that Renault.' His voice was surprisingly steady.

Bonalov crawled out first, still holding his pistol. Tarrent followed him. Apart from some bruises and a few nicks from slivers of glass, they were unharmed. Without speaking, Bonalov handed his gun to Tarrent, and stooped inside the car to retrieve his attaché case. Straightening himself, he said, 'I'm afraid Mr Mont has been injured.'

'What?' From where he stood, Tarrent couldn't see into the front of the car.

Kenmare leant inside and gently shook Mont by the shoulder. 'Damn! I think he's concussed. He must have hit his head.'

'Hell! What a mess! Why on earth did you go into the side?'

'There were distractions, my dear Neil.' Kenmare's sarcasm was heavy. 'I might ask you why you let Colonel Bonalov shoot up the Renault.'

'Yes.' Tarrent acknowledged the justice of the remark. 'I should have searched him for weapons. Sorry.'

'Okay. Let's get Simon out of there and see how much damage had been done. It's not going to be very easy.'

'Wait! Wait!'

The interruption came from Bonalov. If the Englishmen had temporarily forgotten their enemies in the Renault, the KGB Colonel hadn't. He was standing on the edge of the track, pointing down the hill. In the half darkness bits of metal, wheels, a whole car door could faintly be seen. The shattered remains of the Renault itself lay, a black shape, some way further down, smoke wreathing from it.

As they watched flames flowered among the smoke. They heard a dull thud, then a great roar. The petrol tank had gone up, the fire was devouring the car – and its occupants. Tarrent turned away, nauseated by the sight and mindful of Simon Mont, but Bonalov was still intent.

'Look!' he cried. 'Look! Over there.'

Following Bonalov's pointing finger, they saw where the falling Renault had spewed out the big Russian. He lay spreadeagled on a rock. And in the light of the fire he seemed to move. It was possible he was still alive.

EIGHT

For a man in his fifties Alexei Bonalov moved with surprising speed. He had lowered himself over the edge and was sliding and slithering down the side of the hill before either Kenmare or Tarrent had thought to stop him.

'Blast the chap! What the hell's he up to? Get after him, Neil.' Kenmare swore. 'And do your best to neutralize the Russians while you're down there. Find their weapons if you can.'

'What if either of them's still alive?'

Kenmare didn't answer. He merely looked at Bonalov's pistol, which Tarrent was still clutching. Tarrent hesitated. He had no wish to kill an injured man – KGB or otherwise.

'Hurry!' Kenmare said. 'That fire won't go unnoticed for ever, so we'd better get out of here pretty quickly. I'll see what I can do for Simon.'

Tarrent copied Alexei Bonalov and slid down the hillside, mostly on his behind. It was a painful process, but fast. He reached Bonalov within seconds, and found the Colonel leaning over the big Russian, holding the man's head up by the hair. The back of the skull was a bloody mass of bone and brain.

'Yevgeny Zourenko, and very truly dead. It was only the flicker of flames that made him seem to move.' Bonalov let the head drop and, quite unmoved, wiped his hand on the grass. 'KGB, of course. He used to work for me once.'

Tarrent swallowed the bile that threatened to rise in his throat. He was relieved that Zourenko was dead, and thus presented no problem, but he hoped that Bonalov was telling the truth. There hadn't been much time, but enough – Bonalov could readily have lifted the unconscious Zourenko's head and crushed it on the rock.

Tarrent picked up the automatic that lay beside the big

86

man's body. Swiftly he went through his pockets. He took wallet and keys, but left the watch, an expensive Swiss make, and the loose change. It was impossible to strip the Russian completely and sooner or later he would be identified, but even a brief delay might prove an advantage.

'The other one's still in the car, which saves us some trouble,' Bonalov said.

From where he stood Tarrent could feel the heat from the burning wreck. At present he couldn't get any closer, and he couldn't afford to wait. Besides, Bonalov was right. There wouldn't be much to identify in what remained of the Renault.

Bonalov said, 'I'm not sure, but I'd guess the driver was Andrei Kharkov. He was excellent at the wheel, and he was Zourenko's sidekick.'

'Is that why you came down here?' Tarrent couldn't resist the question. 'To see who they were?'

'Yes. Naturally. It's important to know who your enemies are, Mr Tarrent. Those who seem to be your friends are not invariably so. Remember that. It's good advice.' He waved a hand between the blackened flame-licked hulk of the Renault and the sprawling body of Yevgeny Zourenko. 'These two don't matter. They just obeyed orders. But I can tell you who gave those orders.'

'Later,' said Tarrent. 'We'll go into all that later. The first thing is to get back to the others. We've wasted enough time already.'

The climb up to the track was more difficult than the slide down. The side of the hill was steep and potted with holes – perfect traps for an ankle or a leg. The rocky outcrops were slippery with lichen and best avoided, Tarrent soon discovered. So were what seemed to be sandy patches that offered neither foot- nor hand-hold. Nor was the rising moon of assistance. It merely made the darkling shadows appear what they were not.

Tarrent's main problem, however, was Alexei Bonalov. Bonalov was in good physical shape, but he was no longer a young man. As he lagged further and further behind, Tarrent was forced to return and help him. It was a short but hard haul.

87

'For God's sake, hurry up.' Kneeling on the verge, Kenmare gave a hand to pull each of them up and over the edge.

'Simon?' Tarrent asked.

'He's hurt.' Kenmare nodded to where Simon Mont sat, propped against the side of the car. 'He won't be able to walk. We'll have to carry him, Neil, you and I. It must have been a fluke, but that bugger sliced his side with a bullet.'

'God!' Tarrent was across the track and crouching beside Mont. 'How are you, Simon? This is a bloody stupid thing to have happen.'

Simon Mont managed to grin. 'I'll survive.' He seemed to be having some difficulty breathing. 'Neil, get Bonalov away – now – before the authorities arrive. Otherwise, the *Direction de la surveillance du territoire* – our DST chums – they'll get their hands on him.'

'What about you?' Tarrent could see the pallor of Mont's skin and the perspiration on his upper lip. 'We can carry you, but—'

'Yes. Just hurry. I'll be okay.'

Tarrent turned back to Kenmare, who was engaged in an argument with Bonalov. 'John, I'm not sure about Simon. Must we take him?'

'Yes. There's no option.' Kenmare was brisk. 'We can't leave him here and the Jag's useless. I've done the best to clean our prints off it. I'll have to say it was stolen. Which is why, if that story's to have any credibility at all, Colonel Bonalov must carry your two bags, whatever his objections.'

'All right, Mr Kenmare. All right. But it won't be easy with my own heavy case.' Shrugging angrily, Bonalov picked up the baggage and began to hump it up the track, not waiting for the others.

Kenmare looked after him venomously for a moment, then turned to Tarrent. 'And them?' He pointed down the hill.

'Dead. The big man was thrown out and killed. I got his gun and took what I could off him. The other burnt up with the car. Bonalov identified them both as KGB.'

'Fair enough. Now let's shove the Jag over the edge and go. With any luck it'll burn too and cause more confusion.'

Little effort was required to send the Jaguar crashing down the hillside. It was more difficult to lift Simon Mont and arrange him on a three-handed seat that Kenmare and Tarrent formed by gripping each other's wrists, with Tarrent's free arm supporting the injured man's back. But Mont was able to give them some help and, fortunately, though tall he was very thin and light. Nevertheless, it was no easy matter to carry him on the rough track.

By the time they reached the point where the track ran into a minor road, Kenmare and Tarrent were breathing hard and in need of a pause. But the sight of Bonalov, sitting indolently on the bags, awaiting the rest of the party, seemed to infuriate Kenmare.

'I could kill the bastard,' he muttered, loud enough for Mont to hear and make him twist a grimace of pain into a half-smile. 'Not after all this trouble, surely,' he said.

Kenmare made no response. He was wondering what the hell they would do if the aircraft wasn't there, if Peterson had decided they weren't coming. Mont clearly needed medical attention – attention he couldn't get in France, where too many questions would be asked about bullet wounds. And Bonalov wasn't to be trusted an inch. Nor possibly was Tarrent, though for different reasons; he'd be inclined to put Mont's well-being before anything else. Kenmare swore to himself. He'd done everything he possibly could, and this was the result – a complete balls-up. It could be the end of all his hopes, all his ambitions.

'What?' said Kenmare. Tarrent had interrupted his thoughts.

'How much further?'

Kenmare glanced about him. The moon was high in the sky and very bright. That was a blessing. There would be no problem with the take-off – as long as Peterson had waited.

'A hundred yards or so,' he said. 'Round the next bend. There are some big gates. And let's go. Come on, Colonel,' he added. 'Pick up those bags. If the plane leaves without us, the French Government'll soon be sending you back to your chums in Moscow.'

Bonalov shrugged again, but did as he was told. The small

89

procession set off down the road, moving more rapidly now, though Tarrent's arms felt as if they were being pulled out of their sockets. The sight of a pair of iron gates, set in a high stone wall bordering one side of the road, came as an enormous relief.

They were handsome gates, finely wrought, with the design of a peacock carved into the stone pillars that supported them. They were crowned with the coat-of-arms of the de Noirmont family. For security reasons it had been decided earlier that every effort should be made to prevent Bonalov learning the route by which he was leaving France, but such precautions were no longer possible. In fact, he reached the gates first and, after inspecting them carefully, shook them hard.

'They're locked,' he said. 'What do we do, gentlemen?'

'I've got a key,' Simon gasped.

Between them, Kenmare and Tarrent lowered Mont to the grass beside the road. Mont was barely conscious; his eyes were bright and glittering feverishly, and in the moonlight his skin had a greyish sheen. Kenmare supported him, while Tarrent felt in his inside pocket for the key. When Tarrent withdrew his hand it was warm and sticky with dark blood.

'God!' Tarrent swore. 'John, you just said he was hit in the side. I thought it was a flesh wound, but—What did you do for him? Or were you too busy cleaning the Jag to do anything?'

'What could I do? I found a shirt in one of the bags and bandaged him as tight as I could.' Kenmare controlled his temper and spoke almost pleadingly. 'Neil, be reasonable. Whatever his condition, we had to move him. And there was no point in worrying you – or him. Now we're only wasting time. Come on and get these damned gates open.'

It was a sensible remark, and Tarrent responded. But his brain was racing. If Simon was really seriously hurt, and assuming Peterson was still waiting for them, it was a choice of evils. They could take Simon back to the UK, though they had no way of knowing if he was fit to travel. Or they could leave him at the château. The Comte, whose love of

90

England had even extended to an English-born wife, would look after him, arrange for a doctor – and make sure the doctor kept his mouth shut.

By this time the gates were open and they were making their way up a narrow, tree-lined drive. This forked to the left and brought them unexpectedly to flat open ground. There, on the grass runway, sat a Piper Aztec, not far from the hangar in which the Comte kept his own private plane. Bill Peterson, contentedly smoking his pipe, sat with his back against the hangar wall. Tarrent could smell the scent of his tobacco on the night air as Peterson got to his feet and loped towards them.

'Hi! I thought you were never coming.' Peterson was a tall, angular man who still retained traces of his native Australian accent after twenty years in Britain. 'What kept you?'

'Trouble,' Kenmare said, helping Tarrent to set Mont down on the grass.

'One of you hurt?' Peterson took in the situation. 'Bad show. But you're here now. Let's go.'

'Just a minute.' Tarrent spoke quickly. 'How do we know Simon's fit to travel. Maybe we should take him to the house.'

'Hang on! The family aren't there. Some relation of the Countess died and they've all gone off to the funeral.' Peterson tapped out his pipe on the sole of his shoe and carefully extinguished the ashes on the ground. 'No one's there, except servants – French servants. They were given orders about me, but I don't know what they'd say about him.'

'Well, that solves that.' Kenmare was positive. 'Without the family it's too much of a risk. Simon comes with us.'

'But—' Tarrent felt Mont's fingers tighten round his ankle and bent down to him. 'Simon?'

'Take me, Neil. Please. Better off at home.'

Tarrent hesitated. 'Okay. Anyway, with any luck the worst's over. The rest of the trip shouldn't be too bad.' He forced himself to smile and stood up. 'He wants to go with us.'

'Great,' Peterson said. 'Now, I don't want to hurry you

91

guys, but we don't have all night.'

'That is our aircraft?'

It was the first time Bonalov had spoken since they'd entered the de Noirmont estate, and Peterson gave him an unfriendly stare before he nodded. Bonalov promptly picked up his attaché case, made a gesture towards the two other bags and, leaving them, walked off towards the plane. Peterson looked after him.

'Is that the bastard you've collected?' he asked.

'Yes,' Kenmare said shortly as, with Tarrent, he once more lifted Mont. 'The bags. Would you mind?'

'Surely not. I only hope the b's worth all this.'

He hoisted the bags as if they weighed nothing, and strode off after Bonalov. In spite of his concern for Mont, Tarrent found himself grinning. He too hoped the Russian would prove his worth.

'I'm coming to the UK with you,' Kenmare said suddenly. 'Without the Jag I've no means of getting back to Paris, and anyway you'll need me when you land. You can't cope with both Simon and Bonalov.'

Tarrent didn't argue. He had assumed that Kenmare, having seen them safely on to the plane, would find his way to a major road and hitch a ride. There would be plenty of trucks going through to Paris at this time of night. But, if Kenmare preferred to go to England, it was up to him. Tarrent wasn't going to object to the change in plan. It would certainly make things easier. Fleetingly he thought of Helen Kenmare, waiting for her husband.

They reached the aircraft. Bonalov was already seated and strapping himself in. His precious attaché case was at his feet, the two bags stowed behind him. Peterson was standing by the door on the wing. With Kenmare and Tarrent supporting him from the rear, and Peterson pulling from above, Mont was somehow helped to scramble into a seat. But the effort was almost too much for him. His head sagged on his chest and a thin dribble of liquid streaked with blood escaped from the corner of his mouth.

Appalled, Tarrent did up Mont's seat-belt and wiped his face. He felt a little sick himself. He put an arm around

Mont's shoulders and tried to support him.

They were all in the aircraft now, the door shut. Peterson started first one engine, then the other. He taxied to the end of the grass strip and turned into the wind. The moon gave plenty of light, and there was no difficulty about take-off. Peterson said something to Kenmare, who shouted over his shoulder.

'Peterson says he's sorry, but it may be a rough trip. Until we're out over the Channel he'll have to fly low to keep under French radar cover. Once we're clear of the coast we'll be okay – we're expected the other side – but before that it'll be bumpy. So, hold on.'

It was easier said than done. The Piper seemed to have a life of its own. It rose and fell like a leaf in the wind, skimming the dark hedgerows, just clearing a belt of trees, diving into a shadowy valley. It was an exciting but uncertain passage. Occasionally the aircraft juddered fiercely, as if trying to shake itself to bits. Sometimes, for short periods, it flew level and true.

Bill Peterson was in control and there was no real danger, but there was little that could be done for the passengers. Beside him, Kenmare sat brooding, apparently unaffected by the motion. In the seats behind, Tarrent struggled to protect Mont, who had lost consciousness. Held only by his safety-belt, he swayed helplessly around. Fully occupied with doing what he could for Mont, Tarrent had no time to think of himself. Once or twice he heard Bonalov retching drily behind him, but he felt no sympathy. In fact, the Russian, overcome by the turbulence, was wishing himself home in Moscow.

Eventually, their passage became easier. Peterson lifted the nose of the plane and, from a few feet above the level of the waves, they climbed into the sky. Soon they were over the English coast, Peterson making his radio contact.

'Won't be long now,' Kenmare said over his shoulder. 'How's Simon?'

Tarrent didn't answer at once. For the umpteenth time he had wiped Mont's face. A couple of soiled handkerchiefs were already on the floor, and the one he was using was wet

93

and blood-stained. Suddenly Mont's eyes opened. For a moment they gazed into Tarrent's, appealingly, hopelessly. Then they clouded over. A trickle of red blood from the corner of Mont's mouth grew to a stream. It poured over Tarrent's hands, hot and thin, and he stared at it in disbelief.

Kenmare repeated his question, turning in his seat in an attempt to see what was happening. Tarrent was blocking his view. 'How's Simon?'

'Simon—' Neil Tarrent cleared his throat, but when he spoke his voice was perfectly steady. 'Simon,' he said. 'I think he just died.'

NINE

Fifteen minutes later the Piper Aztec made a perfect landing, and taxied to the end of a little-used runway at an RAF base in southern England. Almost before John Kenmare could undo his safety-belt and open the aircraft's door, a large black saloon car drew up beside it and a Squadron Leader got out. The car was closely followed by a Land Rover, driven by a Flight Lieutenant. The two officers saluted as Kenmare jumped down and offered them his hand.

'Good evening, sir. You're a bit later than we expected.'

'Does that matter?'

The sharp retort startled the Squadron Leader, who had only been making polite noises. 'Not at all, sir. Here's your car,' he added hurriedly. 'The tank's full, of course. And there's some coffee and sandwiches on the back seat.'

'Very considerate of you. Thanks.'

'If there's anything else we can do—'

Kenmare was peering through the car's windows. He could see a folded rug inside. Good. They would be able to wrap up Mont's body and put it in the boot. But first he had to get rid of the two RAF officers.

'No. Nothing. The plane will be taking off as soon as we've unloaded. The pilot's in touch with your control tower. A matter of minutes,' Kenmare said authoritatively. 'How do we get off the base?'

'Over there and then turn right.' The Squadron Leader pointed. 'But we'll show you, sir.'

'No need. Just make sure we're cleared with your guard house. Then go to bed or whatever you do here at this time of night. And thanks again.'

The Squadron Leader hesitated and glanced at the aircraft. The door was wide open, but no one else had attempted to get out. And no one was going to, he thought wryly, while the RAF was around. 'Very good, sir,' he said, and turned away to the Land Rover.

Kenmare collected the rug and climbed back into the Aztec. 'Right!' he said.

It was the only word that was spoken for several minutes. In the limited space of the little aircraft Simon Mont's body was, with difficulty, wrapped in the rug. With even greater effort, it was lowered to the ground and arranged in the boot of the car. Alexei Bonalov got somewhat shakily into the back seat. He was still feeling sick, but he grimly clutched his attaché case. Peterson put in the two bags. He was anxious to be gone.

'I'll say goodbye then,' he said, a little awkwardly.

'Goodbye and thanks.' Kenmare and Tarrent shook his hand. 'The blood in the plane, you'll clear it up yourself,' Kenmare reminded, 'and forget about it, of course.'

'Sure. I understand.'

With a brief nod Bill Peterson left them. Kenmare slid behind the wheel, and Tarrent got in beside Bonalov. As the car passed through the gates of the RAF establishment, saluted by the guards and watched from the shadows by the two officers in the Land Rover, Peterson was taking off into the night sky.

'What about that coffee, Neil?' Kenmare asked, after they had been driving for a short time. 'I don't know about you, but I could do with it.'

Tarrent had been thinking of Betty and the Mont children. There would be a pension but, without something to bolster it, it wouldn't be adequate, not for Simon's commitments. His parents would probably suffer; poor Simone might not be able to take up her place at Cheltenham. And as for Betty herself, with her doubtful health . . . It was a dismal prospect for the Monts. He forced his mind away from the subject.

'Yes. Coffee,' he said. 'Let's hope it's good and hot.'

The coffee was hot, the sandwiches fresh and there was some fruit. Parked beside the road, they ate and drank quickly. Tarrent was surprised that any of them could feel hunger, but it was evident they all did. Except for essentials they didn't speak.

It was not until they were moving again, and Kenmare had turned on to the northbound motorway, that Bonalov asked about their destination. 'We are going to London?' he said.

'Fairly close,' Kenmare answered over his shoulder.

'To a "safe house"?'

'Yes.'

'Really safe?' Bonalov was acid. 'I've not been very impressed with your security arrangements so far, Mr Kenmare. And when can I see your Director, Sir Patrick Cordar?'

'In due course!' Kenmare hooted loudly as a truck he was overtaking swayed, without warning, into his lane.

Bonalov didn't press the point. Smiling sardonically, he leant back in his corner, shut his eyes and appeared to sleep. Tarrent stared out of the window, trying not to think. And Kenmare sat stiffly, his mind apparently concentrated on his driving.

Traffic was almost non-existent. They made good progress. Half an hour later they left the motorway and, soon afterwards, reached their destination – a low, rambling house, of no particular architectural merit, set behind a high wall about a mile beyond a village. Within easy commuting distance of London, it nevertheless gave the impression of being in the depths of the country. The gates, though not as imposing as those of the de Noirmont château, were solid and shut.

Kenmare hooted. Tarrent climbed out of the car and immediately was bathed in a powerful beam of light. 'Hello, Mr Smith,' he called involuntarily, screwing up his eyes, but making no attempt to shield his face. 'Sorry we're late.'

'That's all right, sir,' a voice said.

The light went out. In the distance there was a single, sharp bark, and nearby a dog growled deep in its throat. Tarrent got back into the car. The gates swung open and Kenmare drove in, slowly.

Mr Smith appeared at the window. 'Straight ahead, sir. Mrs Smith'll be waiting to welcome you, but stay in the car till I come, please. I've got to shut the dogs up.'

Kenmare acknowledged the request with a wave of his hand, and proceeded circumspectly up the drive. This particular 'safe house' was new to him. He had not been here before. Simon Mont had supervised all the arrangements for Bonalov's reception, and it was lucky that Tarrent had known the location. Certainly Mont had been in no condition to pass on the information before he died. Otherwise they would have been forced to call their headquarters – even the Director – to find out where they were going. And what could look more stupid than that?

'What sort of dogs are they?' Bonalov asked suddenly.

'Dobermann Pinschers,' Tarrent said. 'You'll be introduced to them in the morning. They're very well-trained and won't hurt a friend, but they're excellent protection.'

'Gentlemen, if you would care to come in now.' Mr Smith had reappeared. 'You've got luggage?'

'Only what you see, but—'

Kenmare explained briefly about Mont. Mr Smith, an ex-SAS sergeant, showed no emotion. He gave a slight bow of his head.

'Very good, sir. I'll take care of the matter, sir. We'll fix it in the morning.'

'Thank you.'

Mr Smith picked up the two bags and led the way to the front door; Bonalov insisted on carrying his attaché case. The house, which had been in darkness, suddenly seemed to come to life. A light went on over the door, and the door itself was opened, revealing a wide, oak-panelled hall.

'Good evening, gentlemen. Welcome. I'm Mrs Smith.'

The ex-sergeant's wife was in her late thirties. An attractive, efficient-looking woman, she was responsible for the domestic running of the house where, she prided herself, the 'visitors' were as well cared for as in any luxury hotel.

'What can I get you? Your rooms are ready. There are drinks in the drawing-room. But perhaps you'd like tea, sandwiches, an omelette?'

The question was directed primarily at Kenmare, but it

was Bonalov who answered. 'I wish to go to bed, and sleep without interruption until I awake,' he announced. 'First, however, I would like a hot bath and some vodka.'

'There is ample hot water for everyone.' Mrs Smith's gaze flickered momentarily over Tarrent's blood-stained, torn suit. 'And there is vodka in your sitting-room, sir,' she said to Bonalov.

'What I need is a telephone,' Kenmare said, and to Tarrent, 'If you'll make sure the Colonel's all right.'

'I'll take you to the study, sir,' said Mr Smith. He showed Kenmare the phone and murmured, 'All the lines go through the control room, sir. Just ask if you want a secure link.'

Leaving Kenmare, Mr Smith went back to the hall and led Tarrent and Bonalov upstairs. He opened a door and stood aside. 'The suite,' he said simply. He looked at Tarrent. 'I'll take the bags to the two rooms opposite, shall I, sir, and then attend to the car?'

'That'll be fine. Thanks.' Tarrent didn't bother to explain that one of the bags belonged to Simon Mont. He followed Bonalov. 'Is this to your satisfaction, Colonel?' he asked.

Bonalov had just poked his head into the bedroom. 'There's a connecting bathroom, I presume. Excellent. I'm sure I'll be very comfortable here – assuming the food's up to standard, of course. Even my favourite brand of vodka, I see.'

He stopped abruptly. His mood had changed. Something in Tarrent's expression had warned him how very unwelcome his sardonic humour was at this point. For a reason he couldn't explain, he suddenly felt unbearably lonely.

'I'm sorry,' he said. 'About Mr Mont, I mean. Truly sorry.'

Neil Tarrent nodded. Oddly enough, he believed Bonalov, but he had no wish to discuss the matter with him. He said, 'You'll find toilet articles in the bathroom, Colonel, and there are pyjamas, robe, a few casual clothes in the cupboard. You didn't give us much opportunity to equip you properly, but we'll remedy that in the next few days.'

'Good. Good.' Accepting that his sympathy was

unwanted, Bonalov went across to a side-table and poured himself a large vodka. But he didn't drink it immediately. He glanced enquiringly at Tarrent. 'There is something else?' he asked.

'Your attaché case. I'd like to see the contents, please.'

'Certainly.' Bonalov was impassive. 'I brought a few personal possessions, things dear to me.' He put the case on a chair and opened it. 'You'll find nothing of value to you, Mr Tarrent. The valuables I have for you are all in my head.'

Tarrent smiled, but made no comment. He brought another chair, and unpacked the contents of the case on to it. Bonalov, he realized at once, had told the truth. The case contained a file of personal papers – birth certificates, marriage certificates and so on – an album of family snapshots, an old brooch, a gold wedding-ring, some medals and two silver-framed studio photographs.

'My wife, who died recently, and my son, who was killed in Afghanistan,' Bonalov said simply. 'He was a soldier, an officer in the Soviet Army – but you'll know about that.'

'Yes. We know.'

Against his will Neil Tarrent was moved. Bonalov's possessions – all that a middle-aged man had chosen to bring with him into exile – were somehow touching. But they weren't all that Bonalov had brought, Tarrent reminded himself. Perhaps the contents of the case had been deliberately picked to encourage sympathy and trust. He shrugged mentally, and turned to Bonalov. 'I'll say good night then, Colonel. There's a telephone by your bed. You can order breakfast when you like, or anything else you wish.'

'Thank you, Mr Tarrent, and good night.'

Tarrent went downstairs slowly. He found John Kenmare in the study on the phone to Sir Patrick Cordar. To judge from Kenmare's expression, their dialogue was not going well.

'Yes, sir,' Kenmare was saying. 'Of course. Yes. Yes. I appreciate that, sir, but—' He listened for another couple of minutes, then held out the receiver to Tarrent, his hand firmly over the mouthpiece. 'He wants to talk to you, Neil,

God help you. The old bugger's breathing fire.'

Vaguely amused – Kenmare didn't make a habit of criticizing the Director – Tarrent took the instrument. 'Neil Tarrent, sir.'

'Ah yes, Neil. John has been telling me . . .' Sir Patrick began softly, as if he had exhausted himself abusing Kenmare. 'At least the parcel has been delivered satisfactorily. Otherwise, complete disaster, as I understand it. The DST aren't fools, you know. They're more capable than the next man of putting two and two together. And when they come up with the right answer, the French Government's going to be hopping mad. But I've been into all this with John. I've told him what's to be done. Now, about poor Simon. I think it best that you, Neil, as a friend of the family, should break the sad news to his wife.'

'No!' Tarrent said.

'What?' Sir Patrick took no notice of the interruption. 'You'll say Simon was killed in a car accident in France, that his body's being brought home, that everything will be arranged. Naturally, in due course, I'll call on Mrs Mont myself. Meanwhile . . .'

Tarrent listened dully to the rest of Sir Patrick's instructions. He made no further attempt to protest. Automatically he took the whisky Kenmare put into his hand and raised the glass. He drank to Sir Patrick's eternal damnation, but only half-heartedly. His thoughts were centred on Betty Mont.

'Another drink, Neil?'

Tarrent stared at his empty glass. He couldn't remember drinking the whisky. He smiled wanly. 'Thanks.'

'You look done in.' Kenmare was sympathetic. 'You need a hot bath and bed.'

'What about you?'

'Not till I've phoned Paris and briefed Helen on what she's to tell the police. They won't believe her, of course, once they've inspected the wrecked cars, but if she sticks to the story that the Jag was stolen last night they can't do much. Incidentally, the old man wants me to stay on here, at least for a few days, take Simon's place, as it were, till Bonalov's properly settled in.'

'Fine.' Tarrent wouldn't have chosen Kenmare as his colleague, but he certainly had no reason to object. 'Did he tell you he wants me to break the news to Betty Mont?'

'Oh Lord! No, he didn't. Trust him to get his pound of flesh.' Kenmare glanced at his watch. 'Breakfast in six hours all right with you? We'll make a plan of action then.'

'Sure.' Tarrent put down his glass. He was, he knew, being dismissed. Kenmare didn't want an audience while he was talking to his wife, which was fair enough. 'Good night, John.' He was at the door when he remembered Bonalov's attaché case.

'How very odd,' Kenmare said. 'The way he hung on to it, I thought it contained the Tsar's imperial crown jewels.' He shook his head in disbelief.

As soon as Tarrent had gone, Kenmare put through his call to Paris. He wasn't looking forward to his conversation with Helen. He hated having to involve her, but there was no alternative. The story would come so much better from her than from Anna, who never drove the Jaguar. And Sir Patrick had been very firm; they had made a mess of things and now they must clear it up. No congratulations for having brought Bonalov safely to the UK. Kenmare swore, softly but viciously. He could hear the phone ringing in the apartment in Paris.

'Hello.'

'Anna. This is John. Sorry to wake you up in the middle of the night, but I need to speak to Mrs Kenmare.'

'Mrs Kenmare?'

'Yes. And if my mother happens to be awake, perhaps I'll have a word with her afterwards.'

'Very good, Mr John.'

There was a pause, then Helen came on the line. 'John, honey, where are you? You promised you'd be home and – and I must have fallen asleep. Is something the matter? Are you all right?'

'Helen, darling, I'm perfectly fine and there's nothing seriously wrong, but I had to change my plans. I'm in England.'

'England!'

'Yes, and I'll be here for a few days. I'll let you know as soon as possible when I'll be home. Meanwhile, there's something very important I want you to do for me.'

'Of course, John. What is it?'

Kenmare had given some thought to what he would say, but the words stuck in his throat. He knew that his call was being monitored in the control room of the 'safe house', and he was also pretty certain that by now Anna would have woken his mother, and she would be listening on the extension in her bedroom. He cleared his throat.

'Darling, I had an accident with the Jag this evening, a bad accident, and I simply can't afford to get involved with the French police, so I'd like you—'

'A bad accident? How bad? Was anyone hurt?'

'Yes. Simon—' Kenmare stopped short. There was no need for Helen to know about Simon Mont. 'Listen, darling, and try to understand. I want you to phone the police, first thing, and say the Jag's been stolen. Tell them that yesterday evening, after you dropped me and a couple of friends at the Embassy, you parked the car as usual in the garage under the apartment. But this morning, when you went to get something out of it, you found it had gone. There have been thefts from our garage before, so—'

Helen, who had been in a deep sleep when Anna roughly woke her, had been slow to grasp the full import of what John was saying. She could still scarcely believe it. It was foreign to her nature to lie, and to lie to the police about what she assumed to be some kind of hit-and-run accident seemed quite dreadful. That John Kenmare, her husband, was asking her to do it made it worse.

'No,' she said sharply. 'I can't do that, John, not even for you. You said Simon Mont was hurt. Was anyone else hurt? You haven't told me what happened. Why can't you tell the police the truth?'

'For God's sake, darling!' Kenmare's nerves were already overstretched, and he hadn't expected Helen to be obstinate. His temper flared. 'You've got to do as I say! It's essential!'

'No! Not unless you explain—'

'It's all right, John dear,' Clara Kenmare cut in, astound-

103

ing and infuriating Helen who had no idea Clara had been eavesdropping. 'I'll arrange everything this end. You've no need to worry. Helen and I will have a little talk. Now, is there anything else we should know?'

John Kenmare winced as a sharp click on the line told him that Helen, not even bothering to say goodbye, had replaced her receiver. His mother's intervention had been reassuring, and probably necessary, but it certainly hadn't been tactful. 'You heard everything?' he asked. 'Then there's nothing else at the moment. Mother, be careful how you explain to Helen. She's got to play her part. I'll be in touch when I can.'

'All right, dear. Don't worry. Good night.'

'Good night, Mother. Sorry to have disturbed everyone.'

Miserable at having quarrelled with Helen, but unable to do anything about it, Kenmare put out the light and left the study. There was still one more thing to be done before he could go to bed. He went along the passage to an unmarked door. He knocked and identified himself, and waited for the control room door to be released.

It was a strange room, filled with flickering light, and Kenmare looked around with interest.

'So this is the latest set-up,' he said. 'You're George, aren't you? You'll have to explain it all to me.'

The man in jeans and a polo-necked sweater stood up from the console at which he had been working. 'Of course, sir,' he said. 'The communication equipment's over there, and the secure lines to London terminate here. We monitor all calls, of course, internal and external, incoming and outgoing; those are the recorder banks. Over here are the perimeter alarms and their test racks. I'll go into details later if you like.'

'Very interesting,' said Kenmare. 'And these?' he added, pointing to a row of television monitors, one of which showed the dark shadow of a Dobermann loping down the drive.

'We've got TV surveillance of the gate, a fair area of the grounds and the perimeter, and of course of the suite.'

'And how is our guest?' asked Kenmare.

'Nothing of interest, sir. After he was left alone he undress-ed, bathed, had a second vodka, stared out of the window for a while and went to bed. Would you like to see a replay of the tape?'

'No, thanks. I'm sure it's not necessary.'

'Right now he's sleeping like a baby.'

The man pressed a switch and another screen came to life, with a clear shot of Alexei Bonalov. Wearing the pyjamas provided for him by the British authorities, the Russian defector lay on his back, his mouth slightly open. From the gentle rise and fall of the bedclothes it was obvious that his breathing was even and he was peacefully asleep. He might not have had a care in the world.

TEN

For what remained of the night Helen Kenmare slept fitfully, her snatches of unconsciousness punctuated by frightening dreams. When finally she awoke, she felt tired, depressed and desperately worried about John. Her anger – which anyway had been mainly directed against Clara – had completely evaporated. But she was still determined not to tell the police a concoction of lies about the Jaguar.

She showered and dressed, choosing a favourite green two-piece in an attempt to lift her spirits, and went along to the dining-room. To her surprise Clara, who usually breakfasted in her room, was sitting at the table.

'Good morning, Helen dear. I'm glad you're up so early. It gives us time to talk before you telephone.'

'The only call I intend to make is to John, Clara, if you have his number.' Helen's hand shook as she helped herself to coffee.

'No, I haven't John's number and I don't know where he is.' Clara was firm. 'Nor do I know any more about last night's accident than you do. But I trust my son implicitly, and you must trust him too. If he says you should tell the authorities the Jaguar was stolen, then you should.'

'I'm sorry, but I can't.' Helen was equally firm. 'It's asking too much. He said Simon Mont was badly hurt. There could have been others, perhaps someone killed.'

'Perhaps.'

'And if John was driving, if he was responsible—'

Helen looked hopelessly at the older woman. She didn't understand how Clara could remain so majestically calm and composed when John was obviously in trouble.

'Helen, there's something I must tell you. Please listen carefully. It's very important.' Clara toyed with a piece of toast. Sooner or later, she thought, something like this had been bound to happen. 'My dear, haven't you realized that John's not an ordinary diplomat? For that matter, nor are Simon Mont and Neil Tarrent. That's merely their "cover", as they call it. They're all intelligence officers – secret intelligence officers. Do you understand what I mean?'

Helen stared at her mother-in-law in perplexity. 'Yes. I suppose so. But—'

'Helen, you must accept John's position, and do all you can to help him,' Clara went on. 'His work can be unpleasant. It can be dangerous. But it's vital. You know John's father was one of the youngest VCs in the First World War, and afterwards he had a brilliant career in the army and politics. Well, I'm certain he'd have been proud of his son today – and I can't say more than that.' Clara glanced at the portrait of her late husband that hung on the dining-room wall. 'You should be proud of John too.'

Clara had spoken with absolute conviction, but she'd spoken of a world Helen found hard to accept – a world she'd only met before in television serials and headlines in the press. Maybe she was naive, but she'd never thought of it as part of her own life – and that of her husband. 'But why hasn't John told me this himself?' she asked suddenly.

'Oh, come, my dear. You know the answer to that. The essence of secret intelligence is secrecy. He's forbidden to discuss his work with anyone – his family, even his wife.'

'But then how—' Helen paused.

'Quite right. You may well ask how I know so much. John and I have been so close for so long that there was no way I could be kept in complete ignorance. And there was another reason for keeping it all from you. Rhoda, John's first wife, did get to know about his work – in circumstances rather similar to these. She couldn't take it. She was a rather stupid woman and, once she knew, she made a great fuss if she thought John was engaged in anything – anything untoward or dangerous. She worried dreadfully. We didn't realize how much it was preying on her mind until—'

'Until what?' Helen's voice was small and strained.

'She took her own life. She jumped from an upstairs window when we were staying with friends in Scotland.'

'She jumped!' Helen interrupted. 'John told me it was an accident. I never knew—'

'Scarcely anyone knew. It was all hushed up. But John has always blamed himself, and the last thing he wanted was to worry you about it and the reasons for it. Surely you can see why he's been so very careful to keep his other life apart from you.'

Helen pushed away her plate, her toast and honey uneaten. Her mouth felt dry. She licked her lips with the tip of her tongue.

'Is there anything else I should know?' She was surprised how calm she sounded.

Clara smiled at her. The girl was taking it well, better than she had expected. 'Yes. It's about last night. I'm sure we shouldn't know this, but a high-up Russian delegate to the conference – you know, the meetings John's been at all the week – was planning to defect, to come over to the West. John didn't tell me any details, but I suspect that Simon Mont and Neil Tarrent were taking the Russian to England. Something must have gone wrong.'

'Yes. The car accident. I see—' Helen couldn't go on.

Clara nodded, not unkindly. 'I know you don't want to let John down – he loves you so – but all this must have been a shock to you. Maybe I took too much for granted in telling you, my dear. It would have been better if John had told you before, but he couldn't know it would be necessary. If you really feel you can't help him, I'll get Anna to say she was driving the Jaguar last night and found it gone this morning. It won't be so convincing, but she's devoted to John and she'll do anything for him.'

'No! No, you mustn't ask Anna.' The words escaped before Helen could stop them. Her mind was whirling, but one thing was clear: it was up to her, not Anna, to help John. Clara was right. She couldn't let him down, even though—'I'll call the police,' she said quietly.

While Helen was dialling the local Commissariat in Paris, in Moscow the telephone was ringing in Sergei and Tamara

Dronsky's apartment. The ringing continued for some while, then ceased. The Dronskys were out. Neither of them worked on Saturdays and they had gone shopping.

The ringing was repeated intermittently throughout the morning. The Dronskys heard it as, laden with parcels – for once they had been lucky with their purchases – they climbed the last flight of stairs; the lift was out of order for the second time that week. Dropping everything, Sergei Dronsky thrust his key into the lock and dashed into the apartment. Equally anxious, Tamara bundled together what he had let fall, and hurried after him.

Ever since Maya had been taken from them they had lived for the ring of the telephone, but time and time again they had been disappointed. Either it had been one of Sergei's students or a fellow teacher from the University, or some friend of Tamara's from the laboratory, never the voice they wanted to hear, telling them that Maya was coming home. The days had passed. They had done their best to behave normally, as they'd been ordered, but the strain had told. Now they looked what they were, miserable, dispirited, beaten. Yet they had never completely given up hope.

But this time, his face bright with excitement, Sergei whispered, 'Tamara! It's him! It's him!'

Quickly she said, 'Ask him how she is. Ask him if we can speak to her.'

'Hush!'

Tamara sat down. She felt too weak to stand. Night after night she had cried herself to sleep in Sergei's arms, wondering where Maya was and what she had been doing that day and whether she was very unhappy. Tamara had even tried to pray. She would do anything, anything, to have her little daughter safe and at home.

'I'm not sure I understand,' she heard Sergei say and her heart began to thump loudly.

'Yes. Yes. That I understand. We are to go to Kazan Station, but what train are we to meet? No train?' The line crackled angrily, and Dronsky held the phone away from his ear. 'And what shall I do with these bags?'

Oleg Kerensky explained. Really, the man was stupid, he

thought, especially for a teacher at Moscow University. It was absurd that he was to be promoted next term but, as Alexei Bonalov had instructed, it had been arranged, though not without some difficulty. Of all the orders that the Colonel had given concerning the Dronskys, the arrangement of this promotion had caused the most trouble. All the other things had been simple.

Kerensky suppressed a sigh. It was incomprehensible to him why Alexei Bonalov had bothered with the Dronskys' welfare, when there were other far more pressing problems to consider. It could only be a weakness, a sentimentality, on the Colonel's part. But he had done what Bonalov wanted, and after today, once he'd put the fear of the devil into them, he'd be able to forget the Dronskys.

He said into the phone, 'You will not question the child. What she will have to say, her prattle, will not be inconsistent with the story you've told your friends – that she has been having a holiday with your wife's family. Perhaps in time you may believe it yourself.' He laughed humourlessly. 'Because everything else must be wiped from your mind. Remember – always remember – what has been returned to you can at any moment be removed again – and for ever. Do I make myself clear, Comrade.?'

'Yes.' The word seemed to stick in Sergei Dronsky's throat. 'Absolutely clear,' he stammered.

'Good. I rely on you to make sure your wife understands, too. And be constantly grateful that we have shown you so much mercy.'

The line went dead, but Dronsky continued to stand, the receiver against his ear, as if listening. He was trying to make up his mind. If he told Tamara of the man's threat she would live in constant fear for Maya. But if he didn't tell her, as the months passed and her sense of security grew, she might be tempted to confide in a friend and so unwittingly put Maya at risk. He had to tell her.

Slowly Sergei put down the receiver and held out his arms. Tamara, who had been watching his expression with increasing anxiety, didn't move.

'What is it?' she whispered. 'Has something—Is Maya ill?'

'No. Maya is well and she's coming home to us. We're going to collect her right now.'

'Sergei!' Tamara was out of her chair and had thrown herself at him, tears of joy wetting her cheeks. 'Where is she? Quick. We must go.'

'One moment!' Sergei held her from him and shook her gently. 'Not so much excitement. Maya has just been on a country holiday. That is all. Never, Tamara, never must anyone know the truth. Do you understand, Tamara? If anyone, anyone ever discovers what really happened, she might be taken from us again. And this time it would be for good.'

Some of the happiness faded from Tamara's face. It was replaced by a fierce determination. 'I would die sooner than that,' she said simply.

'Be sensible, and prudent. Keep a watch on your tongue. That's all that's required,' Sergei said. 'And now, come. The taxi will be waiting.'

'The taxi?'

'Yes. Everything has been made easy for us.'

The taxi was parked along the street. Its green light was out. The driver, with a copy of *Pravda* propped open on his wheel, watched the entrance to the apartment building. He had been shown a photograph of the Dronskys, and recognized them at once. As they approached, he folded his paper, leant out of his window and opened the door for them.

'Kazan Station,' Sergei Dronsky said.

The driver nodded. He didn't speak. He revved the cab away from the kerb, tilting the mirror above his head so that he could keep an eye on his passengers. He need not have bothered. They sat close to each other, holding hands rather stiffly, and never uttered a word until they reached Komsomol Square and drew up to one side of the station entrance, in front of a black Zil.

'There she is!'

Sergei spotted Maya first, but Tamara was out of the taxi

before him, dashing across the pavement, almost knocking down an elderly man who turned and shook his stick at her. Tamara didn't see him. She had gathered Maya into her arms, hugging and kissing her.

'Steady! Steady!'

But Sergei was himself shaking with excitement and relief and happiness. Because for the moment he couldn't get at Maya to embrace her, he seized a cuddly toy in the shape of a huge bear – Maya had dropped it on seeing her mother – and hugged that instead. Then, with a struggle, he picked up the three bags that had apparently been left at Maya's feet, and somehow managed to shepherd his family back to the waiting taxi.

None of them spared a glance for the black Zil parked behind the cab, not even Maya, though in it sat the kindly *babushka* who had taken such good care of her and shown her so much affection during the 'holiday'.

'A dear little girl,' the woman said. 'Polite and obedient, but a happy child. I've grown quite attached to her.'

Oleg Kerensky made an inarticulate sound. Ignoring the woman, he leant forward. 'To the office,' he said sharply to the driver, 'and be quick. We've wasted enough time. I've work to do.'

The driver obeyed instantly, and the Zil moved off. The woman was silent, wondering what had caused the Comrade's sudden irritation. And Oleg Kerensky, adjusting his gangling frame more comfortably in the corner of the limousine, tried to suppress his doubts and fears.

The taxi bearing the Dronskys was already on its way. Maya, sunburnt and glowing with health, sat between her parents, clutching the big bear. It was clear she was pleased to be coming home, but it was equally obvious that she'd enjoyed her visit to the country. She chatted happily about her dear *babushka* and the *dacha* with so many rooms and the lovely garden and how she had learnt to swim in the river, and all the presents she had been given.

Above her dark curly head, Sergei and Tamara Dronsky looked at each other, but they said very little. Maya had been returned to them, and nothing else mattered. The taxi drew up immediately in front of their apartment block, and unloaded them and their bags on to the pavement. Tamara went ahead with Maya and her bear.

'How much?' Sergei asked.

'No charge, Comrade.' A smile split the driver's face. 'But I was told to remind you to be careful how you go. You're a lucky man. Don't forget it.'

Sergei stared after the taxi as it drove off. But Tamara and Maya were waiting. He hurried into the building, where Maya was telling the *dezhurnaya* about her lovely holiday. At least it will be something different for the old woman to report, Sergei thought without malice.

Luckily the lift was working again and within minutes they were alone in their apartment, just the three of them. Now they were able to kiss and hug Maya as much as they liked, to stand her on a chair and admire her pretty new dress, to shed a few tears over her, then to hug and kiss her again. The child bore it stoically, returning their love, but it was she who suggested they should open the bags and look at the presents.

Letting her choose, making a game of it, they opened the biggest bag first. It contained toys, an array of bears of different sizes, two dolls with comprehensive wardrobes, a farm with a collection of beautifully carved animals, and other things. Some of them were foreign made. Most of them were unavailable in Moscow shops.

In the second bag were clothes, mostly for Maya, including a new fur coar and hat. Tamara held up the coat against her daughter and was delighted to see that it would fit her for at least two winters to come. Sergei was trying on a pair of boots, made of real leather.

'Super!' Tamara said. 'Super! Are they comfortable?'

'Very comfortable. As you'd expect, they know my size,' Sergei said. 'I'm sure they know yours too.'

'Yes.' Suddenly subdued, Tamara laid aside the fur-lined gloves she had been about to slip on her hands. 'Shall we open the other bag?'

The third bag was by far the smallest. It contained three bottles of vodka and a variety of canned goods, expensive

113

delicacies, difficult if not impossible to come by. There was also a large brown envelope, addressed to 'Sergei Dronsky'. Inside was a thick bundle of fifty-rouble notes, together with an equally thick bundle of a different kind of money.

'What are those?' asked Tamara, her eyes wide.

'They're special roubles,' said Sergei. 'They're called "certificate roubles", I think. Some people at the University have them occasionally, if they've been abroad or they're in contact with foreigners. They're used at the *beryozka* shops – you know, like hard currency. We can buy all sorts of things that aren't in GUM or anywhere else, cheaply too. We could probably even get priority on a car with these, if we went about it the right way.'

'You mean we've got a kind of *blat*? Oh, Sergei!'

'Yes,' said Sergei slowly. 'while the money lasts. And there's a note in the envelope.' He read it and held it out to Tamara.

It was typed, and it said simply, 'Use this circumspectly. Do not arouse comment. Remember your commitment.'

'I don't understand,' said Sergei. 'Why? Why have they been generous? We did what we did because—' He glanced quickly at Maya, but she had seated herself on the floor and was fully occupied playing with her family of bears; she was not in the least interested in what he was saying. 'Because there was no choice,' he continued bitterly. 'They know that. We acted under duress. We love our country. We wouldn't willingly help anyone to betray—' He stopped again, and shrugged. It was useless to speculate.

'Let's have a drink, and some of that caviare, Tamara,' he said. 'We must forget about the KGB defector, whoever he is, and hope that his friends – and his enemies – forget about us.'

Because of the time difference, it was still only mid-morning in England, and Alexei Bonalov was just finishing a late breakfast. He drained his coffee cup and gave a sigh of pleasure. He had slept well. The breakfast had been excellent. And today, he was pretty sure, would be easy. The

114

English would want him to relax and settle in; there would be no formal interrogations. Nor was he in any immediate danger, as far as he could see. Nevertheless, he must insist on talking personally to Sir Patrick Cordar as soon as possible.

'Come,' he said, as there was a tap on the door.

Neil Tarrent came into the room and wished him good-morning. 'I thought you might like a walk in the garden, Colonel, before the doctor comes.'

'The doctor?' Bonalov stroked his neat beard. 'Do you need a doctor?'

'Of course not, Colonel. You know he's for you. He'll give you a complete check-up. There'll be a dentist too. It's all part of the service.'

Bonalov laughed. 'If you insist, but I assure you I'm in perfect health, and I don't have a death-pill in a hollow tooth or stuffed up my arse, if that's what you're afraid of. Nor will you find one among my possessions. So please tell whoever's going to search them while we're in the garden to do no damage.'

'He's always very careful,' Tarrent said, and grinned in spite of himself.

Tarrent showed Bonalov around the drawing-room, the dining-room and the study, and indicated the kitchen regions of the rambling house. Then they went into the garden, which was mostly lawn and flowering shrubs, easy to maintain. Meeting Mr Smith, who had his favourite Dobermann on a leash, they were taken to admire the vegetables and fruit he grew, and afterwards to the kennels.

The visit to the kennels took some time. Mr Smith was insistent that each of the three dogs should know them by voice and by smell. 'At night two are loose,' he explained. 'By day we patrol with just one dog. Sometimes Mrs Smith takes a turn. She's particularly fond of Caspar. And, of course, the others can be released by remote control if there's an alarm of any kind.'

'Very impressive,' Bonalov said. 'What about the local people? And deliveries?'

Mr Smith looked at Tarrent. It was up to him to answer such questions. He had told the visitor about the dogs

115

because that had been Mr Mont's order. The Dobermanns were very fierce, and there must be no accidents. Everyone should be warned.

'The local people don't come here,' Tarrent said. 'A rumour's got around that an elderly recluse has bought the place, and strangers aren't welcome. And of course the dogs scare people off. I doubt they'd want to deliver. Mail, such as it is, and newspapers and milk are left at the gate. The rest comes down from London, though, as you've seen, we've got our own fruit and vegetables, thanks to Mr Smith here.'

They strolled on. 'It all sounds very safe,' Bonalov said, putting a particular emphasis on his last word.

'It's meant to be safe, and it is.' Tarrent gestured at the high stone wall. 'I won't go into details, but we've got alarm systems all round.'

'You've thought of everything.'

Tarrent disregarded the sarcasm. 'I hope so.'

They rounded the corner of the house. In the drive stood a dark blue van. As they watched, two men – Mr Smith and the driver – came out of the front door carrying a stretcher on which lay a form covered by a sheet. They slid their burden carefully into the back of the van and shut the door. The driver got into his seat.

'I'll be back for the doctor about three. Okay?'

'Okay.' Mr Smith nodded, and spoke rapidly into a pocket radio. 'You'll be expected at the gate.'

The man outlined a salute, and drove off. Mr Smith returned to the house. Tarrent would have followed him, but Bonalov caught him by the arm.

'Mr Tarrent. Please will you do something for me?'

'What?'

'Telephone Sir Patrick Cordar and tell him I must talk to him, in person and privately, tomorrow, if not today. It's most important, for all our sakes, and most urgent. I appreciate that you've taken every precaution you can, but I shan't be safe in this place for long. Believe me, my enemies will discover where I am and . . .'

Tarrent freed his arm from Bonalov's grasp. He wasn't surprised. Defectors were always terrified. 'Okay, sir,' he

116

said reassuringly. 'I'll make certain he gets your message. But, in the meantime, don't worry. There's no need. You're in absolutely no danger here.' They were words he was to remember.

ELEVEN

In spite of the care Mrs Smith had taken, lunch was not a success. Only the doctor, napkin tucked into the front of his waistcoat, did it justice. The others pecked at their food.

Alexei Bonalov, who had undergone a rigorous physical examination and was not looking forward to the psychological tests promised for the early afternoon, was feeling tired and jaded. The events of the previous evening seemed suddenly to have caught up with him. John Kenmare, also brooding on the previous night, was wondering how he could put through a call to Paris that would be unmonitored and reasonably private. He knew the rules, but for once, if he could get the chance, he was prepared to break them. As for Neil Tarrent, he had no appetite.

Tarrent's morning had been busy. Even when he had handed Bonalov over to the doctor, he still had his report on the last twenty-four hours to prepare. So it was not until shortly before lunch that he had faced up to what lay ahead of him that afternoon. And the thought of having to tell Betty Mont that Simon was dead overshadowed everything.

Skipping coffee, Tarrent went around to the garage and borrowed a Cortina. Mr Smith let him out through the gates, and he drove slowly across country towards Wimbledon. The weather had changed. The sky was grey and overcast and, as he reached the edge of the Common, great drops of rain began to fall. In the distance, thunder growled. It suited Tarrent's mood. He didn't want to find Betty sitting in the garden in bright sunshine.

It was after three when Tarrent drew up behind the Monts' old Ford parked by the front door, and got out of his car. The garage was open and he could see the new station wagon inside. Unless she had gone for a walk, which was unlikely in the heavy rain, or was visiting a neighbour, Betty

118

was at home. Tarrent rang the doorbell.

He had purposely not considered how he could break the news of Simon's death. He had thought that the unexpected sight of him alone would give Betty some warning, and the rest would follow naturally. What he was dreading was her reaction to the news, the fear that she might break down completely and he wouldn't know how to cope. He steeled himself as the door opened.

'Why, hello! Come on in. We're in the kitchen. Mum's making jam.'

Tarrent swallowed. Silently he cursed himself. Not that he could have done anything about it, but he should have remembered that the day was Saturday, and Simone wouldn't be at school. He managed a wide, mirthless grin.

'Hello, Simone. How nice to see you. How are you?'

'Fine, thanks. Terrific, in fact. Did Dad tell you? I've won a scholarship to Cheltenham. Isn't it super?'

Tarrent winced as if he had bitten into a sour lemon. Fortunately Simone, leading the way down the passage, was talking over her shoulder and couldn't see his expression. And there was no need for him to answer. She went on chatting.

'One thing, the boys will have to show me some respect now. I've proved I'm just as bright as they are, if not brighter.' She broke off as they reached the kitchen, which smelt pleasantly of stewing fruit. 'Mum, guess who's come to tea.'

'Neil! How nice.' Betty Mont, busy ladling newly-made jam into jars, offered him her cheek to kiss. 'You've chosen a good day too. There are scones in the oven.'

'That sounds splendid.'

'Can you stay to supper? We can easily add a few veg, and there'll be heaps for everyone.'

'No. I'm sorry. I can't. I have to get back.'

Betty grinned. 'I'm tempted to ask "back where", but I won't. May I ask if Simon's with you? I mean, in the UK?'

Neil Tarrent looked at her, then at Simone. 'No,' he said. 'But yes. Betty—' They were regarding him expectantly, and he realized they hadn't any idea, any intuition of what

119

he was about to say. 'I'm afraid I've bad news for you. There's been a car accident. Simon was badly hurt.' He paused, but they said nothing, and he hurried on. 'My dears, I'm most terribly sorry, but – but he died soon afterwards.'

'Died? Simon's dead?' Betty continued to fill the remaining jars. She spilt some jam and wiped the table with the end of her apron. She opened the oven and inspected the scones. 'They're nearly done,' she said.

'Mum! Didn't you hear what Neil's just told you?' Simone's voice was shrill. 'He said Dad was dead!'

'Yes, darling. I heard.'

'Oh God!'

Simone flung herself into a chair, pillowed her head on the kitchen table and began to sob. It was hysterical behaviour, but genuine. Tarrent preferred it to Betty's unnatural, unnerving calm.

'The boys must be told,' Betty said, going to her daughter and stroking her hair. 'And Simon's parents, and Valerie, his sister. And Peter Remington. He's our lawyer. Simon always said that if anything happened, Peter would—' She stopped. 'Neil, where is Simon's body now? Is it still in France?'

Betty Mont shouldn't have known Simon had been to France, but Tarrent ignored this. 'No. We – we brought him back with us.'

'Where to – the house?'

'What house?'

Betty made an impatient gesture. 'Neil, he's my husband and he's dead because some bloody Russian decided he wanted—' It was the first time she had shown any emotion and, without warning, she broke. Her face crumpled. Tears streamed down her cheeks. She pulled Simone roughly to her and hugged her tight. 'God knows what we're going to do without him!' She shook her head hopelessly.

'Betty, we can't bring Simon back to life, but everything else that can be done, will be. I promise.'

'Don't make me sick, Neil. You know as well as I do. There'll be an inadequate pension and damn all else.' Angrily Betty wiped away her tears with the back of her hand. 'What a moment to be thinking about money. Any yet we've got to be practical. Tea.' She was getting control of herself again. 'Lord, the scones'll be burnt. Simone!' She shook her daughter, none too gently. 'Come on, darling. You put the kettle on. Neil, would you please do the phoning for me? The Monts, and Val – her married name's Carter – and Peter Remington. The numbers are in the index by the phone. And the boys. Their housemaster's called Waterlow.'

'Yes, of course I will.'

Glad to escape, to be by himself for a minute or two, even with a thankless task ahead, Neil Tarrent went into the hall. He dialled the Carter's number. Bill Carter answered. He was shocked but businesslike. Tarrent heaved a sigh of relief. Carter would telephone the other Monts, and he and his wife would be with Betty within an hour. Westminster School was equally efficient. The boys had gone to Lord's to watch the Test Match, but if the rain didn't stop they would soon be back, and Mr Waterlow would drive them down to Wimbledon himself.

There remained the lawyer. On a Saturday afternoon Remington wouldn't be in his office, but his home number was also in the index. He wasn't pleased to be interrupted at the weekend but, once the situation had been explained to him, he was prepared to do anything he could to help.

Tarrent returned to the kitchen. Tea was ready, bitter, black tea, because Simone hadn't noticed how much she was putting in the pot. Tarrent drank his manfully, and ate two dark brown scones he didn't want. He told them of the calls he'd made, but otherwise conversation was almost nil. He left shortly after the Carters arrived. He had the impression that Betty was glad to see him go.

The storm had passed, though there were still some ominous clouds in the sky. The roads were wet, running with water where a drain was blocked, sometimes slippery with leaves. Tarrent drove carefully, his thoughts heavy. He now had a new problem.

It wasn't unreasonable that Simon should have told Betty

121

he was going to France. But it was a major breach of security to have mentioned a Russian defector. Tarrent wondered how much else Betty knew. She'd mentioned the safe house. Did she know its location? Most probably she did. And in her present desperately fraught mood, she might forget the significance of her knowledge. There was no doubt in Tarrent's mind that he should warn Sir Patrick and Kenmare, but he hated the idea.

Tarrent drew up at the gates of the safe house as a Dobermann loped down the drive towards him. Immediately he was alert, fearing trouble. He recognized the dog – it was Caspar – and, lowering his window, called to it through the ironwork of the gates. The dog pricked its ears at the known voice and barked twice, but didn't growl. Mr Smith came running. He gave Caspar an order, and swung the gates open. Tarrent drove in, still suspicious.

'Why are the dogs loose, Mr Smith? Is there an alarm?'

'No, sir. Just a precaution – in the circumstances.'

The two men eyed each other. The ex-SAS sergeant was the older, but Tarrent was the officer. Mr Smith knew about officers; they stuck together. Nevertheless, he was prepared to trust Tarrent. Besides, if he told Tarrent he would have done his duty, without making a big thing of it. Kenmare had annoyed him with his highhanded manner, but there were no grounds for official complaint.

'When we have a visitor in the house, sir, we're meant to have an officer available at all times. That's the rule.'

'Yes, I know.'

'Well, sir, this afternoon, immediately after the doctor had gone, Mr Kenmare left.'

'Left?'

'Went for a walk, like. He insisted. He said he must have some real exercise. Pottering around the garden wasn't enough.'

'Where's the visitor?'

'In his suite, sir, where Mr Kenmare put him. He seems a bit restless. He watched the cricket on telly for a bit. Then he had a brief snooze. Then he tried to read. Now he's pacing up and down or staring out of the window.'

122

'Right. I'll go and see what's bothering him. Thanks, Mr Smith. You call the dogs in. Mr Kenmare'll be back soon, and anyway I'm here.'

'Very good, sir.'

Thoughtfully Tarrent drove the car up to the garage and went into the house. Where the hell was John Kenmare? What had possessed him to leave Bonalov alone like that? When would he be back? First Simon, spewing out all his secrets to Betty, oblivious of security, of need to know. Then John, who had a reputation for being a stickler for the rules, breaking an important one for no apparent reason. Christ! What was the matter with everyone?

Having checked on Bonalov from the control room, Tarrent went up to Bonalov's suite. The television set was on, but Bonalov wasn't watching it. He turned away from the window as Tarrent came in.

'Ah, Mr Tarrent, good. Have you telephoned Sir Patrick yet? Have you impressed on him that I must see him without delay?'

'Colonel, this is the weekend, and Sir Patrick has other engagements. I'm afraid he won't be able to visit you.'

'But he must. I insist.'

'I'm sorry.' Tarrent was curt.

'You told him it was essential to my safety that I should speak to him personally?'

Tarrent didn't bother to lie. In fact, he had made no attempt to phone Sir Patrick, who had already agreed that it would be undesirable for him to meet Bonalov for some days. Tarrent merely repeated he was sorry.

Bonalov shot him an angry glance. 'You'll be even more sorry when I'm kidnapped – or killed,' he said with some venom.

Tarrent disregarded the remark. 'Would you like to have supper here or downstairs?' he asked.

'What does it matter?' Bonalov shrugged.

'I thought you might be getting bored with this room.'

'All right, downstairs then.'

'Fine. I'll be along in about half an hour. We can have a drink or two before we eat.'

123

Alexei Bonalov made a wry face as the door closed behind Tarrent. It had been an unexpectedly trying day. He had taken an instant dislike to the doctor, and had resented the examination and tests he'd been forced to endure. He certainly wasn't going to wait half an hour for a drink. He went across to the side table and poured himself a healthy shot of vodka. He tossed it down his throat and felt the warmth spread through him. It gave him some comfort.

Tarrent found John Kenmare in the study, just completing a telephone call. He gestured to Tarrent to give them each a drink, but Tarrent didn't move.

'That's all right then,' Kenmare said into the phone. 'Thanks a lot, darling. I'll be in touch when I can. Goodbye.' Frowning, he cut the connection. 'That was Helen. I was asking her about the Jaguar. The French have been too bloody clever, as usual. They'd already traced the Jag to me by the time she phoned to say it was stolen. It didn't burn up, evidently, and they got the number. Simple.'

'Does it matter?'

'Not really, I suppose. It was inevitable. But I don't like them quite so hot on my tail, especially with two unidentified bodies lying around.' Kenmare looked about him. 'Where's that drink you were pouring me?'

'I wasn't.'

Kenmare smiled understandingly. 'A bad time at the Monts'?'

'As you'd expect. The daughter was there, which made it worse. She's only twelve.'

Tarrent hesitated. It really wasn't any of his business to explain the Monts' financial problems to Kenmare. But someone in the Department should know, and maybe Kenmare could help to arrange some kind of assistance. Picking his words carefully, he outlined something of the Monts' situation as he understood it.

'I'm sorry. That's pretty tough,' John Kenmare said when Tarrent finished, but it was only a casual remark. Kenmare was obviously distrait, his mind on other things.

124

Tarrent, regretting he had been so forthcoming, abruptly changed the subject. There was no reason why Kenmare should interest himself in the Monts' affairs; he had never been particularly friendly with Simon.

He said, 'I must go and get Bonalov.'

'Bonalov? Why?'

'I promised him drinks and dinner with us. He's been shut up in his rooms most of the afternoon, and he's very edgy.'

'Oh dear!' Kenmare laughed ruefully. '*Mea culpa*. I was always taught my sins would find me out, and over the years how right that maxim's proved. I confess. I sneaked down to the village to telephone.'

'Telephone? Who to? Why couldn't you call from here?'

'I could say "my business", Neil, but I won't.' Kenmare wasn't feeling as good-tempered as he wished to appear. He didn't appreciate Tarrent's implied criticism of his actions. He poured some whisky into a glass and added a splash of soda, but didn't offer to do the same for the other man. 'I wanted to speak to Helen.'

'But you were just speaking to her.'

'Yes. She was out this afternoon. She'd gone to Vincennes with some friends, to see the trotting races. So I had to phone again from here, where of course the whole call was monitored.' Kenmare took a long gulp of whisky. 'Look, Neil, try to understand. Helen and I had a pretty acrimonious conversation last night. She didn't like Sir Patrick's idea that she should lie to the French police about the Jag. And I wanted to make it up with her without Mr Smith or one of his henchmen listening avidly to every word. After all, we've hardly been married a year, you know, and it's not easy to combine a happy marriage with our kind of job.'

'No. I imagine not.' Thinking that Simon Mont seemed to have solved the problem by confiding everything to his wife, Tarrent grinned reluctantly. He wasn't exactly satisfied with the situation, but he had no desire to take the matter further. 'Okay, John. I've forgotten about it. I'll go and get Bonalov.'

'Thanks,' Kenmare called after him as he went out of the door. 'I'm grateful.' And indeed, he thought, he was.

TWELVE

Sunday was a quiet day. John Kenmare decided that the household needed to relax a little. Security had to be maintained, but conditions would be better if individuals were less tense. He made his peace with Mr Smith, paid a special visit to the kitchen to compliment Mrs Smith on her domestic arrangements and her cooking and spent a while chatting with the rest of the staff in the control room.

Alexei Bonalov was allowed to do as he pleased. He chose to sleep late, and then walk in the garden with Neil Tarrent; by mutual consent they confined their conversation to general topics, though Bonalov, seemingly resigned to the weekend lull, reiterated his demand that Sir Patrick should see him as soon as possible in the coming week. In the afternoon he watched a movie on television and later, after supper, played snooker with Kenmare. It was, Bonalov thought with a certain bitter amusement, very close to his idea of a traditional English country-house party.

There were differences, of course. The siege conditions weren't obtrusive, though in a curious way the surface normality of life served to emphasize the true facts of the situation. A casual glance through a window would too often show a man patrolling with a dog on the end of a leash. The knowledge that it was impossible to walk at will down the drive and through the gates caused frustration, irrational though that might be. The sudden, heart-stopping vigilant jerk, merely because a door had banged shut, was an overreaction that wasn't normal. All such things combined to prevent Bonalov and those who watched over him from being completely at ease. But, in the course of that Sunday, some of the tension drained out of them.

The formal interrogation of Alexei Bonalov was to commence the next day. There were two immediate objectives.

126

The first, quite simply, was to find a basis for deciding whether Bonalov was a genuine defector or a KGB plant. The second was to determine how he had obtained the JIC paper he had used as bait, and what other information he might have received from the same source. The lengthy full debriefing would follow later, and its detail would depend to some extent upon the assessment of the first results. All this was routine, but at the backs of the SIS officers' minds lurked the ugly facts of the possible next step – the potentially explosive damage assessment exercise that would inevitably follow if Bonalov were judged genuine and his source had proved prolific.

The day began badly. Mr Smith appeared as Kenmare and Tarrent were finishing their breakfast. He looked grim.

'I'm sorry to interrupt you, gentlemen, but something odd's happened. Two of the dogs are sick – Jason and Sinbad.'

'How sick?'

Mr Smith frowned. 'They're sleepy like. Lethargic. Too tired to stand up. They were loose in the grounds last night, but there was no trouble. Though we did have a problem once, when a couple of lads from the village threw stuff over the wall.'

'What sort of stuff?'

'Old bones those were, sir. But there was no real harm intended. The police gave the lads a warning, and we've had no bother since. That was over a year ago.'

'You're suggesting the same thing might have happened again?'

'I'm suggesting someone might have copied the idea, sir.'

'But surely any villain would simply have poisoned the dogs. Why just make them sleepy?' Kenmare was thinking aloud. 'Have they vomited?'

'Not that I know of, but they're right off their feed. Percy was on duty with them last night. He says that when he brought them in they were very slow in obeying the whistle, and they wouldn't touch the little treat – a bit of raw liver we always give them.,

Kenmare took another piece of toast and buttered it

slowly. Mr Smith fidgeted. He was worried about Jason and Sinbad, both for their own sakes and for security reasons. If they didn't brighten up, Caspar would have to do their work as well as his own, and that was too much for one dog. Moreover, as Mr Smith had learnt from experience, inexplicable happenings were often warnings, and shouldn't be disregarded. He didn't want to rely on Caspar alone. He looked hopefully at Tarrent.

'Would you like the vet to see them?' Tarrent asked.

'Yes, I would, sir.' Mr Smith was eager. 'I'm not happy about tonight. If anyone was—'

Kenmare interrupted him. 'There was no alarm, was there?'

'No, sir.'

'And no sign of anything unusual?'

'Percy's having a good look round now, sir. But I don't think so.'

'Well, then, let's forget about the vet for the moment.' Kenmare pushed away his plate, his last piece of toast uneaten. 'Keep an eye on the dogs. If they get any worse, we'll send for the vet, but we don't want outsiders coming here unless it's absolutely essential. You know that, Mr Smith. All right?'

'If you say so, sir.'

Mr Smith went reluctantly. The responsibility was Kenmare's, not his, but he didn't like the situation. Apart from Mrs Smith and himself, there were three security men on the premises, but one of them was always in the control room, where a round-the-clock watch had to be maintained. They were heavily dependent on the dogs. If Caspar were to fall ill too . . .

Tarrent wasn't happy either. He waited till Mr Smith had gone, then tried to protest. 'John, surely it can't be just chance that two dogs have gone sick at this moment. And if they're so dopey now, they could have slept during the night. Someone could have sneaked over the wall.'

'Where is he, then? And what about the alarm system?' Kenmare was impatient. He stood up. 'The most likely explanation is that the dogs killed a mole or a rabbit that had

128

picked up some poison, and ate it.'

In spite of his doubts, Tarrent didn't argue further. 'So we go ahead as planned?'

'Sure. Once Bonalov's had a little air and exercise, we'll start on him. It's a long time since I've conducted an interrogation session. I suggested to the Director he should send some experts down, but he wants this thing held so tight that he won't – not till he's seen what we can get by ourselves. Okay?'

'Okay, John. Half an hour, then.'

As Kenmare went out of the room, Tarrent poured himself another cup of coffee. He took it to the study and had settled down with *The Times* crossword when the door suddenly opened and Mr Smith came in quickly and without knocking.

'Oh, there you are, sir.'

'Yes. What is it? Are the dogs worse?'

'No. It's Percy. I can't find him. He's disappeared.'

'What?'

'Disappeared, sir. He was inspecting the perimeter, sir, as I said. He's not come back and he doesn't answer his call. Mr Kenmare's just taken the visitor out, and I've got to get Caspar and I wondered—'

Tarrent had thrown aside his paper and was already on his feet. He didn't let Mr Smith finish his sentence. 'Of course, I'll go and look for him.'

'I'd rather you came with me, sir.'

Tarrent nodded. He knew at once what was in Mr Smith's mind. If one man could disappear, so could another. Two men with a trained Dobermann were a different matter. But in these circumstances Bonalov shouldn't be out in the garden; he ought to be in the security of his suite.

'You say Mr Kenmare's taken the visitor out?'

'Yes, sir. I saw them go through the drawing-room.'

They had themselves left the house, and were hurrying across the grass to the kennels. Mr Smith, calling to Caspar, went into the enclosure, and put a leash on the dog.

Tarrent swore. Kenmare had once again broken the rules by taking Bonalov outside without another man and a dog on watch. He said, 'Call Mr Kenmare at once. Get them both inside till we're sure all's well.'

Mr Smith tried. 'No reply, sir.'

'Hell!' Tarrent hesitated. Kenmare and Bonalov might have returned indoors. That would explain why there was no response; Kenmare would have turned off his pocket transceiver when he was back in the house. Or he might have neglected to take it out with him, or simply forgotten to switch the thing on. Or he might be in no position to use it.

'Call control at once, and warn the others,' he said. 'Quick! We need a proper search.'

'And London?' said Mr Smith. 'And the police?'

Again Tarrent paused. 'No,' he said. 'Not yet. Let's give ourselves a minute or two. After all . . .'

As Mr Smith spoke into his radio, they ran together in the direction of the house. But Caspar had other ideas. Swerving sideways, almost pulling Mr Smith over, he headed for an outbuilding that was used as a garden shed. Mr Smith slipped the leash, and the dog bounded forward, whining and pawing at the door.

'It's all right,' Mr Smith said. 'Caspar wouldn't behave like that if it weren't a friend inside.'

Percy was lying on his back behind a pile of seed trays. His face was white and there was a nasty swelling on his head, but his eyes were open and he was obviously alive.

'Tell control to send one of the others,' said Tarrent. 'And leave the door open so he can get some air.'

At that moment Caspar pricked his ears and growled. Mr Smith looked at Tarrent, and said sharply, 'Fetch! Fetch, Caspar!'

The command was scarcely necessary. As if he had heard himself called, the Dobermann was already streaking across the grass. Tarrent and Mr Smith raced after him. But Caspar easily outdistanced them.

The dog ran almost straight, leaping the low hedge that cut off the kitchen garden and burrowing through the shrubbery. The two men, forced to make detours, were left behind. But they were able to follow his excited barking and, in the far corner of the garden, finally caught up with him.

130

Caspar was leaping again and again at the wall, doing his utmost to pull down a man who clung tenaciously near the top of a curious V-shaped aluminium structure, that straddled the wall like a pair of steps and was high enough, Tarrent noticed, to avoid the alarm wires and beam on top of it. The man, in a greenish brown track suit, a stocking mask over his face, was kicking at the dog's head. Another man, in the same outlandish garb, was perched on top of the structure. As he hesitated between trying to help his chum and jumping to safety, Caspar received a heavy blow in the eye.

The dog fell back with a howl of pain, and the man on the ladder seized his chance. By the time Mr Smith had reached the top of the step ladder, both men were running towards the lane where a car was parked, awaiting them. Mr Smith was about to follow them over the wall, but Tarrent restrained him.

'Let them go,' he shouted. 'You'll never catch them now, and there's enough to do here.'

Tarrent had gone first to Alexei Bonalov, who was sitting on the grass, propped against a tree with his legs straight out in front of him. He had been thrown heavily to the ground, but seemed no more than slightly shocked. Tarrent helped him to his feet.

'Are you all right, Colonel?'

'Yes, but no thanks to you. No thanks to any of you,' Bonalov said, as Tarrent left him and went across to John Kenmare who was lying, face downwards and unmoving, a few feet away. The Russian showed no concern for Kenmare, but his expression softened as he looked towards Caspar. 'It was the dog that saved me. If it hadn't been for him, I'd be half way to London and the Soviet Embassy by now. And even he wouldn't have found me in time if I hadn't—'

'Later!'

Tarrent's sharp command temporarily silenced Bonalov. Together Tarrent and Mr Smith turned Kenmare over. He groaned, but his eyelids flickered as he regained consciousness.

'They're on their way from the house, sir,' said Mr Smith.

'Good. Get that damned contraption back over this side of

131

the wall.' Tarrent turned to Kenmare who was making an effort to sit up. 'What happened, John? Are you all right?'

'They knocked me out, I think, but I'll be okay in a minute.' Kenmare looked at Bonalov. 'They didn't get him.'

'No, they didn't get me.' By this time, Bonalov was almost spitting with rage. 'But don't expect me to be grateful, Mr Kenmare. You're meant to be responsible for my safety, and a thoroughly bad job you've made of it. As for you, Mr Tarrent, I warned you. Why wouldn't you believe me? I tell you, you'll get nothing from me, nothing, till I've seen Sir Patrick Cordar.'

'All right, sir.' Tarrent refused to be provoked, and John Kenmare had taken no notice of Bonalov's outburst. 'But, please, let's get our priorities right. Inquests later. The first thing is for all of us to get back to the house.'

Twenty minutes later Tarrent was reasonably content. He felt he had the situation under control. He went along to the study, where he had left Kenmare lying on a sofa. Kenmare had refused to go to bed. He had been knocked out by a blow to the jaw and the side of his face was already swelling but, apart from some miscellaneous bruises, had seemed otherwise unhurt. When Tarrent entered the room, he was standing up and pouring himself a whisky.

'Ought you to be drinking that stuff, John?'

'Why the hell not? It may be too early in the morning, but I need it.' Kenmare flung himself back on the sofa. His jaw hurt and it wasn't easy to speak. He had a splitting headache. He was sure that at least one tooth was loose. And he was furious about the events in the garden.

'What the hell's the situation now?' he demanded.

'Bonalov's in his suite, and safe, I think, short of something like a rocket attack,' said Tarrent. 'Percy's got a nasty head wound, and Mrs Smith says he's concussed, but in no danger. I've been on to London, but I couldn't get the Director. He'll call back as soon as they can trace him. I didn't like to say too much to anyone but Sir Patrick, but I requested a replacement for Percy, laid on a couple of extra security men and asked them to send the doctor back as soon as possible. We don't want to tackle a local man about Percy unless we have to, do we? And our MO can have a look at you too, when he gets here.'

'Oh, I'm all right,' said Kenmare, holding his jaw. 'And immediate security?'

At that moment there was a knock at the door, and Mr Smith came in. Tarrent repeated Kenmare's question to him.

'Well, sir,' Mr Smith replied. 'Bill's outside making a thorough search. He's got Caspar with him. The man on the ladder must have had soft shoes, because the kick in the eye's done the dog no harm. And George is in the control room.'

'But we're still one man short for the moment,' said Kenmare.

'Yes – excluding yourself – and two Dobermanns.' Tarrent grinned. 'But we should be all right till reinforcements arrive. Having failed once, they're hardly likely to have another go right away.'

'As to what actually happened,' he went on, 'it's not hard to work out, though it doesn't help much. Percy was hit from behind – presumably he interrupted the operation – and he's got no idea who or what hit him. Nor do you, I imagine, John?'

Kenmare shook his head. 'All I saw was a face in a mask, and all I felt was this damned punch.'

'There's one thing,' said Tarrent. 'That ladder structure they used might have been made for the job. It was just the right height to clear the alarm, wasn't it, Mr Smith? It was collapsible, I suppose?'

'Yes, sir. It was a very neat job. It would easily go on a car roof rack. And what's more, sir, they knew about the pressure alarm system inside the wall. You can see their footprints in the cleared strip where they stepped over the buried wires.'

'That's pretty suggestive,' said Tarrent. He looked enquiringly at Kenmare.

'I suppose so,' said Kenmare. 'Though I don't see what we can do about it. Anyway they didn't get Bonalov. What's

133

the wretched Commie got to say about it all?'

Tarrent looked at him in surprise. It was a totally uncharacteristic remark, but he supposed that John could be excused for reacting sharply to the shock of the attack.

'He's livid,' Tarrent replied. 'He says all he knows is that he heard you cry out, and was grabbed from behind as he turned. He was being hustled towards the wall when the dog arrived. He keeps saying we guaranteed his safety and we've been hopelessly incompetent. They'd have taken him this morning if Caspar hadn't stopped them, and Caspar was only there in time because he heard the whistle.'

'What whistle?'

Tarrent took the glass that Kenmare was holding out to him. He splashed in some whisky and added a lot of soda. It wasn't going to help if Kenmare got drunk. He looked at Mr Smith, who shook his head. As he returned the glass he gave Kenmare a searching glance. Kenmare looked ghastly, and Tarrent decided he was possibly hurt more than he had admitted.

'John, don't you think you should go to bed till the doctor arrives?'

'What whistle, Neil?'

'Yesterday, when he was being shown round the kennels, Bonalov pinched one of those high-pitched whistles – you know, the kind that only dogs can hear. Luckily he had it in his hand in his pocket, and somehow he managed to blow it during the struggle as they were hustling him off. Simple as that.'

'How very, very clever of him!'

There was venom in the words that startled Tarrent. 'Yes,' he said mildly. 'He thinks so too. And I'm not sure he hasn't got a point. Look,' he went on, 'if you won't go to bed, Mr Smith and I'll go and scare up some coffee, while you wait for Sir Patrick to call.' It was meant as a hint. If Kenmare insisted he was fit, it was his responsibility to report formally to Sir Patrick as soon as he had the opportunity.

*　　*　　*

134

As the door closed behind them, Kenmare swung his legs to the floor and slowly sat up. The whisky had helped the pain in his jaw, but had done nothing for his head. Tentatively, with the tip of his tongue, he probed at the loose tooth, and winced sharply as pain jabbed at him. Swearing under his breath, he went to sit at the desk.

What on earth was he going to say to Sir Patrick? What excuses could he make? The morning had been a disaster in every way, and he couldn't fail to come out of it badly. At the very least, his chances of succeeding Sir Patrick had decreased, though probably that was the least of his worries. That damned Russian! Everything had been going so well for him until Bonalov had decided to defect. Now . . . The phone rang, and reluctantly Kenmare lifted the receiver.

Sir Patrick Cordar arrived at the safe house in the late afternoon. The 'safe house'? What a misnomer that had turned out to be, he thought as he climbed somewhat stiffly from the car. The house was blown, its 'visitor' no longer safe, the entire operation at risk.

Kenmare and Tarrent were waiting to greet him. He regarded them both with a jaundiced eye, and made a mental note to tell Tarrent to get his hair cut. That red hair of his was absurdly long. Then he remembered he was no longer in the army. His officers' haircuts were no longer any real concern of his. His gaze flickered over Kenmare, who looked ill, his face swollen. Sir Patrick frowned.

'You were hurt this morning, John? You didn't mention it on the phone.'

'It's not important, sir. I'm all right.' Kenmare started to grin, but it turned into a grimace and involuntarily he put his hand to his mouth. 'Sorry, sir. I was going to say, the worst I really suffered was getting my suit ripped. Having come here without any luggage, I've been wearing poor Simon's shirts. Now I'm reduced to his jacket too.'

Sir Patrick made a noncommittal sound, but he patted Kenmare sympathetically on the arm before leading the way to the study. Perhaps without thinking, he sat himself behind the desk. It gave their meeting a somewhat formal air.

'Now,' he said, as if calling them to order. 'Tell me it all in detail.'

'The first warning we got was from the dogs,' Kenmare began. 'The two who'd been out during the night were sick this morning. We thought they might have been poisoned. In fact, they were just drugged – presumably thrown some doped food – because they're fine again now . . .'

With Tarrent's help, Kenmare gave a full account of what had occurred. He made no excuses for himself and laid no blame on anyone else. Sir Patrick listened attentively, rarely interrupting.

'. . . and that's as much as we can tell you, sir,' Kenmare concluded.

Sir Patrick nodded. 'At least you didn't lose Bonalov. We must be thankful for that. It's about all we have to be thankful for. The attempt to get him back was well-planned. The Russians seem to have known not only where their man was, but exactly what they'd be up against. And I find that a most unpleasant thought.'

There was silence, and it lengthened, while Sir Patrick allowed Kenmare and Tarrent to consider the implications of what he had said. Not that the idea was new to either of them. The betrayal of the safe house and Bonalov's presence there was self-evident. It had been nagging at their minds throughout the day.

Tarrent broke the silence. 'Sir, there are two things that might be relevant. One is that Bonalov expected that an attempt would be made to capture or kill him. He was quite positive about it. He swore he wasn't safe here. Incidentally, he's demanding to see you personally, sir.'

'I'll see him before I go.' Sir Patrick dismissed Bonalov's importunity and, when Tarrent didn't continue, said sharply, 'What's the other thing, Neil?'

'It's a question of who knew about the house, sir.' Tarrent picked his words carefully. 'I think it's possible that Simon Mont told Betty, his wife.'

'And what makes you say that?'

Tarrent kept his explanation brief and factual. He knew he'd been stupid in not reporting it before, and he waited for

Sir Patrick's wrath to descend on him. He didn't have to wait long.

'You told John about this, of course?'

'No, sir.'

'Then whom did you tell?' Sir Patrick was very precise.

'No one, sir. At the time it didn't seem—' Tarrent stopped. He wasn't going to lie. He had nothing against lying when necessary, but it wasn't necessary now. He said firmly, 'I find it very difficult to accept that Betty Mont could be the source of the leak.'

'Very praiseworthy of you to stand up for your friends, Neil, but may I remind you there are other loyalties.'

'As a matter of fact, sir,' Kenmare said. 'I rather agree with Neil. Even if Simon did tell her where the house is, this morning's attack was well-planned, as we agreed, and the planning was based on accurate knowledge of our security and alarm systems. I doubt if that's the sort of thing he'd have mentioned casually.'

'Maybe not, but—' Sir Patrick shrugged. 'Anyway, Bonalov will have to be moved, though where to I'm not sure at the moment. We'll discuss it later. I'll have a word with the staff now. You come with me, John. Then afterwards you can take me along and introduce me to our precious guest.'

The two men shook hands. Sir Patrick would have preferred to avoid the physical contact – he had no liking for defectors of any kind, least of all if they happened to be KGB – but Alexei Bonalov had given him no choice. He couldn't deliberately refuse to take the Russian's proffered hand.

'Sir Patrick, I am delighted to meet you at last. We have private matters to discuss, urgent matters.'

'Colonel Bonalov—'

'Sir Patrick, I said private matters. I wish to speak to you alone. It is essential – for your sake as well as mine.'

'Certainly, if you must.' Sir Patrick's smile had no warmth. 'John—'

'Of course, sir. I'll be in the study, if you need me.'

Sir Patrick nodded his thanks. 'Now, Colonel,' he said as the door shut.

Bonalov, his eyes bright with anger, let his temper rip. He had made a bargain with the British and they had let him down. He had trusted them with his safety and twice – once in France and again in this so-called safe house – he had been forced to save himself. The British had proved themselves inefficient, untrustworthy, traitorous. He was beginning to regret he had approached them.

'Why did you?' asked Sir Patrick suddenly. The Russian, he thought astutely, was over-playing his hand; he wasn't nearly as angry as he was pretending.

'Not because I think your system's so wonderful,' said Bonalov, suddenly thoughtful. 'But after my son was killed in Afghanistan in a stupid, unnecessary war, and my wife died, I had only myself to think of. As Head of Directorate T, I had reached my plateau. The way ahead was barred. There was nothing more for me in the Soviet Union – and always there were enemies. No, it may be cynical, Sir Patrick, but with Pavel and Olga gone I decided I'd be altogether better off in the West – in the United Kingdom.' Suddenly his anger, which had apparently subsided, seemed to flare again. 'It appears I was wrong, however. Trusting in your promises, I find myself at serious risk – and nothing gained.'

'Oh, come, Colonel,' Sir Patrick protested. 'It's not quite as bad as that. You're still with us, after all.'

'That is a stupid remark, Sir Patrick. Why do you think that from the moment I walked out of the Soviet Embassy in Paris, everything has gone wrong?' Bonalov stepped forward and confronted the Director. 'I will tell you. It is because the operation was betrayed, and every move you make is known to your – our – adversaries. From the very beginning it was betrayed, though I didn't realize this myself until it was too late and I couldn't go back.'

'Nonsense. Our security's been as tight as a drum.'

Alexei Bonalov laughed aloud. 'My dear Sir Patrick, I know you don't believe that, and you know I know you don't believe that. Start the operation over again. Move me to a really safe house – one that no one so far connected to this fiasco is aware of – and I'll tell you the name of your traitor.'

THIRTEEN

Sir Patrick Cordar was not given to indecision. By the time he had arrived back in London and been dropped at his Kensington house, he had decided on a course of action.

It was more than likely that Alexei Bonalov was trying to deceive him. The Russian was probably lying in his teeth. The original misfortunes in France could easily have been due to his own carelessness, and the safe house could have been blown by accident. If this were so, there was no reason to suspect the existence of a traitor among Sir Patrick's own men. Nevertheless, as the Director knew well, it was a natural tendency to believe what one wanted to believe, to avoid unpleasant conclusions. He wasn't going to be caught in that sort of trap. He would humour the ex-KGB Colonel, and see what came of it.

The next morning he returned, without warning, to the safe house. 'Everything under control, Mr Smith?' he asked as his car crawled through the gates.

'Yes, sir. A quiet night. No alarms.'

'Splendid.'

Sir Patrick met Neil Tarrent jogging, rather disconsolately, down the drive. 'Good morning, Neil. Taking some exercise?'

'Yes, sir. It seems a pity to waste such a lovely day.'

Sir Patrick nodded. 'I want to talk to you and John.'

'He's in the study, sir.' Tarrent glanced at his watch. 'Shall I get Mrs Smith to bring us some coffee?'

'Yes. Do that.'

Sir Patrick found John Kenmare lying on the sofa, and gestured to him to stay where he was, but Kenmare struggled to sit up. His face was very swollen and he looked exhausted. The pain-killing tablets he had taken on going to bed had drugged him, but without giving him the benefit of sleep.

'How are you, John?'

'Not too bad, thank you, sir. But I've got to see a dentist as soon as possible.' He spoke out of the side of his mouth.

'I'm sorry.' As yesterday, Sir Patrick seated himself behind the desk. He opened his briefcase and took out some notes he didn't need. What he had to say was quite clear in his mind. He looked round as Tarrent brought in a tray. 'Ah, coffee. Good.'

'It was all ready,' Tarrent said. 'Mrs Smith only had to add another cup.'

In spite of the casual, genial conversation, there was tension in the room. All three of them were aware of it. Sir Patrick did nothing to relieve it.

Steepling his hands, he said, 'I've reached some decisions which concern you both. First, I'm taking you off the Bonalov operation.'

It was unexpected. Admittedly they hadn't had much luck, but the Director rarely changed horses in midstream like this. Tarrent found himself resenting it.

'May we ask why, sir?'

'I was about to tell you, Neil.'

Tarrent swallowed the implied rebuke. He looked at Kenmare, who was stirring his coffee as if the process required all his concentration. Otherwise he appeared unmoved.

Sir Patrick unbent a little. 'Perhaps I should say that it's not because I've lost faith in either of you. But it's quite obvious the present situation is unsatisfactory. So I'm bringing down two fresh interrogators who will move with Bonalov to a new safe house as soon as it's ready. That should be in the course of the next few days.'

'Can't he be moved immediately, sir?' Kenmare said, frowning. 'I mean, this place isn't exactly secure any more, is it?'

'Unfortunately there's nowhere suitable that's available at the moment. But I hope by the beginning of next week . . .' Sir Patrick left the sentence unfinished.

'And us, sir? Do I go back to Paris?'

'I was coming to that.' Sir Patrick shifted in his chair. 'The answer to your question, John is no. You're posted back to

Headquarters as of today. I don't want you to return to France at all. If you're not there the DST can't question you about your car or your movements last Friday. I've heard the Soviets claim that three of their people were kidnapped, and by now the French must have a pretty good idea of what actually happened. There's damn all they can do, of course. But there's no knowing when the Russians will try to make public capital out of the affair, and it's best you're out of the country.'

Kenmare nodded. 'Right. I'll lay on my move, then.'

'I hope it won't inconvenience your mother or your wife too much.' Sir Patrick was sympathetic. 'I'll have a word with the Ambassador myself, and explain some of the circumstances.'

'Thank you very much, sir.'

'Your London house is available?'

'Oh yes, we never let it. But – I was wondering. There'll be a fair amount to arrange. Unless you want me for something particular, I should like to take two or three days off, sir.'

'Certainly. Just make sure we know where you are, in case we need you.' Sir Patrick looked at his notes. 'I think that's all for you, John.' He turned to Tarrent. 'And now you, Neil.'

Tarrent didn't expect such consideration – he was a more junior officer, after all – and he didn't get it. He too was to stay in London, at least temporarily. He might or might not be going back to Moscow. Leave wasn't mentioned, and Sir Patrick didn't enquire about his domestic arrangements.

'There's one other thing,' Sir Patrick concluded. 'Simon Mont's funeral is tomorrow. I've arranged for wreaths to be sent from the Department, and from his colleagues. But I think it would be best if neither of you attended. It's a family affair, and your presence might possibly cause some comment.'

Tarrent was tempted to ask if it was permitted to telephone Betty, to enquire how she was. Instead he said, 'When do we leave here, sir?'

'As soon as you're ready. One of the staff can drive you, then bring the car back.'

'You don't want us to wait for our replacements.'

'No need, John. I shall be here myself. I want to have another talk to Bonalov.' Sir Patrick spoke pleasantly enough, but it was obvious to both Kenmare and Tarrent that he was leaving a lot unsaid, and that they were no longer fully in the Director's confidence.

It took them half an hour to pack and depart. Twenty minutes later, Alexei Bonalov joined Sir Patrick in the hall of the safe house. He was carrying the attaché case he had brought with him from Moscow.

'You know the form, Colonel,' Sir Patrick said. 'The object of the exercise is to start afresh – to provide as complete a cut-out as possible between now and the future, as it were. The officers so far concerned with the operation don't know when you're moving, or where to. The staff here will continue to behave as if you were still in residence. My driver will know you're leaving, but even he won't know where you're going. We've got to trust some people a little, and you know the staff and you've seen my driver. You agree to the plan?'

Bonalov nodded.

'And,' went on the Director, 'just in case of surveillance, I'm afraid the first part of your journey may not be very comfortable.'

'I'm more concerned with my safety than my comfort,' said Bonalov brusquely. 'I've had two narrow escapes. I don't want a third.'

The Director made no reply. But he assisted Bonalov into the back of the big Daimler and helped him to settle on some cushions on the floor. Then, stepping carefully, he climbed in after him, and allowed his driver to arrange a light rug over his lap, so that it also hid the Russian.

They drove at a modest speed and, except for his cramped position, Bonalov experienced little discomfort, though it grew warm under the rug, and the car's motion was slightly sick-making. He was glad when, after about half an hour, the car drew off the road and stopped. With Sir Patrick's help he struggled up on to the seat, and looked curiously about him.

In the Soviet Union, he thought, blinds would have been

drawn across the car windows, but here no attempt had been made to obstruct his view. They had turned off what must be a minor road – the only traffic he could hear was light – and had come to a halt in a clearing, protected on all sides by dusty trees.

'Why have we stopped? What do we do here?' he asked.

Sir Patrick consulted his watch. 'In five minutes another car will arrive. In it will be a couple of my most trusted officers. They are replacements for Mr Kenmare and Mr Tarrent, and I hope you will have complete faith in them.' From his wallet he extracted two photographs, and handed them to Bonalov. 'Tell me now if you have any objections to either of them. Their names and dates of birth are on the backs.'

Bonalov regarded the photographs with interest, and shook his head. 'No objections, Sir Patrick. I know little of the younger man. Hasn't he been in Washington, though? The other was a thorn in our flesh when he was operating in the German Democratic Republic some years ago, but I can't hold that against him, can I?'

'Hardly.' Sir Patrick refused to show his annoyance at the nonchalant way in which Bonalov had revealed how much he knew of the SIS officers. 'I'll tell them where to take you. They've not yet been informed. And the staff at the safe house to which you're being transferred only know that they're to expect a visitor. Arrangements will be made so that you have the absolute minimum of contact with them, and they will remain unaware of your identity. So, apart from my two officers and myself, no one will know your whereabouts. That should be satisfactory, Colonel Bonalov.'

'Perfectly satisfactory, Sir Patrick.'

Sir Patrick's last remark had been intended as a statement, not a question, and the Director greeted Bonalov's reply with a blank face. Then he looked impatiently at his watch. As the thought crossed his mind that the other car was overdue, a dark-coloured Cortina drove into the clearing and parked a few yards ahead of them. A man in his early forties, recognizable from the photograph the Russian had been shown, got out and walked back to the Daimler. Sir

Patrick wound down his window.

'Good morning, Dermot.'

'Good morning, sir.'

'Mr and Mrs Graham are expecting you.'

'The Grahams?' The man smiled his pleasure. 'Yes, sir.'
He went round to the other side of the Daimler and opened
the door for Bonalov. No introductions seemed to be expected, and the man simply said, 'We're ready when you are,
sir.'

Sir Patrick said sharply, 'One moment.' Then. 'Colonel?'

'Yes, Sir Patrick. I've not forgotten our agreement.' From
the inner pocket of his jacket Bonalov produced a folded
piece of paper and offered it to the Director. 'The name you
want, and the date on which the man was recruited by us.'
He hesitated, then added, speaking slowly and seriously,
'Believe me, Sir Patrick, I give you this name, not to cause
havoc in your organization, though inevitably it will do that,
but to protect myself and to prove to you my good faith. I beg
you not to disregard it.'

'Thank you.'

Sir Patrick took the piece of paper between two fingers as if
it were something untouchable, and waited for Bonalov to
leave his car. He was not prepared to give the Russian the
satisfaction of watching him unfold the paper and read the
name. Not that he expected to be surprised. He was fairly
sure whom Bonalov would accuse.

Turning to retrieve his attaché case, Alexei Bonalov said
softly, 'There is one more thing I must tell you, Sir Patrick.
You have there more than we agreed. The name I have given
you is not only that of the man who betrayed this current
operation. The same agent provided us with that JIC paper,
and over the years has given us much else.'

With that, Bonalov strode off to the Cortina. Sir Patrick,
watching him, found that his fist was crushing the paper.
Bonalov's parting remark, if true, had added a new and
appalling dimension to the situation.

Sir Patrick forced his fingers to relax. Leaning across the
seat, he relieved his temper by slamming the Daimler's door
with unnecessary violence. He waited until the Cortina had

144

turned and driven out of the clearing. Then he unfolded the crumpled ball in his hand.

His face expressionless, he stared at the name and the date. He didn't believe Bonalov. He refused to believe Bonalov. But he knew he couldn't ignore the Russian's accusation. For some minutes he sat, deep in thought. Then he pushed the button that lowered the window dividing him from the driver, and said, 'Wimbledon next, please. I'll direct you when we get there.'

Betty Mont opened the door herself. It was some time since Sir Patrick had seen her, and momentarily he didn't recognize her. She looked thinner than he remembered, more fragile, and there were dark shadows painted under her eyes. She was holding a duster, and somehow she made it an excuse not to offer him her hand.

'Sir Patrick, good morning. This is a surprise.'

'I hope I'm not disturbing you, but I was passing quite close.'

'I never mind being disturbed when I'm doing housework. Come in.'

Sir Patrick followed her through the sitting-room, which was in some disarray, and out on to the terrace. It was cool and peaceful here. He sat in the comfortable old basket chair to which Betty Mont had pointed, and gazed across the grass to the child's swing suspended from the branch of a tree. He thought of Simon Mont with real sorrow.

'Can I get you some coffee, Sir Patrick? Or would you prefer sherry?'

'Neither, thank you. Mrs Mont—' This was more difficult than he had imagined. Sir Patrick cleared his throat and began again. 'Mrs Mont, I want to talk to you about Simon.'

'Yes.' She waited for him to express his condolences, but he remained silent, and she said, 'It's the funeral tomorrow, which is why I'm tidying up the place. Everyone'll be coming back here afterwards.'

'But you're alone at the moment?'

'Right now, yes. I made Simone go to school, though she

145

didn't want to. She'll be home later, and the two boys. Simon's parents are staying with his sister. She lives—' Betty's voice tailed away. 'Why did you ask that?' she said sharply.

'I hoped we wouldn't be interrupted.'

Sir Patrick hesitated again. He thought of making some specious excuse for his visit, having a glass of sherry and leaving. But, if he went, he would have to send someone else to interrogate Simon's wife officially, and he didn't want to do that, not yet. Apart from the blowing of the safe house there was nothing to suggest the traitor was in his Department – Bonalov's lies could be discounted – and the last thing he wanted when he was on the verge of retirement, was the suggestion of a scandal. The more people involved, the greater the likelihood that the media might sniff the story, get a whiff of treachery . . . Sir Patrick shook his head. It was being a bad day.

He said carefully, 'Mrs Mont, what I have to say – to ask you – is highly confidential.'

'Money?' Betty Mont smiled wryly. Simon was dead but what was uppermost in everyone's mind – including her own – was money. 'I know we're going to have a lot of problems, Sir Patrick, but I really haven't tried to face them yet. There'll be a pension, I understand.'

'Nothing to do with money. It's a question of security.' Sir Patrick hadn't intended to be so blunt. 'Simon confided in you a great deal, didn't he? It's not unnatural. Husbands often tell their wives more than they should, strictly speaking – especially if it's a close marriage. And we're not in an easy business. From time to time wives become involved, and inevitably they learn things.'

'They also learn to keep their mouths shut, Sir Patrick.'

'Yes, of course. But, Mrs Mont, I have to ask you. How much did Simon tell you about the last operation he was on?'

There was a bowl containing freshly-picked peas on the garden table between them, and a colander. Betty Mont pulled them towards her and began shelling the peas. It was a full minute before she spoke.

'Neil Tarrent,' she said. 'He told you. I lost my temper

when I heard about Simon. I let fly. But it was the first time it's ever happened, I swear, so you don't have to worry about your precious security, Sir Patrick. There was no one else there, except Simone, and she was far too upset at her father's death to take in what I was saying.'

'You've never mentioned the operation to anyone else – even the children?'

'No!' Mechanically Betty continued to shell peas. 'Look, Sir Patrick, aren't you making rather a fuss about nothing? Simon told me he was going to France to collect some bloody Russian defector. That's all – literally all. Okay, he shouldn't have told me, but it's too late to reprimand him now. As for me, surely I'm allowed one minor indiscretion after all these years.'

'Simon told you about the safe house, too.'

'He did not.' Betty frowned, then her face cleared. 'I remember. I asked Neil if they'd taken Simon – Simon's body there. For God's sake, it was a reasonable question in the circumstances.'

'But you knew about the safe house?' Sir Patrick persisted. 'Where it was. The security arrangements. The dogs. Simon supervised the preparations.'

'I didn't know that. I didn't know anything about it. Simon never mentioned it. I just assumed—Oh, in novels and films the defector's always taken to a "safe house".'

Sir Patrick nodded. Rightly or wrongly, he believed her. Her candour, her sincerity, were transparent. He was prepared to accept that Simon's careless talk to his wife had been trivial, and was almost certainly irrelevant. But that left the other obvious possibility. The question was how to approach it.

'Mrs Mont, thank you for being so frank,' he said, to gain time. 'I'm sorry I've had to question you like this. I'm sure you understand.'

'Yes, I understand. It was my fault. That outburst.' Betty Mont shook her head. 'I hoped Neil would forget it. I thought he was my friend – Simon's friend – and he'd keep quiet about it.'

Again Sir Patrick hesitated. But there was no point in

147

leaving matters here. He said, 'I'm afraid it's a little more serious than that. Neil did keep quiet about it at first, and that was quite wrong of him. But he had to tell me, he had no option, when it became clear the house was blown.'

'What?'

'Blown, as we say. Our – er – our opponents learnt a good deal about the place. I'm sorry, Mrs Mont, but your husband was one of the few people with the necessary knowledge. So there are some more questions I've got to ask – about Simon.'

Betty Mont stared at him, her mouth very slightly open. Sir Patrick hadn't come to express his regrets about Simon or to discuss her financial situation, not even to give her a fussy warning about security. He'd come because he suspected her – or Simon, or both of them – of betraying the safe house.

'Get out!' she said suddenly, her voice thick with tears. 'Get out of my house! I don't give a damn what you think about me. But Simon was one of the most honest, hard-working, loyal men there's ever been. If you can believe he was a traitor, you'd believe anything.'

Immediately Sir Patrick returned to his office he told his secretary he was not to be disturbed. For a while he sat silently behind his desk, thinking about his interview with Betty Mont. Maybe he'd been wrong to tackle it by himself; perhaps he should have called in the professionals. In any case, it was water under the bridge.

He rose from his desk and went to a filing cabinet, taking from it again the list of those who had official access to the JIC paper that had come into Bonalov's possession. Once more he checked through it carefully.

He knew only too well the problems with such access lists. Named recipients of documents would pass them to their juniors; in defiance of regulations, photocopying for convenience was not infrequent, especially with papers of such a category that return of the original was demanded. Secretaries had to type papers, and printers run them off. Nevertheless, one had to start somewhere, and it was a fact that, although this list included the names of several of his staff, only two of them had been involved in any way with Bonalov's defection and reception. Theoretically, therefore, and excluding himself, only John Kenmare and Simon Mont could have both copied the JIC paper, and attempted to betray Bonalov. Neil Tarrent's name was not on the access list.

Sighing, Sir Patrick took from his pocket the crumpled paper that Bonalov had given him. With fingers that trembled slightly he smoothed it out. Betty Mont was wrong, he thought sadly: there were some things he couldn't bring himself to believe.

He had been sure Bonalov would name Simon Mont. It was so obvious. Dead, he couldn't defend himself. Dead, he couldn't be interrogated, so the damage assessment would be that much more difficult. By naming Mont, Bonalov would cause great disruption and embarrassment to the British, and ultimately to all Western intelligence services.

But Alexei Bonalov had denied himself this opportunity. To protect himself, as he said, and to establish his credibility as a genuine defector, he had done the incredible. He had named John Kenmare.

FOURTEEN

The bank draft arrived on Thursday morning.

The announcement of Simon Mont's death – 'suddenly, as the result of a motoring accident' – had appeared in *The Times* and the *Daily Telegraph* on Monday. Since then Betty had received a sheaf of sympathetic letters, many of them from people she had never heard of but who had either worked with Simon or known him in one way or another. She was surprised at their number.

On Thursday, having sent Simone off to school, Betty sat down at the kitchen table and sorted the obvious bills from the personal mail. There were a lot of bills – the Monts' creditors had also read of Simon's death, she thought cynically – and she pushed them to one side. They could wait. She began to open the letters.

The bank draft was in the fourth or fifth envelope. She looked at it, at first with mild interest, then with amazement. The cheque was for twenty-five thousand pounds sterling. It was payable to Simon Mont, and drawn on the City of London branch of a Swiss bank. No letter was enclosed with it.

Twenty-five thousand pounds. Betty's immediate reaction was one of joy. It was a wonderful sum of money. It would make all the difference to the family, save them all from immediate financial worry. Then, in the flick of a second, joy gave way to doubt. Where had the money come from?

Suddenly cold, though it was a warm humid day, Betty Mont shivered. It was absurd to receive twenty-five thousand pounds like this, with no indication of its source. She looked again in the envelope, on the table, on the floor. But she hadn't missed anything; there was no enclosure.

She tried to think logically. Why did people give other

people money? The most usual reason was because they'd earned it. She wondered for a moment if the FCO could possibly have sent Simon – or rather Simon's estate – some kind of *ex gratia* payment, and the letter that should have been enclosed inadvertently forgotten. She knew that Simon's Department could be devious if necessary, but this seemed an extraordinary way of making any such gesture, even from secret funds. Surely it would be less equivocal to explain. She looked at the envelope again. It was plain manilla, with an ordinary first-class stamp, not OHMS, not franked, and postmarked London W1.

If it weren't from the Department, what else could it be? Certainly not the repayment of a debt; Simon had never been in a position to lend anyone such a sum. And it wasn't a gift from a rich friend; they had none with that sort of money to give away. It had arrived out of the blue, at a time when she desperately needed it, but she was far from sure she should accept it.

Finally, reluctantly, she forced herself to think of Sir Patrick Cordar's extraordinary visit two days ago. In the end, he had practically accused Simon of passing secret information to a foreign power – of espionage, of treason.

Betty knew enough of the system to be aware that the matter would not end with her vehement denials. Any security trouble almost inevitably led to detailed enquiries, renewed positive vettings, investigations of all those involved and their families – and their finances. In the past, such prospects had never troubled her. The security chaps – the dogs, as Simon called them – could do as they damn well pleased; she had plenty of other things to worry about. But now . . . What was she to do with this bank draft – this sudden wealth? Any display of affluence would be certain to be noted, and she wouldn't be able to offer any credible explanation. She knew what the security men would make of that.

She sighed unhappily. It was hard to have her hopes raised, and then immediately dashed. But there was no way she could keep the money, not till she had discovered its source. She wished she'd never seen the cheque. She wondered if she could destroy it, forget about it and, if questioned, deny all knowledge of it. She knew at once that wasn't possible. It would look as if she doubted Simon. And she didn't doubt him. Nothing on earth would ever make her believe that Simon had worked for the Soviet Union – or for any nation except Britain.

'Mr Remington shouldn't be long now,' his secretary said. 'Would you like a cup of coffee while you're waiting.'

'Yes, please.' Betty Mont smiled with a false brightness. She picked up the newspaper that lay on the table in front of her and glanced at the front page. She tried to read, but she couldn't concentrate. Her eyes flicked from one headline to the next. They all seemed equally meaningless. Then her attention was caught, riveted.

It was just a brief news item. It said that three members of the Soviet Delegation attending the Conference on Arms Limitation in Paris had mysteriously disappeared. The bodies of two had later been found some distance from the French capital. They appeared to have died in a car accident, probably in an attempt to prevent the third man, a Colonel Alexei Bonalov, from either being kidnapped or defecting to the West. Tass, the Soviet news agency, had picked up the story and reacted with unusual speed but, unsurprisingly, had strongly hinted at the kidnapping theory.

Betty Mont was re-reading the story when Remington's secretary brought her the coffee. She gave the girl only perfunctory thanks, her mind elsewhere. She now knew, or thought she knew, how Simon had died, and it strengthened her resolve. Simon was not going to be made a scapegoat for anyone or anything.

'Betty! What a surprise. I didn't expect to see you again so soon.' Peter Remington, already behind schedule, tried to sound pleased. A client was due any minute – the man should have arrived by now – and he had not yet looked at the morning's mail. 'Come along in.'

Pausing to give his secretary some instructions, Remington led Betty into his office. 'I'm not usually as late as this,' he explained, motioning her to a chair and riffling through the letters on his desk. They, like the contents of his briefcase, would have to wait. 'I had to call on an elderly client. She's always changing her will, and she insists I go to her.'

Remington stopped abruptly. He was not by nature a verbose man, but Betty's face, pinched and white around the mouth, had jolted him. She looked far more tense now, he thought, than yesterday at the funeral.

He said gently, 'What can I do for you, Betty? Is there some problem?'

'Yes.' She pushed the envelope containing the bank draft across the desk, and watched him study it.

Remington gave a long whistle. 'My dear, I wouldn't call this much of a problem.'

'But it is.' Betty leant forward. 'Peter, I believe this money's supposed to have come from the Russians – from the Soviet Embassy, perhaps. I think someone's trying to frame Simon, to suggest he was a traitor.'

Remington smiled weakly. He had been a good friend of Simon Mont for years, and knew that he worked in some branch of the Foreign and Commonwealth Office. Simon rarely talked about his job, and then only in general terms, and Remington had assumed it was confidential and probably technical. He had never associated Simon with spies or counter-espionage or anything of that kind.

Wondering if the strain of the last few days had been too much for Betty, he said, 'Why on earth should anyone want to do that?'

'I don't know. Perhaps to divert suspicion from himself.' Betty shrugged. 'But I don't intend to let him get away with it.'

'No. No, quite.' Peter Remington took off his spectacles and polished them. It was more a nervous gesture than a necessity. 'Why have you come to me about this, Betty? Wouldn't one of Simon's colleagues be more help? That man, Tarrent, I spoke to on the phone? He said he was a friend.'

153

'I'm not so sure he is.' Betty was still angry with Neil Tarrent. He had telephoned, but she had hung up on him. And he hadn't bothered to come to the funeral, though Simon had been good to him. 'No. It's you I want to help me, Peter. I want you to go and see Sir Patrick Cordar.'

In fact, Sir Patrick was having a trying day himself. With uncharacteristic indecision, he had so far taken no action on Bonalov's accusation against Kenmare, though at the back of his mind he had the outline of a plan that might test it. The accusation still seemed utterly incredible. Of course he knew of traitors in the past – the recent past – with impeccable backgrounds and brilliant careers, but he still found hard to accept even the remote possibility that the son of General Sir Peter Kenmare – dear Clara's son – could be one of their number.

Sir Patrick paced up and down his office as once more he considered the matter. In the first place, Bonalov was a highly suspect source of information; he might well prove to be an active source of intentional disinformation. And against him there was at least some evidence to support the assumption of Kenmare's innocence.

For example, Kenmare's arrival in the UK, accompanying Mont and Tarrent and Bonalov, had resulted from a last-minute change of plan, occasioned by Mont's injury. Until his arrival in England – or at least his departure from France – it was unlikely that Kenmare knew the location of the safe house prepared for Bonalov's reception. Even if Mont, or Tarrent, had told him where it was, only Mont was fully in the picture about the alarm and intrusion systems, and as Kenmare himself had pointed out, this kind of detail had been crucial to the attack. It was almost impossible that Mont should have discussed technical data of this kind in casual conversation with Kenmare; such questions simply would not have arisen. Kenmare therefore could not have passed on the vital information in France.

And in the UK, thought Sir Patrick, they had all gone straight from the airfield to the house. Once there, where the

154

rules were strict and even staff phone calls were monitored, Kenmare would have had no opportunity to make any untoward contacts.

Sir Patrick shook his head. It was good, but not nearly watertight. Even he could see holes in what, after all, was largely conjecture. There was nothing for it. Bonalov's accusation must be put to the test. He asked his secretary to get hold of Kenmare.

A few minutes later he came on the line. 'Hello, sir. You just got me. I'm spending most of the rest of the day at the dentist's.'

'I'm sorry about that, but I'd like to see you – not today, but tomorrow. Could you come in to the office for half an hour or so? Say ten o'clock?'

'Yes, of course, sir.'

'Good. Tomorrow then. And good luck.'

Sir Patrick had hardly put down the phone when it rang again. His secretary said, 'I've a Mr Peter Remington calling, sir. He's Mrs Mont's legal representative, and he wants to make an appointment to see you. He says it's very urgent.'

The Director hesitated. He had an unpleasant feeling that any such interview would spell more trouble, more complexities, but he could hardly refuse. Better to get it over as soon as possible.

What time can I manage?'

'You're free at five this afternoon, sir.'

'See if that'll suit him, then.'

It was exactly five o'clock when Peter Remington was shown into Sir Patrick's office. He was a smallish man, in his forties, going bald, with humourous eyes behind large spectacles. A typical lawyer, Sir Patrick summed him up. Then, rising, he offered his hand across the desk.

Remington didn't waste time. 'Sir Patrick, as you know I represent Mrs Mont and the estate of the late Simon Mont. First, I must admit that I find the reason for my visit a little bizarre. However, I'll proceed. Please ask whatever questions you like. Mrs Mont has instructed me to answer anything and everything with total frankness, and to the best of my ability I will.'

Sir Patrick bowed his head in acknowledgement, but didn't reply. Remington then gave him photocopies of the bank draft and the envelope in which it had arrived. He explained how and when Betty had received it – and her misgivings about accepting it.

'It could be the gift of a friend who wishes to remain anonymous, but Mrs Mont considers that extremely unlikely.' Remington paused, to add emphasis to his next point. 'My first question is this, Sir Patrick: May we assume that this draft does not originate from your Department, or any other department or agency of the British Government?'

'Ah, now I understand.' Sir Patrick was bland. 'I was wondering how you imagined I was involved. Yes, Mr Remington, as far as I know, I think you may safely assume that.'

'Thank you.' Peter Remington took off his spectacles, polished them on a corner of his handkerchief and replaced them. He smiled apologetically. 'This is where I'm afraid I dive in out of my depth, Sir Patrick. I have to tell you that Mrs Mont believes that this money might have been sent in an attempt to implicate her husband in some kind of an – er – an espionage plot or undertaking, perhaps in order to draw suspicion from the real culprit. I have tried to put her suspicions in as neutral terms as possible. I hope I make myself clear.'

'Quite clear, Mr Remington. Your suggestion is that the money originated with a foreign agency, in furtherance of some kind of conspiracy.'

'Yes, Sir Patrick. But let's not mince words more than we have to. We're both thinking of the Soviet Union, or one of its satellites, aren't we?'

Remington waited, but Sir Patrick remained silent. He seemed to be contemplating a painting on the wall behind Remington's head. Sir Patrick won the contest to see who could wait the longer.

Remington said, 'Mrs Mont thinks that you may have some means of tracing the source of this bank draft. May I ask if this is so?'

'If it were necessary, we might try.'

'It would be a kindness, Sir Patrick – and to my mind

156

possibly also a duty. I tell you in confidence that the Monts could make good use of the money. But as long as there's any question of it being – tainted, shall we say? – Mrs Mont insists that the original draft remains in my safe-keeping.'

'Mr Remington, I understand what you say, and I'm most grateful for all you've told me.' Sir Patrick produced a wintry smile. 'I would like to help Mrs Mont if I could, but I shall have to give the matter some thought. I'll be in touch with you in a few days.'

'Thank you, sir.' Peter Remington picked up his briefcase. He knew when he was dismissed. 'I'll give your secretary my card, with my business and home addresses and phone numbers.'

'Splendid.' Sir Patrick was opening the door for him. 'There is one thing. I'm not quite clear why Mrs Mont bothered you, why she didn't come straight to me herself.'

'Well, Sir Patrick, we discussed the matter, and she thought it best, in view of any possible accusations against her late husband, that this conversation should be formal, if I may put it like that – between you as his superior and me as her legal representative.' Remington left it at that.

'I see. Yes, I understand. Good day to you, Mr Remington. If you'll give my secretary your pass – the slip of paper they gave you when you entered the building – she'll sign it and call a messenger to show you out.'

The Director shut the door of his office with exaggerated gentleness. He was restraining his temper with difficulty. He'd been inveigled – trapped, if you like – into what that wretched lawyer had called a 'formal interview' – almost a matter of record. He could just see the man sitting in his car making notes of it while it was fresh in his mind. What on earth was the Mont woman thinking of? Suppose the money were traced to a Soviet source. She'd have only herself to blame for branding her late husband a traitor.

If that was what they wanted, he could easily put the dogs on, and see what emerged. But would that necessarily be the best course? This business of the bank draft was odd, very odd. Could Betty Mont conceivably be right? Was someone trying to frame Simon? No. The first thing to do was to go through with his half-formulated plan . . . Sir Patrick called his secretary.

'I want Neil Tarrent, just as soon as you can get him.'

Tarrent, however, had already left the office. He had killed the day reading old files and preparing a report on a part of the world that might, just might, become important in the nearer future. He knew that if he had not been there, the job wouldn't have been done. It had been created to keep him occupied, and served no purpose other than to bore him.

He didn't have a car in London, and decided to walk off his frustrations. Crossing Westminster Bridge, he went through Parliament Square and into St James's Park. He walked fast, lost in thought, unhappy that Betty Mont had refused to speak to him when he had phoned, pausing only to admire the Whitehall skyline from the bridge over the lake. He wouldn't have noticed Helen Kenmare if she hadn't called to him.

'Hi there, Neil – Mr Tarrent!'

'Hello!'

She was sitting by herself on a bench, just the other side of the bridge. In a bright yellow dress, with her dark curly hair and bare tanned arms, she looked young, full of vitality, delightful. Tarrent was surprised that he had almost passed her by without a glance. He went to sit beside her.

'What are you doing here? I thought you'd still be in Paris, helping with the packing.'

'No. There's really not much for me to do. We rented the apartment three-quarters furnished. The movers are doing the rest – except for the precious things, like the General's portrait, that I wouldn't be allowed to touch anyway. They'll all come in the car with Clara, my mother-in-law. I flew over yesterday.'

'To keep John company?'

'Ye – es, and in theory to get the house here ready.'

'Only in theory?' There had been a tinge of bitterness in Helen's words, and Tarrent kept his tone light. 'Has John coped with everything already? I know he was taking a few days' leave.'

158

'Leave?' Helen smoothed the skirt of her dress over her knees. John hadn't even met her at the airport. He had said he was desperately busy at the office. She smiled doubtfully. 'No. It's not John. We've got a married couple who live in an apartment in the basement, and take care of the house. It's all very easy and opulent.'

'And lets you come and sit in the Park. Which is my luck, as I happened to meet you.'

'My luck too.' Helen noticed again the attractive slight Scots burr in his voice. 'I'm sorry. I haven't asked how you are. You weren't hurt in the automobile accident?'

'Not more than a bruise or two. I was sitting in the back.'

Helen nodded. 'I'm so glad. I did ask John about you and Mr Mont, but he said he didn't want to talk about any of it. You can't blame him. It must have been a dreadful experience. He's still feeling it, I'm sure. He looks dreadful and he's frightfully nervy. I was quite startled when I saw him yesterday.'

Tarrent felt no particular sympathy for John Kenmare. Nor did he wish to discuss him. Kenmare's reactions – his nerves – were probably due more to the attack on the safe house than to the car accident and the events in France, but he couldn't tell Helen that.

He said quietly, 'You mentioned Simon Mont. You know he died?'

'Died! No, no. I'd no idea. John never told me.' Helen hesitated. 'He was married, wasn't he? I remember he spoke of his wife and children when we were having dinner that night.'

'Yes. So are a lot of people. The trouble is that being married doesn't give one immunity.' There was a short silence. Then he added without thinking, almost to himself, 'I'm not sure the job's compatible with marriage.'

'No. I'm beginning to realize that.'

Tarrent glanced sharply at the girl beside him. His remark had been incautious, almost insecure, but her reply had been unexpected. He could think of no adequate response. Better to change the subject. He looked at his watch.

'There's a very pleasant pub just off St James's Street,

159

over there. If we started to stroll now we'd arrive at opening time, and I could buy you a drink. What about it?'

'It sounds great.' The frown cleared from Helen's brow. She had been alone all day, and was feeling lonely and miserable when Neil Tarrent appeared. She gave him a wide smile. 'Why are we waiting?'

It was half past seven when Helen paid off the taxi and used her key to open the front door of the Kenmares' house in a quiet square off Knightsbridge. She could hear the chimes of the grandfather clock in the hall. They made her feel slightly guilty. She hadn't meant to be so late. But she'd enjoyed the pub, though she'd refused to have more than one drink, and she had enjoyed Neil Tarrent's company. Time had passed with surprising speed.

She ran upstairs to the sitting-room, which stretched across the front of the house on the first floor. John Kenmare was standing with his back to one of the long windows. His mouth was set and there was a dull flush high on his cheekbones. He didn't give Helen a chance to speak.

'Where the hell have you been? What have you been doing? Do you realize what time it is?'

Helen stared at him. For a moment she wondered if he could be drunk. Then, as he strode towards her, she thought he was about to hit her. She was horrified, but not afraid.

'John!'

It was her expression more than anything else that stopped him. John Kenmare stood, his arms at his sides, his teeth clenched, every muscle in his body taut. He was breathing deeply. Gradually he relaxed. He managed the travesty of a smile.

'I'm sorry. Darling, I'm sorry. But I've been so worried about you. I was terrified something had happened. You don't know London, and it – it's not always the safest of places.'

Helen forced a laugh. 'Sweetie, you've forgotten. I'm a true New Yorker, born and bred in Manhattan. I'm even used to Paris – more or less. London's a lot easier, except the

160

traffic goes the wrong way. At least they speak the lingo here.'

'Yes. Yes, of course. Darling, I'm sorry. Forgive me.'

John Kenmare held out his arms and, with some reluctance, Helen came to him. She returned his kisses. But, when he repeated his questions and asked her where she'd been and what she'd been doing, she said nothing about her meeting with Neil Tarrent. Somehow it seemed wiser not to mention it.

FIFTEEN

It was a cheap kitchen alarm clock, and no one could have slept through the clamour that it made. Neil Tarrent put out an arm and brushed the clock off the bedside table. Swearing, he leant out of bed, fumbling among a pair of shoes, a pile of underclothes, a glass, a couple of books, but the clock eluded him.

'Turn that damn thing off!'

'I'm trying, my pet. I'm trying.'

'Then try bloody harder.'

Reluctantly Tarrent got out of bed, found the clock, turned off the alarm. He grinned at the girl who lay back on her pillow, glaring at him. She was a very pretty girl, with long fair hair and wide violet eyes.

'Success,' he said, putting on a robe.

'Where are you going?'

'To make us some breakfast, if it's possible to find the ingredients in that shambles you call a kitchen.'

'If you don't like it, you can leave. It's jolly generous of me to put you up at all, considering.'

'Considering what?'

Tarrent was searching for some slippers. The carpet was thick, but anything from a drawing-pin to a piece of walnut shell could be lurking in the pile. A woman came in to clean once a week. Otherwise the flat was untended. Amanda Price didn't believe in housework.

'Considering the last time you stayed here you went to your office one fine morning and I didn't see you again for six months.'

'And when I did get back, there was your new boy-friend wearing my bathrobe.'

Amanda laughed, and Tarrent, having found a pair of slippers, went off to the kitchen. He was very fond of Amanda. He had once thought quite seriously of marrying her, and had only been put off by her father's wealth. He had decided, not without regret, that he wouldn't fit in with her family's style.

Grinding coffee beans, popping bread into the toaster, laying a tray with a variegated collection of china, Tarrent caught his thoughts straying to Helen Kenmare. From what she had said, and left unsaid, he guessed that the Kenmares' way of life was tending to overwhelm her. From the little he'd seen of her, this didn't surprise him, and he sympathized. But she was John Kenmare's wife. It was a fact, Tarrent told himself, that he shouldn't forget.

He carried the breakfast tray back to the bedroom. Amanda was sitting up, happily displaying her naked breasts. She clapped her hands as she smelt the coffee.

'Neil, darling, I've just realized. It's Saturday. We can spend the morning here – in bed. Isn't that fun?'

'It would be if it was possible.'

'Why not? Don't tell me you've got to work.'

'I do. Tell you, I mean. And have to work. That's why I set the alarm.'

'You set the damn thing! I thought it had gone off by mistake. Oh, hell!'

Amanda was annoyed, but she didn't argue and she didn't ask questions. She was already planning a different sort of day for herself, and she wasn't curious about Neil. She believed he worked for some kind of export firm, and accepted that he had to work at odd hours and go abroad at short notice. From Tarrent's point of view, she was the ideal girl-friend and, wanting a bed in London for a few nights, he hadn't hesitated to phone her. Their relationship had long since ceased to have any serious implications but he knew that, if it weren't inconvenient, she would be glad to see him.

'I'm sorry, Amanda. You know I'd much rather stay with you, but it would probably mean my job.'

And that was true enough, Tarrent thought, as he went along to the bathroom. There was no doubt he'd have preferred to spend the day with Amanda – in or out of bed – rather than undertake the task that Sir Patrick had given him. At best it would be tedious, a waste of time. At worst . . . In imagination he saw himself being systematically beaten up

163

by a couple of thugs, when they realized they'd been tricked. He stared at his reflection in the mirror. The role he was to play wasn't to his liking, and he doubted if he'd be much good at it. But Sir Patrick had insisted.

Tarrent finished dressing, kissed Amanda a fond goodbye and left the flat. In the Fulham Road he caught a taxi that took him to the far side of Westminster Bridge. He walked from there, but made no attempt to approach the main entrance of the tower block. Instead he went in by the garage entrance, a steep ramp to the basement. His pass was carefully scrutinized, and a man in mechanic's overalls took him to a waiting truck.

It was a small Ford Transit van, blue, very clean and new-looking. Tarrent walked round it and then opened the back doors. The interior was furnished as a kind of rudimentary ambulance, with two cots and some neatly folded blankets. Again, everything was spotless and appeared unused.

'Okay, sir?' said the man who had shown him to the van. 'I checked her out first thing this morning.'

'Thanks.' Tarrent climbed into the driver's seat and fastened his seat-belt. 'I'll see you later.' I hope, he added under his breath.

The man outlined a salute, and Tarrent drove across the garage, up the ramp and into the London traffic. He didn't hurry. He had allowed himself plenty of time to get to the safe house by eleven, as Sir Patrick had stipulated. The Director's briefing had been quite explicit. 'Bonalov's being moved,' he had said. 'I shan't tell you how or when – or where to. Your job is to take the ambulance van down to the house, wait there an hour, and then come back to London by a fairly circuitous route. In fact, your van will be the decoy vehicle. And remember how tightly we're holding this operation. Not a word to anyone.'

'And how do I react if they attack me?' Tarrent had asked.

'Do your best to play the innocent,' Sir Patrick had said. 'Say you've been delivering a doctor and some medical equipment. That should make them think. But if I'm right, you should have no trouble. If you do, I want a full report as soon as possible. But, as I say . . .'

164

Sir Patrick had repeated his reassurances, which was unusual for him, and Tarrent hadn't liked it. He didn't like it now. The Director had been almost too positive, had over-stressed the point. Maybe he had been reassuring himself.

Tarrent shifted his weight in the driving seat. There was a lot of traffic on the outskirts of London, and it was not until a minute of two after eleven that he approached the safe house through the village. Mr Smith, accompanied by Caspar, opened the gates for him. 'Good morning, sir. Nice to see you again.'

Tarrent returned the greeting, and enquired after Mrs Smith and Percy. Though he knew he shouldn't ask – it was no longer his direct concern – he said casually, 'Any more excitement since I left?'

'No, sir. All very quiet. Too quiet really.' Mr Smith responded to Tarrent's easy grin. 'We're here to look after visitors, and it gets a bit boring when we don't have any.'

'I expect it does.'

With a wave of his hand Tarrent drove on towards the house. He had asked an innocent question, and been reward-ed by an indiscretion. Alexei Bonalov had already left, and from what Mr Smith had said it seemed that no visitor had been in residence for some days. On the face of it Tarrent's role now seemed pointless, but the Director didn't go in for pointless operations. Clearly without taking Tarrent into his confidence, he had devised some kind of ploy.

Thoughtfully, Neil Tarrent went along to the kitchen, where Mrs Smith made him welcome. He had coffee and homemade biscuits, and wondered what to do. He had an unpleasant feeling that he was being set up for something. He thought fleetingly of trying to put a spanner in the works by leaving at once and not waiting an hour as he'd been instructed, but he knew he couldn't do that.

At noon precisely Tarrent drove his van through the gates of the safe house and, watched by Mr Smith, turned left towards London, following the route he'd been told and avoiding the village. He maintained an even speed, and kept an eye on his rear-view mirror. He wished for a moment he had a radio transceiver, but Sir Patrick had vetoed any compromising equipment.

165

It was a little more than five minutes after leaving the house that Tarrent heard and saw a black Rover approaching from behind him. The roads were very quiet on this Saturday morning, and there was no other traffic in sight. Tarrent kept well in to the verge as the car drew out to pass him. He caught a glimpse of the man at the wheel, and a passenger in the seat beside him. There was nothing obviously suspicious about them. But suddenly, as they were almost past, the driver swung in, carefully side-swiping the front of the van with the rear of his heavier vehicle.

There was little that Tarrent could do. Instinctively he braked and swung the wheel hard over. The van crashed into the nearside ditch. Tarrent was thrown forward but, restrained by his seat-belt, he wasn't hurt, just momentarily shocked. Because he hadn't been taken completely by surprise, he was quick to recover.

The two men were even quicker. They were both out of their car, which had come to a halt a few yards in front of the van, and were running back, before Tarrent could free himself from his belt and climb out of the cab. By the time he had his feet on the ground, one man was crowding him up against the side of the van, and the other was opening the rear doors.

'What the hell d'you think you're doing? I might have been killed!'

Tarrent was furious. He eyed the man pushing against him with extreme dislike. He could feel the hard muscles, and the even harder bulge under the shoulder that could only be a gun. The man's breath was foetid. But suddenly mindful of Sir Patrick's instructions, Tarrent forced himself to smile, ingratiatingly he hoped. He said, 'Now look, I don't want to make too much of a fuss, but it was your fault, you know. Your insurance—'

There was a shout from the rear of the van, and the second man appeared, his gun in full view. 'It's empty. There's no one in there!' he cried angrily. He spoke in English, heavily accented.

The first man thrust himself away from Tarrent so that, while he was still very close, there was no longer any bodily contact. For a few seconds he regarded Tarrent speculatively. Then he struck him a back-handed blow across the face with all the force he could muster.

It was too much for Tarrent's temper and, what was more, Tarrent's attacker had made a tactical error. His moment of withdrawal, of speculation, had given Tarrent time to anticipate the blow. He swung with it, and thus diminished its effect. He had no doubt that the two hoods were the same men who had tried to abduct Bonalov last Monday. And they were clearly after Bonalov again.

As these thoughts flashed through his mind Tarrent, Sir Patrick's instructions forgotten, brought up his knee into his opponent's groin with a vicious jerk. Then, as the man doubled forwards, he chopped him across the side of the neck with the ridge of his hand. Retching, the man collapsed on the ground.

Tarrent looked up. He found himself staring down the barrel of a pistol, held in a very steady hand. Instinctively he judged the distance. It was too far. There was no immediate hope of jumping this character. His best chance was bluff.

'You stupid shit! Didn't you understand your orders? You've made a balls-up of the whole thing. It was the second van you were meant to stop, not mine. And it'll be well away by this time. You've lost it. You son of a . . .'

Tarrent let his anger blaze, but it was not this that affected the man with the gun. It was surprise. For Tarrent, threatened as he was, had not only sworn at him with authority, but had sworn at him in Russian. It didn't make sense. Slowly, he lowered his pistol.

Then, in the quiet country lane, there came clearly the warning hoot of a car, and the answering ring of a bicycle bell. Tarrent seized his opportunity. He kicked the man who still lay groaning at his feet with the sort of contempt he hoped a KGB officer would have shown.

'Quick! Someone's coming. Get your comrade out of here,' he snapped.

Thrusting his pistol into his pocket, the man obeyed. He was used to taking orders, and the present situation was beyond his understanding; it certainly hadn't been covered in his briefing. Best to get clear, while they could. He seized his companion under the shoulders and dragged him, groaning and protesting, to the car. With some help from Tarrent,

167

who was equally anxious to get rid of them both before witnesses arrived, he managed to bundle him into the back seat.

As Tarrent had subconsciously noticed at the time, the accident had been carefully engineered, and the only damage to the Rover was a dent in the rear wing. The car was fully roadworthy. Tarrent heaved a sigh of relief as it gathered speed towards a red Mini which came bustling round the far corner. He was thankful the incident was over, and that it had ended so well. He grinned at the thought of the Russians explaining what had happened to their bosses, but his grin faded as he was reminded of his own superior, Sir Patrick.

'Good morning. Can I be of any help?' The driver of the Mini, an elderly, white-haired lady, was regarding the van with interest.

'That's awfully good of you. If you're going through the village, I'd be glad of a lift.'

'Of course. Jump in.' She moved various shopping-bags to the back seat, and he got in beside her. 'Was it that big black car that hit you?' she asked.

'It was an accident, not really their fault,' Tarrent said mildly.

'They might have done something more to help than just abandon you here.'

'They did offer, but they were in a hurry and going in the wrong direction.'

It was a weak explanation, but the white-haired lady seemed satisfied. She nodded. 'I'll drop you at the garage. All right?'

'Thank you very much.'

The village garage consisted of a couple of petrol pumps, a small office where a middle-aged man could be seen brooding over some paperwork, and a large, ramshackle shed. In the forecourt a youth was working on a dilapidated coupé. Tarrent went into the office, and arranged for the van to be hauled out of the ditch and kept at the garage until he could organize its collection. He asked about means of getting back to London. He had decided it would be best not to return to the safe house. His face was now known in the village, and the association might be noted.

The garage man was helpful. 'My boy could drive you to the station this afternoon, if you could wait till then. You can get a good meal at the White Hart.'

'That sounds splendid,' Tarrent said.

It was splendid, in fact. A surprisingly good bottle of wine and an imaginative lunch gave him time to think. Later, he was driven eight miles to the nearest station to catch a train to London. He arrived at Amanda's flat soon after four.

No one was there. Tarrent made himself a pot of tea, and sat drinking it at the kitchen table. His orders had been to report to Sir Patrick as soon as possible, but he didn't intend to hurry himself. After all, he thought, he might be lying dead in that ditch, and Sir Patrick had probably been quite aware of the possibility. Tarrent had no objection to taking risks – it was part of his job – but he liked to have them spelt out for him. In this case, as far as he could see, the Director had deliberately misled him.

Tarrent finished his second cup of tea, and went to the phone. He dialled the Director's home number. The receiver was picked up after the second ring. He recognized Sir Patrick's voice.

'Hello. Yes?'

'Neil Tarrent, sir.'

'Ah yes. At last.' There was no doubt that the Director had been waiting for this call; each word was bitten off sharply. 'Where are you?'

'Back in London, sir. In Fulham, where I'm staying.'

'And this morning?'

'It was – eventful, sir,' said Tarrent carefully. 'I was forced off the road on the way home. I'm afraid I had to leave the van in a ditch.' Tarrent waited for a comment, but none came. The silence grew. 'Are you there, sir?'

'Yes, yes. I'm here.' Again there was a pause, then: 'We must meet at once. I'll see you in my Whitehall office as soon as you can get there.'

SIXTEEN

Sir Patrick was the first to arrive at his office, and he turned away from the window as Tarrent came in. The Director took a deep breath and visibly straightened his shoulders, but he couldn't hide the fact that today he looked his age. He was tired and spent, and perhaps a little afraid.

'Not a good way to spend a summer evening,' he said rather sadly. 'I should be in the country with my wife. And you—' He motioned to Tarrent to sit down. 'You're all right, Neil? I should have asked on the phone. You weren't hurt?'

'No, sir. They hit me once, but I'm okay. Better than one of them, in fact.'

'Tell me what happened, in detail.'

Even in detail, it was briefly told. 'I called the duty officer and got the car number checked,' Tarrent concluded. 'Rented, of course. But there was no doubt who they were, sir. Or who they were after.'

Sir Patrick didn't interrupt the story, and asked no questions. Instead, he said simply, 'It was a trap, Neil. Apart from you and me, only one person was told that Bonalov would be moved this morning, and he wasn't told of any decoy plan. In fact, Bonalov was moved last Tuesday. I drove him myself.' Sir Patrick stopped short. Something in Tarrent's expression had alerted him. 'You knew,' he said accusingly. 'You knew Bonalov had already gone.'

'Not until this morning, sir, when I got to the safe house,' Tarrent said hurriedly. At least the old man had come clean about Bonalov, he thought, but the situation was still obscure and full of pitfalls. Who was this other man, and what on earth had made the Director devise such an amateurish plan to try and catch him out? 'I guessed from something Mr Smith said,' he explained, 'but it made no difference to your plan. I just went ahead.'

As if he couldn't bear to stay still, Sir Patrick pushed back his chair and began to pace the office, six strides in one direction, six in the other. Tarrent watched him doubtfully. 'When Bonalov produced that JIC paper, it was clear we had a bad leak. But there was no reason why it should be from this Department. Then the safe house was blown. Not by chance. We could pretty well rule that out. So, another traitor – or the same one?' Sir Patrick was speaking in staccato phrases, as if he were thinking aloud. He turned to Tarrent, and added, 'Bonalov told me it was the same man – and he named him: John Kenmare.'

'Kenmare?' Tarrent was astounded. 'But – but that's absurd.'

'Yes,' Sir Patrick agreed. 'Absurd. That was my first reaction.' He resumed his pacing, not looking directly at Tarrent. 'As you know, Neil, I'm an old friend of the Kenmares, and John is the last man – the last man—' He seemed to find it hard to continue. He cleared his throat.

'Bonalov could easily be lying, sir,' said Tarrent. 'If he's a plant, it would be an obvious move – almost routine. You know better than I do, sir – disinformation, to cause chaos and confusion.'

'Quite. I told myself all that. But after what happened today—'

'It was John you set your trap for?'

'Yes.' Sir Patrick looked almost appealingly at Tarrent, as if seeking his support. 'It was all I could think of doing, without – without—'

'—without making the whole thing official, and setting the dogs on.' Tarrent completed the sentence for him.

Sir Patrick nodded. 'Of course, I know it's not foolproof. The case against him isn't a hundred per cent watertight. The safe house could have been under surveillance – in some ways it would be odd if they weren't watching it—'

'But—'

'Yes?'

'Don't we know, sir? If the house was under surveillance, I mean. Weren't we watching for watchers?'

'Smith and the staff were keeping their eyes open, yes.

They saw nothing, and you know the place – it would be hard to maintain a round the clock watch without being noticed. But we can't be sure; there's still an element of doubt. And if they were waiting for signs of movement and recognized you, the attack could be explained. There's also the point that it's difficult to see how John could have blown the house in the first place. He had no opportunity once he was there, and he didn't know its location in advance – or did he?'

'No. To the best of my knowledge he didn't. I never told him, and I'm sure Simon wouldn't have. The question didn't arise, and he had no need to know. But, sir—'

Tarrent's thoughts were fierce. Christ, what a mess! A horrendous security leak. A defector who might or might not be a plant. A safe house blown. Two physical attacks on SIS officers in the UK, on home territory. And the old man's main worry seemed to be the possibility that one of his precious Kenmares might turn out to be a traitor. Instead of following the rules, as he'd have done unhesitatingly if suspicion had fallen on anyone else, he'd tried to tackle the problem and disprove Bonalov's accusation on his own. It was incredible. And now . . .

'But what, Neil?'

Tarrent gathered his wits together, and spoke crisply. 'John did have one opportunity to pass a message. On the Saturday, while I was visiting Betty Mont, he went for a walk. He said he went to the village to phone his wife. I gather they'd had a disagreement, and he wanted to speak to her privately.'

'I see. Well, that confirms my decision.' Sir Patrick sighed. 'It's out of my hands. The Security Service are already enquiring into Simon Mont. They must include Kenmare.'

'Simon!' It was an involuntary exclamation.

Sir Patrick explained about the bank draft, and Tarrent hesitated. 'In that case I think there's something else you should know, sir,' he said at length. 'Though the Monts have apparently been very short of money – school fees, doctors' bills and so on – Simon managed to buy a new station wagon a few weeks ago. He told me it took the last of his savings.'

'Which may or may not be the truth,' said Sir Patrick sadly. 'I must say, if the Russians are trying to spread doubt and confusion in the Service they must be happy at the moment. I only wish they'd waited till after I'd retired.'

'And until either Kenmare or Mont became Director, sir?'

'The point hadn't escaped me.'

Almost absent-mindedly, Sir Patrick produced a sherry decanter and poured two glasses. He handed one to Tarrent, who murmured his thanks. For a moment or two they sat in silence.

'Sir,' Tarrent said at last. 'May I ask you something? Why have you told me all this?'

'That's a fair question. I know I took you off the case, Neil, but luckily you now seem to be above suspicion. Certainly you could have blown the safe house, but there's no way you could have got hold of that JIC paper while you were in Moscow. And you've been involved in the operation from the beginning, so you're the obvious man to go on working on it from the SIS point of view. Even though it's primarily a security matter, it's still the job of this Department to decide if Bonalov's a plant.'

'I see. Thank you, sir.'

The Director shifted in his chair. 'Now let's get down to work and make some plans. To my mind, one of the keys to this affair could still be in Moscow.'

'You want me to go back, sir?'

'Yes. As soon as possible. I know Ken Palfrey's there, but you've had personal dealings with the man Dronsky, and you've met Bonalov's aide, Kerensky. You should be in a vastly better position than Palfrey to tackle the job, quite apart from the undesirability of briefing another officer at this stage. No, you must give it a try yourself. Perhaps on these lines . . .'

It was getting late when his meeting with the Director ended, and Tarrent returned to the flat, hoping that Amanda would be there. Tomorrow, Moscow. But in the interval he wanted to take his mind off the convoluted mess. Amanda, however, was not at home.

173

Time passed. The level in the whisky bottle sank. The telephone rang twice, but each time it was for Amanda. What a bloody job, Neil Tarrent thought. Not only was it incompatible with marriage, as he'd told Helen Kenmare in an incautious moment, it was also incompatible with a girl-friend, or any sort of normal life.

Amanda had still not appeared by half past nine, and Tarrent cooked himself a steak he found in the freezer, made a salad and opened a bottle of wine. He played a couple of tapes. He tried television. He glanced at some of the magazines that littered the flat; serious reading was impossible, and the single shelf of books contained nothing inviting. Anyway, he couldn't concentrate. His thoughts kept slipping away to Alexei Bonalov, to Simon Mont and his family, to Sir Patrick, to John Kenmare and Helen – especially to Helen.

As the Director had said, from the security point of view, he was only on the periphery of the affair. He was above suspicion, or perhaps below it. He was too junior for the eventual outcome to affect his career more than marginally. He should be able to regard the events with some detachment. Yet, quite apart from the official role the Director had thrust upon him, he felt himself deeply and personally involved.

Eventually he went to bed, to sleep almost at once. He woke just after two in the morning. Amanda had returned with a party of friends. He was at first shattered by the noise they were making. Then, dragged from a warm cocoon of bedclothes, he was forced to join them, to drink champagne, to dance. Still later he fell into bed again, this time with Amanda.

The alarm jolted him awake once more. He grabbed it quickly and turned it off. As he did so, he groaned aloud. His head ached abominably. His mouth was dry, his sinuses blocked, his stomach uncertain. He felt like hell. There was nothing he wanted to do more than go back to sleep. But he had a flight to catch.

Very carefully he got out of bed, thankful that Amanda, her head half under the pillow, seemed to have slept through the shrilling bell. He went to the bathroom, taking his clothes with him so as not to disturb her. He washed, shaved, dressed, all very slowly. The bathroom cabinet was full of cosmetics, women's and men's, but it didn't contain as much as an aspirin.

'Here you are, darling.'

Standing in the doorway was Amanda. Tarrent gasped at her in amazement. She looked clear-eyed and fresh, as if she'd slept for nine hours.

'What's that?' He pointed to the glass of reddish liquid she was holding out to him.

'My special. Guaranteed to abolish any hangover. Drink it while I make breakfast. The coffee's on.'

'I couldn't eat any breakfast.'

'You can. You must. You should always eat before a journey.'

'What journey?'

'Darling! Your bags are packed and in the hall.'

Tarrent managed to grin. 'Thank God I did something sensible last night.'

Two hours later Tarrent boarded his flight for Moscow. If Amanda's 'special' hadn't completely cured his head, he was feeling in reasonably good form. He could at least think fairly clearly, and he set his mind to considering what lay ahead.

Ken Palfrey would be meeting him at Sheremetyevo, and they could have a preliminary talk on the way into the city. But it was unlikely that Palfrey would be able to add much to the information he had already signalled to London. There had been no mention of Colonel Bonalov in the press within the Soviet Union. The Tass release, with its hint of kidnapping, had been strictly for foreign consumption, and the ordinary Soviet citizen knew nothing of Bonalov's disappearance. A small paragraph in *Pravda* had announced the deaths of the two KGB men, Yevgeny Zourenko and Andrei Kharkov, in a motor accident. The similarity to the British announcement of Simon Mont's death had struck Tarrent as bitterly ironic.

'Today?' Ken Palfrey said in some surprise. The formalities at the Moscow airport had been reasonably rapid and the two SIS officers had met outside the Customs area no more than twenty minutes after the flight had landed.

'Why not?' Tarrent was a little impatient. 'It's vital I see Dronsky, assuming he's available, and I don't want him spirited away just because the KGB know I'm back.'

'Well,' said Palfrey doubtfully. 'We'll do our best. We may be lucky, though it's hard to believe they won't have time to pick him up if they really want to. Shall I come with you?' he added.

Tarrent hesitated. There were some questions he might have to ask Dronsky that Palfrey shouldn't hear. Palfrey knew nothing of the Kenmare angle, and must continue to be kept in ignorance. On the other hand, the situation was pretty dicey.

'Yes, I'd be glad of some back-up, Ken,' Tarrent said. 'But there's no point in exposing ourselves till we're sure Dronsky's not in the Lubyanka. Let's go to my apartment and phone first.'

As soon as they reached his flat, which looked tired and neglected even after his short absence, Tarrent dialled the Dronsky's number. There was no answer, but he could hear the ringing tone.

'That probably means something,' he said to Palfrey. 'At least his phone's not been disconnected, and the call wasn't intercepted by a KGB switchboard.'

'What now?' said Palfrey.

'I'll unpack and have a wash, and then we'll try again.'

Palfrey waited while Tarrent changed his shirt, and poured whiskies for both of them, as Tarrent tried the Dronsky's number again. This time the receiver was picked up quickly.

'Hello.'

The voice was readily identifiable as that of Sergei Dronsky, and Tarrent broke the connection at once. Unless something very devious was going on, it seemed that Dronsky was alive and well and still living in the same apartment. The next step was to see him, Tarrent thought.

He'd been over the arguments in detail with the Director last night. It was quite clear that Dronsky had been used by Bonalov as a go-between, under duress. Tarrent had recalled the passion with which Dronsky had said, 'Did you ever have to choose between betraying your country and losing all you love?' Only a man who believed that Bonalov was a genuine defector could have asked the question with such conviction. Yet, if John Kenmare were indeed a Soviet agent, the authorities must have known of the part that Dronsky had played. Kenmare had been told about Dronsky early in the negotiations, and would certainly have passed a warning to his controller. Yet Dronsky was still free, so presumably Kenmare hadn't taken such action, and therefore was in the clear.

'Another drink, Neil?' said Palfrey, interrupting his thoughts.

'No, thanks,' Tarrent said. 'Just a minute, Ken. I'm trying to plan how to play it.' He shook his head in irritation.

This was where things got complex, as he and the Director had agreed. There could in reality be a handful of reasons why the KGB should leave Dronsky at large. The obvious one was that Bonalov was a plant, and Dronsky had been an unwitting part of a KGB conspiracy; in this case the argument for Kenmare's innocence fell to the ground. Alternatively, they could simply be protecting their own source, which might or might not be Kenmare. Or they might well be inviting the sort of approach to Dronsky that he – Tarrent – was about to make. Tarrent mentally shrugged his shoulders. Anyway, an approach must be made, though exactly how he was going to manage the interview neither he nor Sir Patrick had been able to decide.

Tarrent looked up, to find Palfrey regarding him curiously. 'It's all right, Ken,' he said. 'Let's go.'

The two young Russian guards at the gate of the compound – supposedly there for the foreigners' protection, but really to report on their movements – stared after Tarrent and Palfrey with blank faces. Palfrey was driving, and five minutes later

Tarrent spotted the Volga tailing them. Tarrent was no longer concerned with the fact that his visit would probably cause more trouble for the Dronskys – the stakes had become much too high for such considerations – but he had no wish to have his meeting with them interrupted by the KGB.

'We'll have to try and lose it,' he said resignedly.

'Okay.' Palfrey grinned. 'It'll be a change. No one's bothered me for weeks. It must be you that's causing all the trouble.'

'I dare say. I expect they phoned from the airport. They're certainly pretty quick off the mark.'

'The next lights?'

Tarrent nodded. He could see the traffic lights ahead, and he tried to visualize the layout of the streets around the next corner. He wasn't sure, but he though he could remember a taxi rank. He undid his seat-belt and prepared to jump.

Palfrey timed it well. He approached the lights at a moderate speed, slowed as if expecting them to change, then accelerated through on the beginning of the red. The driver of the Volga did his best to follow, but he failed to take into account the swinging rear of a tram that had the right of way across the intersection. There was a loud crash as the tram side-swiped the Volga, and a cacophony of hooting.

'That's great!' Tarrent said with satisfaction. He fastened his seat-belt again. There was no longer any need to bail out of Palfrey's car and hope to find a taxi. What was more, this was a pleasant revenge for the Rover that had forced him into the ditch yesterday. Only yesterday? He sighed. 'Well done, Ken! Now for the Dronskys.'

Palfrey drove Tarrent to within fifty yards of the block where the Dronskys lived, and Tarrent walked from there. Luckily the *dezhurnaya* was arguing with another old woman in the hall, and barely gave Tarrent a glance. He walked past them into the lift. On the fifth floor he rang the Dronskys' bell, and Tamara opened the door.

'Hello, Tamara. Remember me? Neil Tarrent. Is Sergei at home?'

Tamara Dronsky didn't speak. At the sight of Tarrent her eyes had widened in disbelief, almost horror. Instinctively

178

she made to slam the door in his face but Tarrent, who had half expected such a reception, was too quick for her. He thrust his foot in the narrowing gap and, heaving with his shoulder, pushed his way into the apartment.

'Sergei! Sergei! Here! Here!'

Sergei came running from the bedroom, but he stopped dead when he saw Tarrent. He looked as appalled as Tamara. 'Go. Please go,' he said roughly. 'You mustn't be here. It's bad for us.'

'I just want to speak to you for a few minutes.'

'No. You must go. At once.' Tamara was vehement. 'You heard what Sergei said. It's bad for us that you should come here at all – it's dangerous. Go – now!'

Tarrent stood with his back against the door. There was no hall to the apartment and they were in the living-room. Tarrent looked about him with growing interest. He had only once before been in the Dronskys' home, but he remembered it well, the thin curtains, the cheap rug, the shoddy furniture.

Today it was different. Everything was new, clean and bright and of much better quality. There was a big television set in one corner. A hugh stuffed bear occupied an armchair. A small girl with dark, curly hair and wide eyes sat on the floor, surrounded by dolls and more bears and a variety of carved animals. The toys were obviously expensive, and probably of foreign origin. The Dronskys were clearly doing well.

Tarrent said mildly, 'You mean you're not going to offer me a drink? Surely you've got some vodka.' He smiled from Sergei to Tamara, to Maya.

Tamara saw his glance move to Maya, and suddenly something in her snapped. 'Get out! Get out!' Screaming, she flung herself at Tarrent. Her hands were outstretched. Her nails raked his face. Startled by the attack, Tarrent reacted without thought. He threw Tamara from him, and she staggered back and fell, knocking the side of her head against a table leg. Blood trickled from her cheek. Maya, clutching a horse that Tamara had broken in her fall, began to cry loudly.

'Shut that child up!' Tarrent said curtly. He turned on Sergei. 'Do you want all the neighbours in? Get them both to the other room.'

Tamara sat on the floor and hugged Maya to her, meaning to comfort her, though the fierceness of the embrace merely frightened the child still more. 'If anything happens to Maya because of you, I'll kill you,' she spat at Tarrent. 'I don't know how, but I'll do it. I'll kill you!'

Tarrent hardly heard her. He too was angry – partly with himself – and uncertain how to proceed. Finally he said, quietly and calmly, 'All I want are the answers to some questions, but I want them now and I want the truth.' He thought for a moment, and added, 'If you won't talk to me, I'll fix it so that you talk to the KGB. Which is it to be?'

Dronsky's reaction was unexpected. He stared at Tarrent. He was very pale. His skin had an unhealthy, greenish tinge as if he might vomit at any moment. The unexpected violence had shocked him, and Tarrent's words had clearly been a surprise. 'A minute. A little minute. Please,' he pleaded in a hoarse whisper. He helped his wife to her feet and began to shepherd her and the little girl towards the bedroom. 'You don't understand, Mr Tarrent. I don't think you mean us any harm, but you don't understand . . .'

Neil Tarrent watched them go. He took out a handkerchief and wiped his face. He was sweating, and Tamara's nails had drawn blood. Christ! He certainly didn't understand. True, he'd forced his way into their home. He'd struck Tamara, but only after she'd attacked him. He'd threatened them, though only in the vaguest terms. But surely they were showing excessive fear. Did they really believe he'd report them to the KGB in some covert way? Perhaps they did, though God knew what good they thought that would do him if they were already under KGB control.

Sergei Dronsky came back into the room. He still looked shocked, but he had himself under better control. Tarrent suspected that a swig of vodka had helped to steady him.

Tarrent decided to change the subject. 'You seem to be doing very well for yourself these days, Sergei. Have you been promoted?'

180

'No. I mean—'

'Well?'

'I have been promised promotion from next term,' Dronsky said with some dignity.

'Really? Congratulations. And all these new things? Furniture? Toys? Have you won a big prize in a lottery?'

The reply Tarrent half expected was a curt 'Mind your own business', or its equivalent. Instead, Dronsky hesitated, and then said. 'No – though that is what we've told our friends.'

'Then what's the truth, Sergei?' Tarrent pursued what seemed to be an advantage. 'Obviously you've acquired a lot of money and *blat* from somewhere. What did you do to deserve it?'

'I – I can't tell you.'

'You can't tell me! Of course you can. Anyway, I know already.'

Dronsky eyed him apprehensively. 'What do you mean by that?'

'You got these favours for helping that defector, didn't you? We both know you were acting for him, so why should you mind admitting it to me?'

'You don't understand,' Dronsky repeated. In his ignorance of the true situation, the foreigner might do anything. 'You don't understand,' he said again. There was no alternative to telling him the whole story, throwing himself – and Tamara, and Maya – on his mercy.

'Perhaps you'd better explain,' said Tarrent gently, sensing a change in the atmosphere. 'But I want the truth – the whole truth.'

Tarrent listened to the broken, stumbling sentences, occasionally asking questions. He'd known that Dronsky had acted under duress, but he had believed it to be some kind of general threat. He'd had no idea of the callous way in which Maya had been used, almost as a continuing, permanent hostage. Now that he understood the Dronskys' predicament, they had all his sympathy. But it was the detail of the operation that fascinated him.

The removal of Maya Dronsky from the kindergarten, her

holiday in the country, her return to Moscow, the rewards heaped on the family – all this had required a great deal of organization, and surely some official backing. The big question was could Bonalov have swung it by himself, without KGB cooperation.

Unfortunately this was a question that Dronsky couldn't help to answer. He had no idea of the identity of the defector, or of his importance. Shown photographs of Bonalov and Kerensky, he swore that he had never seen Bonalov, but was less certain about Kerensky, who might or might not have been the contact he had come to fear so much.

And that was all. Tarrent did his best to reassure Sergei Dronsky, and returned to the waiting car. He was tired after his journey and drained by the emotional interview he had just conducted, but as they drove quickly to the Embassy he gave Palfrey a brief and edited account of the meeting.

'So I've got nothing for or against Bonalov,' he concluded. 'Nothing to show conclusively whether or not he's a plant.' But I have achieved a stick to tackle him with, he added to himself.

SEVENTEEN

There was the usual cheerful babble of conversation, a tangible release of tension, when the British Airways captain announced that the flight was leaving Soviet airspace. Neil Tarrent's reaction was no different from that of anyone else. He relaxed. Three days in Moscow, and once more he was on his way back to London; it had been pointless to stay longer.

After his visit to Sergei Dronsky, Tarrent had been able to achieve little. Of necessity his enquiries had been circumspect and incomplete, and such gossip as he had been able to gather was inconclusive, but it seemed fairly certain that Oleg Kerensky had disappeared from Moscow – God and the KGB knew where or why. Nevertheless, Tarrent thought, his mission had been less unsatisfactory than he had expected. Dronsky had provided enough information to present Alexei Bonalov with a nasty choice. He grinned to himself. He would be disappointed if Sir Patrick didn't let him sit in on the confrontation with Bonalov.

In the event, there was no question. Sir Patrick took it for granted that Tarrent would accompany him, and even conduct a part of the interview. 'It's too late today, Neil. We need to be fresh to deal with Bonalov. Whatever else he is, he's a wily customer. But what we can do now is think about tactics . . .'

An hour later, Sir Patrick looked at his watch and said. 'Fair enough. Tomorrow morning, then. Nine o'clock. If you're staying in the Fulham area I'll pick you up. We'll be going out that way. What's the address?'

'Thank you, sir.' Tarrent wrote down Amanda Price's address on the pad that Sir Patrick pushed across the desk to him. He had no idea if he'd be spending the night there, and he had a fleeting vision of himself dashing half way across London to be at the appointed meeting-place on time. 'It's a block of flats. I'll be waiting outside.'

'Right. You've done well, Neil.' Sir Patrick nodded his dismissal. 'Just how well, we'll know tomorrow.'

We hope, Tarrent added to himself as he said good-night to the Director, and went in search of a phone. In one of his bags was a bottle of vodka and a jar of caviare. He wouldn't be arriving on Amanda's doorstep empty-handed. Hurrying along the corridor he rounded a corner, and almost bumped into John Kenmare. Both men were a little taken aback.

Kenmare recovered first. 'Neil, what a surprise! I heard you'd gone back to Moscow.'

'Only briefly. I got home again today.'

'You're not still on the old job? I thought . . .'

It was almost a direct question, and Tarrent wasn't sure how he should answer it. He shrugged. 'For a day or two. And you?'

'Some ghastly routine stuff at the moment. How I miss Paris.' Kenmare smiled ruefully. 'Incidentally, Neil, we're having a few people in for drinks this evening, to celebrate our return. Six-thirty. We'd love to see you if you can make it.'

'Thank you.' Tarrent hesitated. Except for that one time in Paris on the night of Bonalov's defection, he had never received an invitation from John Kenmare. 'Unfortunately I may not be free. I'm hoping to stay with a friend, and until—'

Kenmare didn't let him finish. 'Come if you can. Bring your friend. It'll all be very informal.'

Tarrent didn't repeat his thanks. He wasn't particularly grateful; in fact, he rather wished he'd not been asked. He watched Kenmare's back in its beautifully-tailored suit recede down the corridor. The arrogant bastard hadn't even bothered to provide an address. He'd just assumed that Tarrent would know where he lived.

Restraining his thoughts, Tarrent continued on his way to the small office he had last used. It was unlocked and unoccupied. He dialled Amanda's number.

'Neil, darling, you've just caught me.' Amanda sounded excited. 'I'm all packed, and I'm being picked up any minute.'

184

'You're going somewhere?' Tarrent swore under his breath, hiding his disappointment.

'Yes. Old England's rather a bore at the moment. All cricket. I'm flying down to Nice. A friend's got a boat and we're going to explore the Greek islands.'

'Sounds fun. But surely there's no flight to Nice at this time of night?'

'Daddy's exec. jet, darling.'

'Yes, of course.' God! Tarrent thought, I'm getting suspicious of Amanda now – as if she'd bother to lie to me. 'Well, have a good time, my pet.'

'Thanks. If you want to use the flat, do. Keep the burglars away. I'll leave a spare key with the porter. Use the car too, if you like. Now, 'bye, darling. I must fly.'

'Goodbye, and bless you.'

The flat would be a godsend, but Tarrent still had a vague sense of disappointment. He had hoped that Amanda would be free for the evening. Now he would have to consider alternatives, and none of them seemed attractive, not even the theatre, his favourite amusement when he was in London.

It was not until he had reached the flat and made a couple of unsuccessful phone calls that he thought seriously of John Kenmare's invitation. He found the address in the phone book readily enough. He wondered why Kenmare had bothered to ask him and whether, in the present circumstances, he ought to go. Curiosity prompted him a little. But it was the idea of meeting Helen Kenmare again that finally decided him.

John Kenmare's description of the party as informal was somewhat misleading. Lady Kenmare was once more in residence in London, and she wanted her friends to know it. She had spent a large part of yesterday on the telephone. 'My dear, yes, we're back in England. Just a few people in for drinks. Do come. It would be lovely to see you again, and you must meet John's new wife.'

Helen was not looking forward to it. She could not understand why they had to give a party so soon after their arrival, and while John was seemingly so troubled – indeed, not one, but a succession of parties: Clara was already arranging a couple of dinners in the following week. Helen had even brought herself to expostulate with Clara, but her objections had been brushed aside.

'Nonsense,' Clara had said. 'You're imagining things. There's nothing wrong with John. He may be a little on edge. That accident in France upset him. But he's perfectly all right, and it's good for his career to entertain.'

Helen had given up. She couldn't explain to her mother-in-law how desperately, almost violently, John made love to her these days, how he tossed and turned and muttered in his sleep, how twice she had woken up in the middle of the night to find him sitting by the window, staring out into the square. And it had been impossible to talk seriously to John himself.

This evening, though he had promised to be home early, he had arrived only ten minutes ago. Clearly tired and preoccupied, he had given Helen the most perfunctory of kisses, been surprisingly abrupt with Clara and gone to change. He had still not reappeared, though the guests were almost due. The last thing he wanted, Helen felt, was the noise and effort of a cocktail-party.

Yet, when the doorbell rang and the first people appeared, John was there, laughing and joking as he greeted them. 'Terribly good of you to come, sir. I've just got in myself, and if I'm busy at the office, I hate to think what you must be.'

The distinguished elderly man bent over Lady Kenmare's wheelchair to kiss her on the cheek. And John said, 'May I introduce my wife, sir?'

During the next half-hour, John introduced Helen to a couple of dozen people, none of them young, none of them – she suspected – undistinguished, the majority connected in one way or another with government. They were politicians and senior civil servants, with a leavening of lawyers and a banker. One was the editor of a leading newspaper and another a governor of the BBC. Only about a third of them had brought their wives.

The wives were welcoming. They asked Helen about her family and her life in New York City. They admired her dress. They said how glad they were that John had married again. They hoped she would be happy in London. They were all very pleasant. But, oddly, they made her feel more of a stranger than she had ever felt in Paris. It was with a sudden lightening of heart that she saw Neil Tarrent arrive.

'Neil! Great!' Impulsively she held out both her hands to him. 'John never said you were coming.'

'He didn't really know.' Tarrent squeezed her fingers, then abruptly released them. 'I wasn't sure I could make it.'

'I'm glad you could.'

'She so obviously meant what she said that Tarrent was touched. 'So am I.' He smiled at her.

Across the room Helen caught sight of her husband. He was staring straight at her, his face expressionless, and though she knew there was no cause she had a sudden feeling of guilt. In the distance she heard the telephone. It was a good excuse.

'I must answer that,' she said untruthfully. 'Forgive me, Neil. You'll find my mother-in-law over by the mantelpiece.'

Tarrent collected a drink and went over to Lady Kenmare. He stood chatting to her, commenting on how well organized they were after so few days back in London.

'Oh, we've always kept this house open,' she said. 'It's so convenient, with the lift for me, and everything. A few of our possessions are still on the way from Paris, but we're fully equipped.'

Tarrent looked curiously around, watching the other guests. Some of them he knew officially, others by sight, but none would he have described as friends. He accepted that it was not what Kenmare might call a formal party, but there was nothing casual about it. With a few possible exceptions, the guests were an influential lot and, he surmised, chosen for that influence.

Helen Kenmare returned to the room and came straight to her mother-in-law. 'That was Lady Cordar on the phone,' she said.

'For you?' Clara showed her surprise.

187

'I answered it. Anna was busy. Lady Cordar asked me to give you a message. She didn't want to disturb you.'

'Yes?'

'She sends her apologies, but she and Sir Patrick won't be able to dine here next week. Evidently she made a mistake. Sir Patrick had engagements she'd forgotten to put in her diary.'

'I see.' Clara smiled thinly. 'Dear Mary. And I always thought she was so efficient.'

Tarrent had moved away, as politeness demanded, when it became evident that Helen had a private message for Lady Kenmare. But by chance he hadn't moved far. While supposedly listening with interest to two gentlemen discussing life in the Soviet Union – a subject on which both seemed thoroughly ill-informed – he took in the gist of what Helen had said. It was obvious what had happened. Sir Patrick Cordar had decided that it was at present inadvisable to know the Kenmares socially.

Wishing he had never come, Tarrent went across to John Kenmare, to whom he had so far given only a friendly wave. He wondered if Kenmare was yet aware that he was under surveillance, and what his feelings were. One thing Kenmare certainly couldn't appreciate, Tarrent thought unhappily, seeing Helen on the far side of the room in animated conversation with a well-known Member of Parliament, was how important tomorrow might be for him and for his future.

At ten minutes to nine the following morning, Neil Tarrent was standing on the pavement outside Amanda Price's flat. Sir Patrick might easily be early. In fact, the official car was delayed in the heavy commuting traffic, and Tarrent had a longish wait.

When the car eventually arrived, he got in, to be greeted by a gruff good-morning. Sir Patrick, he was relieved to see, had his briefcase open and papers spread on his lap, a sign that conversation would not be necessary. Tarrent had wondered what they were going to talk about during the long drive; in the event, Sir Patrick continued to work throughout the journey, and very little was said.

An hour and a half later they arrived at Bonalov's new abode. It was a smaller, less imposing, version of the safe house to which Bonalov had originally been taken, but it was a good deal more isolated and set in more open country. Tarrent had been there before. He knew that 'visitors' usually felt a greater sense of freedom but, intentionally, were permitted to live in less luxury than when in Mr Smith's care. He wondered which location Bonalov preferred.

Certainly the Russian appeared more relaxed here. He greeted Sir Patrick warmly, and seemed genuinely pleased to see Tarrent. In accordance with their previous agreement on tactics, Sir Patrick maintained a correct but cold manner, while Tarrent was less reserved.

Formalities completed, they were taken by a uniformed NCO to a bare but comfortable interrogation room that Bonalov had not seen before. Sir Patrick seated himself at the head of a small table, Tarrent on his right and Bonalov on his left. As if casually, he remarked that Tarrent had been back in Moscow for a few days. Immediately Bonalov was interested.

'That's wonderful, Mr Tarrent. Did you hear anything of Oleg Kerensky? I've been a little worried about him. He was my assistant – my colleague – and, as you know, he was a great help in my anonymous negotiations with you. Though I hope my former fellow KGB officers aren't aware of the part he played.'

'I've no news of him, Colonel.' Tarrent glanced at Sir Patrick. This was not quite how they had planned the interview, but Bonalov had unexpectedly seized the initiative. Sir Patrick gave an almost imperceptible nod. 'You can imagine how difficult it was for me to make direct enquiries about him. But I did ask around a bit. He's not been seen in Moscow for some days.'

Bonalov pulled at his beard. 'I see. Well, I expect he's all right. He's got influential connections, and that counts in the Soviet Union, just like anywhere else. But I wouldn't want anything to happen to him because of me. He was a friend of my son, Pavel, and something of a protégé of mine. That was why he helped me – out of a sense of personal loyalty. Privately, he thought I was crazy to want to come over.'

'Would anyone be in a position to know of his – negotiations – on your behalf?' asked Sir Patrick.

Bonalov hesitated for a moment. 'No one of importance. No one he couldn't control. I chose the people I used with some care, Sir Patrick.' He smiled.

'Such as Sergei Dronsky?'

'You could say that Dronsky was chosen for me. He put himself at risk by associating with Mr Tarrent. He should have known better.' Bonalov turned to Tarrent. 'Incidentally, how is Dronsky – and his family?'

'Flourishing,' said Tarrent. 'Materially he seems to be doing very well. New furniture, new clothes, toys for the child. And he's due for a promotion it seems.'

'Splendid! I told Kerensky to arrange all this but, once I'd gone, I had to trust him to carry out my instructions.'

'You ordered all this?'

'Yes. Why not? It was a sort of recompense for the Dronskys.'

'Because you'd abducted their child as a hostage.' Sir Patrick's voice was scornful. 'And why did you need to do that, Colonel? Especially if Dronsky was already compromised because of his contacts with Mr Tarrent.'

'I had no choice. I had to have some hold over him of my own – a hold that was personal, quite apart from my organization. Dronsky's file told me that he was a patriot. His contacts with Mr Tarrent were quite harmless, though naturally they were kept under observation. And I certainly couldn't be sure he'd help a defector without informing the authorities, unless he was under some major compulsion. Admittedly he didn't know my identity – my rank or my importance – but he might have caused a lot of trouble.'

'I see,' said Sir Patrick. 'I'm not sure that argument's entirely convincing, Colonel.'

'Come, sir,' said Tarrent, playing his part well. 'You must admit that Colonel Bonalov's done his best to redress the wrong he did the Dronskys.'

'I suppose so, Neil. But a few consumer goods can scarcely compensate for the misery they must have suffered – and must still be suffering.' He turned to the Russian. 'I assume they're still living under some kind of threat, and will continue to do so. Isn't that so, Colonel?' he said abruptly.

'Why do you ask that?' replied Bonalov. 'Tarrent said they were flourishing."

Sir Patrick ignored him, and addressed himself to Neil. 'It must be pretty ghastly, never knowing when the knock on the door at two in the morning means that you, or your wife – or your child – will be dragged away.'

Alexei Bonalov pushed back his chair and stood up, cloaking sudden apprehension with a show of anger. 'Sir Patrick, Mr Tarrent, what do you speak of? Why should the Dronskys be fearful? The authorities have nothing on them. How can they?'

Sir Patrick regarded Bonalov in silence for a minute. Then he shrugged. 'Kerensky?' he asked.

'Kerensky? Oleg?' Bonalov repeated contemptuously, visibly relaxing. 'My dear Sir Patrick, why should Kerensky inform on Dronsky? Indeed, how could he, without betraying himself?'

'No. I suppose not.' Sir Patrick's reply was almost apologetic. Tarrent gave him full marks for his conduct of the interview. Now it was his own turn again. 'What about John Kenmare?' he said casually.

'Kenmare?' Bonalov hesitated, apparently puzzled, looking from Tarrent to Sir Patrick. He sat down and crossed his legs, perhaps to give himself time to think. Then he addressed himself to Sir Patrick. 'You've told Tarrent about Kenmare?' he said somewhat accusingly.

'Why not?' said Sir Patrick coldly. 'Colonel Bonalov, the use we make of any information you may provide is no concern of yours. But yes, Mr Tarrent has my complete confidence.'

'I see.' By this time Bonalov had recovered his composure. 'You thought Kenmare might have named Dronsky? And therefore Dronsky would be in the Lubyanka?'

'Something like that,' said Tarrent.

191

Sir Patrick intervened. 'You still maintain that Mr Kenmare's a Soviet agent, Colonel?'

'Of course I do. What nonsense is this? He's been one of ours for years.' Bonalov was curt. 'And if you don't arrest him soon, he'll make a break for the Soviet Union. I warn you. Don't you understand?'

'I understand what you say, Colonel Bonalov. But I'm not sure I understand the workings of your Service.'

'My Service? How is this? What do you mean?'

Sir Patrick caught Tarrent's eye. In a sense this was the kill, almost literally a moment of truth. He paused, aware of the chatter of sparrows outside the open window and the drone of a light aircraft passing overhead. Then he said, 'Look, Colonel. You say Mr Kenmare's one of yours. What you may not know is that Kenmare – one of yours – was fully briefed on all the negotiations with Dronsky from the moment Paris was first mentioned. This means that one of your agents knew that a defection was being planned, before any of us knew who the supposed defector was. Yet your organization took no action before the event, and has apparently permitted an accomplice to be handsomely rewarded after the event. All it has done is make two attempts – attempts that some might call unconvincing – to recapture you.'

'Ah, now I see where you're leading. Supposed defector! You've decided I'm a plant.'

'It's a choice, Colonel,' Tarrent said, pressing their advantage. 'Knowing what we know now, we must accept one of two things. Either Kenmare isn't a traitor. Or he denounced Dronsky and warned your authorities, who took no action because your defection was a put-up job. Those are the alternatives, Colonel.'

For a moment the room was silent. Then Alexei Bonalov laughed. Spreading his hands in a characteristically Russian gesture of resignation, he said, 'Congratulations! It would seem you've outsmarted me. I admit it. I was intended as a plant. So, what now? Deep interrogation? Truth drugs? Back to Mother Russia?'

'Perhaps, Colonel.'

'*Nyet*.' Bonalov shook his head. 'You'd be sending me to my death, Sir Patrick, and you know it.'

'Should I mind, Colonel? If it weren't for you, Simon Mont would still be alive. Remember that.'

'I do. Mr Mont's death upset everything.'

'Indeed. Don't you think you should explain.'

'Very well. I've no longer any choice. I'll have to tell you the truth.' Bonalov's expression changed. 'After my wife's death the future looked grim and hopeless, until I had an idea. I put a plan to certain senior officers in the KGB, and they accepted it. Briefly, I would defect to the United Kingdom. Once here, I would name Simon Mont as a traitor. This would ensure that our man – Kenmare – would become Director of the SIS when you retired, Sir Patrick. It would also create yet another British security scandal, with all that implies for cooperation within the West. Eventually I would return to the Soviet Union with any marginal information I had been able to acquire, leaving behind a lot of red faces.'

'So Simon – Simon Mont – was completely innocent?'

'Yes, Mr Tarrent. Your friend was, as you say, completely innocent. I'm sure you're pleased.' Bonalov favoured Tarrent with an understanding smile.

Neil Tarrent found himself returning the smile. 'Thank you,' he said. The interview seemed to be going well, though he had an unpleasant feeling that things might not be as simple as they appeared.

Sir Patrick said, 'A large sum of money has been sent anonymously to Mont's widow. Did that come from Soviet sources?'

'I don't know, but I suspect so. Kenmare would have had an emergency fund, and his controller probably told him to use it to lay a false trail to Mont.'

'I expect you're right,' said Sir Patrick. 'But it was a bank cashier's draft, so they can't stop it. I'd better get that lawyer man to tell Mrs Mont to cash it at once. Maybe she can use some of it to replace the savings they spent on that station wagon.'

'Let me tell her, sir,' said Tarrent. 'Maybe I can make my peace with Betty Mont. I think she still believes I'm to blame for the suspicions about Simon.'

Bonalov was irritated by these irrelevancies. He moved restlessly in his chair. 'Sir Patrick, I haven't finished yet. There's more. When Mont was killed, the KGB decided to abort my plan. After all, its main object was already achieved. With Mont out of the way, it was a near certainty that Kenmare would succeed you. But by then I was in your country, so they had to – to retrieve me.'

'But you prevented them,' Tarrent said sharply.

'Yes. It was like this. Kenmare telephoned his report on the safe house from the village nearby. It was then that for the first time he was told of the conspiracy—'

'You mean—'

'Yes. Till then Kenmare had thought I was a genuine defector. They had to put him in the picture so that he could play his part in the attack on the house. That was when he became dangerous. I had no intention of letting myself be – retrieved or recaptured, or going back to the Soviet Union.'

'What?'

'It's true, Sir Patrick.' Bonalov smiled, rather weakly. 'I had another plan – a private plan of my own, a plan I hoped neither my old Soviet masters nor my new British ones would discover. I proposed to live comfortably in the West – in the United Kingdom – serving both West and East. When Moscow eventually demanded my return, I would make my final decision. Till then I meant to keep my options open, as they say. Unfortunately, this was not to be. I had to make my choice when I refused to accept the orders that Kenmare relayed to me. And when I denounced him, the choice became irreversible. Sir Patrick, I'm all yours now.'

EIGHTEEN

'Is there any doubt?'

'I don't think so, Prime Minister, unfortunately.'

'Thinking's not enough, Sir Patrick. We must know. Otherwise we could be doing the Soviets' work for them, and creating a major security scandal where none exists.'

'We know someone provided Moscow with a copy of that JIC paper, Prime Minister.' Sir Patrick restrained himself with difficulty.

'Someone, yes. But apart from the accusations of this man Bonalov, what evidence have we that John Kenmare's the someone?'

The Director of the Security Service intervened. 'No hard evidence as yet, Prime Minister. Nothing that would stand up in court. It takes a lot of time to get that sort of positive evidence. As you know, it's often not possible at all, and we have to rely on the man breaking and confessing, or trying to make a run for it.'

'And what do you think is likely to happen in this case?' The Prime Minister was icy. The Government was in mid-term, and far from popular. It could easily be toppled as a result of a scandal in high places. 'Surely I don't need to remind you gentlemen – John Kenmare may not be well-known in his own right, but he carries a very famous name. The media will go to town at the first hint of his involvement. We've got to play this very carefully, and be ready for them. We can't afford doubts.'

The Director of the Security Service looked down his long, thin nose. He had no wish to catch Sir Patrick's eye. They certainly weren't enemies; rather, they were unwilling collaborators, always eager to score off each other on behalf of their Departments. But on one thing they were agreed: politicians of whatever colour invariably failed to appreciate the difficulties and requirements and doubts of intelligence operations, internal or external, active or passive.

'We're doing our best, Prime Minister,' he said mildly. 'Meanwhile Kenmare's under strict surveillance. There's no chance he can leave the country. And he can't do us any more damage – assuming he's guilty, of course,' he added hastily. 'Sir Patrick assures me that he's been put on routine duties, and has no access to classified material of any kind. And we're keeping a sharp eye on his contacts in the Service.'

'That's so, Prime Minister,' Sir Patrick hurried to agree.

'He's aware of the situation?'

'Kenmare? Yes, of course. He can't fail to be, by now. Intentionally, we're making no attempt to hide our interest.'

'We need to put more pressure on him, Prime Minister – call him in for interrogation.'

The Prime Minister sighed. 'Yes. I understand that. But it's all very difficult. This business could blow up in the Government's face any moment. I shall have to inform the Cabinet Committee.'

Not that, the security chief thought. He said quickly, 'Prime Minister, I would suggest, if Sir Patrick supports me, that we wait a day or two in the hope that we get a break.'

'Sir Patrick?'

'I'm prepared to agree, Prime Minister. I can't see that we've anything to lose, if it's only a short delay.'

'Certainly we must keep it short.' The Head of the Security Service nodded his confirmation. 'Otherwise we might get a leak rather than a break.'

The Prime Minister gave a thin smile. It was useless to resent the implied warning. Everyone knew that Cabinet security was not as good as it should be.

'Very well.' The Prime Minister reached a decision. 'We'll give it forty-eight hours. But I'll expect to be kept informed and, after that—'

After that, Sir Patrick thought grimly, as he came out of Number Ten and hurried across the wet pavement to his waiting car, after that John Kenmare would be pulled in, and all hell could break loose. Poor Clara! She was such a proud woman. God alone knew how she would bear the disgrace. For that matter, it wasn't going to be easy for himself and his own family. Sir Patrick stared, unseeing, out of the car window at the handful of people who, regardless of the weather, always seemed to gather at the end of Downing Street.

John Kenmare was walking along the Embankment. The rain was falling steadily now, heavy rain, thundery rain, but he scarcely noticed it. The rain wasn't cold, and his suit was already soaked through. He walked slowly, almost as if he were taking an evening stroll.

A few people, in raincoats, umbrellas up, intent on getting to their destinations, glanced at him doubtfully as they hurried past. Some even went a step or two out of their way to give him a wide berth. One couldn't be too careful these days, and only a crazy character, a nutter, would loiter beside the river in weather like this.

Kenmare was unaware of them. He was cocooned in his thoughts. The passers-by, the rumble of traffic, the mournful hoot of a tug on the river, the strident note of an ambulance, none of it meant anything to him. Even his own miserable state, with water dripping down his neck and squelching in his shoes, had no significance. Completely preoccupied, he leant on the balustrade by Cleopatra's Needle and looked down into the mud-green depths of the Thames.

Indecision, he thought, could tear a man apart. Surely the time had come to act, before it was too late – if it wasn't already too late. Why had he delayed so long? Why had he hoped against hope? Was it because he couldn't face up to the future? He wondered what would happen if he climbed quickly over the parapet and let himself drop into the dark water below. Probably some hero would dive in and save him, or a police launch would pick him up. Then there would be explanations. Sir Patrick would be called. Nothing would have been achieved, and the matter would be hushed up, until they were ready . . . Kenmare gave a short, hissing laugh.

'You okay, sir? Want any help?'

Gradually the world about him intruded. Kenmare turned slowly as the older of the two young policemen repeated his question. 'I'm fine, thank you, Constable. Any reason I shouldn't be?' His voice was perfectly steady.

'No, sir, but it's a miserable night to be out when you don't need to.'

The man came close. Kenmare fleetingly regretted the smell of whisky on his breath; he had called in at a couple of pubs before he began his walk beside the river. Now the damn fuzz wouldn't let him alone, wouldn't be satisfied till he'd left the Embankment.

'I suppose you're right, Constable. I'd better be getting home.'

'That's a good idea, sir. Do you live far from here?'

'Off Knightsbridge.'

'That's quite a ways to walk in this downpour,' the policeman said. 'Would you like us to see if we can find a cab for you?'

'Thanks. I'd be most grateful.' John Kenmare tried not to sound ironic. Though he had already decided to go home, and it was true that a taxi-driver might think twice before stopping to pick up such a disreputable-looking fare, he resented the interference. 'Thanks again,' he said, as the second policeman successfully hailed a cab. 'And good night to you both.'

Ten minutes later he was home. The Special Branch men, sitting in their unmarked car a few yards along the street, heaved a concerted sigh of relief as Kenmare let himself into the house. They'd lost Kenmare two hours ago – or rather he'd lost them, by the simple process of going into his very superior London club and leaving by the tradesmen's entrance. They reported hurriedly. The alert at all ports and airports could be called off. The quarry had gone to ground.

'My God, John, what happened to you?'

'I got caught in the rain, Helen.'

Kenmare stood in the doorway of the drawing-room, a pool of water beginning to form on the carpet around his feet.

He stared at his wife as if she were a stranger, as if he were seeing her for the first time. He had made no attempt to kiss her and, though she had got up and come towards him, she was restrained by his appearance and the oddness of his behaviour.

'Sweetie, what's wrong? Please tell me. Even if I can't help, it—'

'Later. I'll tell you later.' Kenmare's voice was harsh. 'I must talk to Mother first. Where is she?'

'In her room, with Anna. She was worried about you. We all were.'

The unspoken appeal went unheeded. Kenmare turned his back and left her. Helen heard his knock, and the door of Clara's room open and close. It was very quiet in the house. Desolate, she went over to the window. Drawing aside the heavy velvet curtains, she looked down into the square below. There were no stars. The cloud cover was low. Except for the patches of brightness thrown by the street lamps, everything was dark and dank, the trees in the small railed-in garden in the centre of the square dripping with rain.

She was about to turn away when a car drove up fast, and stopped in the middle of the road a few yards short of the Kenmare's front door. A man got out and ran across to another car parked at the kerb, from which a second man was climbing, stretching himself. The two of them had the briefest of conversations. Then, making no attempt at concealment, they gazed up at her lighted window.

Hurriedly Helen stepped back into the room and drew the curtains. She found herself shaking. She was sure, without being told, that the men were concerned with John. Standing to one side so that she wouldn't be seen, she moved the curtain fractionally and peered through the slit.

The men were no longer standing there. They had got back into their respective cars. But, as she watched, the car by the kerb drove off, while the car that had just arrived backed neatly into the parking space left for it. There was only one explanation. The house was under observation. But why? Who were these men? Either John knew, or if he didn't he should be told of them at once.

Purposefully Helen left the drawing-room. She was fearful, but determined. Whatever was happening she wanted to know about it, now. She wouldn't be put off, treated like a child, while John confided only in his mother. But, as she reached Clara's door, her resolution failed.

From inside she could hear the sound of sobbing. John? Clara? The hand that had been about to knock dropped to her side. She couldn't bring herself to intrude on them. Unnerved, she went upstairs and into her bedroom. She had never felt more alone. If only, she thought, she had a friend in London, someone she could talk to, someone she could trust. Without volition, her mind turned to Neil Tarrent.

It was more than an hour later that John Kenmare came to their bedroom. He was wearing a robe over pyjamas and he had shaved. Helen could smell the after-shave lotion as he bent over and kissed her. She moved her head on the pillow so that his lips just brushed her cheek.

'Helen, darling, I'm sorry.'

'What for, John? What for? What's happened?' He looked normal, but she could feel his tension.

'I'll tell you in a minute.' He took her hand, and she let it lie in his without returning the pressure of his fingers. 'Helen, I love you very much, darling. When I married you I hoped, I believed, I'd be able to make you happy.'

'You have, John.' She felt a sudden surge of love for him, and almost believed her own lie. 'Really you have. It's been a wonderful year.'

'A year, yes. I'd expected much longer than that.'

'John, you're not ill, are you?' She sat up in sudden alarm, but then she remembered the men waiting and watching outside the house. Even before he reassured her, she knew his trouble had nothing to do with his health. 'What is it then?' she asked sharply.

'Alexei Bonalov, the Russian defector we brought from Paris, has denounced me to the British as a Soviet agent. Or I'm pretty sure he has.'

'But – what does that mean?'

200

'It means I'm under serious suspicion – and surveillance. The Security Service and the police are looking for evidence against me. When they think they're ready, they'll pull me in for interrogation – and arrest me, if you like. Eventually they may charge me and put me on trial, but—'

'That's mad! How can they find evidence when there isn't any?'

'Ah, but there is, darling. And when they dig deep, they'll find enough. That's what I'm trying to tell you, Helen. I've worked for the Soviet Union the best part of my life. Now, at last, the British have caught up with me.'

'I – I can't believe it.'

John Kenmare laughed harshly. 'I bet you're not the only one. Patrick Cordar must have found it a bitter pill to take.'

'But why, John? Goddammit, why? Why you?'

'Oh yes, I know what you're going to say. Old and famous family. Son of that great man, Sir Peter Kenmare. Eton and Oxford. Not even Cambridge. What better cover could anyone want?'

'You resented your father? Was that it?'

'No, it was not! He was unimportant.' With an effort John Kenmare restrained his irritation. This was no time for amateur psychiatry. He had to make her understand. He had to convince her. 'Darling,' he said. 'I realize this has been a shock, but try to accept it. We must think about the future.'

'The future! What future?'

Helen hugged her knees close to her body as she used to do when she was a small girl, and had wanted to comfort herself. Tonight, in this new world, the magic didn't work. She felt cold all through, as though she'd never be warm again. And the cold had atrophied her brain. She couldn't think. Tears pricked her eyes. She heard the word Moscow.

'Moscow?'

'You weren't listening'

'No. I'm sorry. What were you saying?'

The words came in a rush, and Helen caught only the gist of them. A boat in some small south coast port. A train or a hired car. They might have to split. With her American

201

passport she should have no trouble, and he had another passport, in a different name, for just such an emergency. They'd meet up in East Europe, where he'd be safe, and travel together to Moscow. It was a fascinating city, and they'd be together. They'd have a good life, not what he'd hoped, perhaps, but good. He'd served the Communist cause well, and the Soviets would look after him. If she got tired of the place she'd be able to go back to the States for a holiday. No one would stop her. There was a lot of rubbish talked about the Soviet Union by people who knew nothing . . .

Helen stopped listening. Instead she remembered the reception in Paris where she'd met Neil Tarrent. She remembered telling him how much she would like to see Moscow. But not like this. Dear God, not like this!

'Darling, tell me you'll come with me. Please. I'll make you happy. I swear it.'

'What – what about your mother?'

'My mother?' Kenmare seemed surprised by the question. 'She won't come. I asked her – and Anna. They refused. Mother says she's too old to uproot herself, and anyway—' He dismissed the subject with an impatient wave of his hand. 'Helen, it's you I want.'

Helen gave him a long, searching glance. She knew now she didn't love him. She wouldn't – couldn't – go to Russia with him. But she didn't have the courage to tell him, not immediately, not at the moment.

'John I need time to think'

'Time's what I can't give you, darling. At least, not much.' He got off the bed and stood looking down at her. 'I go tomorrow, Helen. And you must be with me.'

NINETEEN

Helen Kenmare hadn't expected to sleep. For some time after her husband left her she lay on their bed, weeping, enormously grateful he hadn't attempted to make love to her. Then she cursed, and wept again. Finally, exhausted, curled up in a foetal position, she slept.

It was light when she woke. A watery sun failed to penetrate the room, but where the ruffles of the curtains met the ceiling there was a band of brightness. She pushed herself off the pillows and sat upright. It wasn't the light that had woken her. A car back-firing? A banging door? Her heart missed a beat. A shot?

Helen had no lack of courage. She slid out of bed, put on robe and slippers and drew the curtains. The muted roar of London's traffic seemed closer. A helicopter was passing overhead. But the square below was an oasis of calm, an elderly man walking his dog, a boy delivering the daily newspapers, the familiar jangle of milk bottles. There was no obvious explanation for whatever had shattered her sleep – and filled her with fear.

The time by the bedside clock was seven fifty-five. Helen went to the door of the room, opened it and listened. The house was quiet, peaceful. On a normal day Anna would be in the kitchen at this time, making early morning tea for Clara, still in bed. John would be in their bathroom, shaving and showering. She herself might be getting up slowly, thinking of orange juice and gallons of coffee and buttered toast with honey. But this was not a normal day.

In the first place, where was John? Helen started downstairs to find him. She didn't intentionally avoid making any sound, but her feet were slippered, the carpet deep, and she moved lightly. In the small room on the next floor that John used as a study, Clara and Anna were unaware of her approach. The door was half open.

'Wipe it! Wipe it, you fool' Clara's voice was high and sharp. It reached Helen clearly.

'That's what I'm about to do. Have patience.' Anna's reply was fierce and curt, quite different from her normal manner to her mistress.

'Patience! Don't talk to me of patience now! He was mine. I made him. I loved him.'

'I loved him too.'

'I know.' Clara was suddenly understanding. 'I know, dear Anna.'

Helen stood on the landing, one hand on the banisters, about to go down the next flight of stairs. Lady Kenmare and Anna. Not John. John wasn't there. They were just talking about him. She gave no thought to her next move. She turned from the stairs and went straight into John's study.

She saw at once that she had been mistaken. John was there, but something was dreadfully wrong with him. He had slumped over his desk, as if he had intended to write a letter and fallen asleep while doing so. He was wearing the robe and pyjamas he had worn the previous night. One side of his head was missing.

Helen choked back her scream, tearing her eyes from the mess of blood and brains splattering the wall behind him. She looked quickly from her mother-in-law, sitting regally still in her wheelchair, to Anna and to the gun in Anna's hand.

'You've shot him!' she said involuntarily.

The tableau came to life. 'Don't be stupid!' Clara's wheelchair moved towards Helen, quietly, almost menacingly. 'Why should Anna shoot John? She was devoted to him. Devoted!'

'But what – what happened?' Helen stuttered. Lady Kenmare was now close to her. 'Helen,' she said. 'John's dead. He killed himself. Accept it. Nothing can alter it. Nothing will bring him back. Neither tears, nor hysteria, nor—'

'Nor what?' cried Helen wildly. 'Nor grief? How can you sit there so calmly as if – as if—?' Suddenly she felt sick and forced herself to swallow the bile that rose in her throat.

'Because calmness is vital if we are to preserve the formalities – the appearances—'

'Appearances! Formalities! What in heaven's name do you mean? John's killed himself! Why didn't you call me? Where are the police—?'

'Helen, take a lesson from me and calm yourself,' Clara said quietly. 'John Kenmare may have killed himself, but the name of Kenmare remains important, very important. Remember you bear it too, Helen. The least we can do – all of us – is preserve its honour.'

Helen laughed mirthlessly. 'You must be out of your mind,' she said. 'After what he told us last night. How can you talk about honour?' She forced herself to look again at what had once been John Kenmare. Anna had wiped the gun and was now kneeling beside the body, pressing one of the hands carefully around it, then letting the arm drop so that the gun fell to the desk.

'And what's Anna doing?' Helen said desperately. 'We must call the police, an ambulance – the authorities,' she repeated.

'Anna is doing exactly what I told her to do,' Clara said firmly. 'She was silly enough to pick up the gun when she found the – John, so her fingerprints were on it. She is now arranging things as they should be – making it appear that John's death was an accident.'

'Accident! But you can't do that! It's not right. The truth—'

'The truth is that John Kenmare committed suicide because he was afraid. His superiors had discovered he was a Soviet agent, and he couldn't face the obvious consequences. You know that, and I know that, and so does Anna. But do you want the police to know, Helen – and the newspapers and the magazines and the rest of the media? Is that what you want: every man and woman and child gossiping about John Kenmare, so that the name of Kenmare becomes synonymous with treason?'

'No. Of course not, but—' Helen was shaken by Clara's vehemence. She even felt a pang of pity for her. She herself could go away somewhere, back home to the States perhaps, and forget she'd ever been a Kenmare, but for Clara the disgrace would be unending and intolerable. Nevertheless . . .

She said more gently, 'Clara, it's not possible. The police won't wear it. They're not fools.'

'You don't understand, Helen. I have no intention of calling the police. I shall telephone Sir Patrick Cordar. I shall tell him that John must have had an accident. There have been a lot of burglaries around here recently. Perhaps John heard something. That could have been why he came in here to get the gun.'

Helen shook her head, disbelieving. 'He'll never buy that,' she said. 'There are too many—'

'I don't expect him to "buy it", as you say, my dear. But Patrick's a good, kind man. He's always been very fond of me. He'll pretend to believe it, for my sake and because it's the best solution for him too – and, I suspect, for everyone concerned, from the Prime Minister down. I doubt if the Government can afford a major spy scandal at present. Nor can poor Patrick, when he's so near retiring. You'll see. Don't worry. Everyone will cooperate in covering things up.'

Helen looked doubtfully at her mother-in-law. They were outside the study now. By manoeuvring her wheelchair Clara had made Helen back out onto the landing.

'You think so?'

'I know so, Helen.' Clara was positive, reassuring. 'My dear, you go and get dressed while I telephone Patrick. The next little while won't be easy for any of us. But however you feel at the moment, remember that John was your husband, and he loved you very much indeed. Poor, dear John! Whatever he did, he's dead now. We can't let his death become a *cause célèbre* in the gutter press.'

Twenty minutes later Helen, fully dressed, sat on the edge of her bed, her arms wrapped around her body as if to hold herself together. She felt empty, exhausted. She tried to concentrate her thoughts, but her mind would work only at random.

Poor, dear John, Clara had said. Nothing else. No other expression of grief, no weeping, no sign of emotion from Anna. The only thing that seemed to matter to either of them was preserving the good name of Kenmare.

For that matter, she hadn't wept herself. But after last

night she had no tears left. She was appalled and horrified, but as yet she could feel no sorrow. She wondered if she ever would. And she was shocked at herself for not caring more about the man she'd married.

Why had he done it? He had given her no hint of desperation. He had been reasonably calm, and had talked clearly and logically of his plans. Trying to persuade her to come to Russia with him, he had sounded almost enthusiastic. And, in fact, she hadn't turned him down, though eventually she would have done. She was thankful for that now. At least she needn't blame herself that her refusal had caused his death.

She looked up, startled, as the door of her bedroom opened. Anna stood there. She hadn't knocked. She regarded Helen appraisingly.

'Good! You're dressed. That's very suitable.' She nodded her approval at the black and white silk dress. 'Come along, then. They've arrived, Sir Patrick and the young man with red hair, Mr Tarrent.'

'Neil Tarrent?' Helen, at first annoyed by the unusually commanding manner that Anna had adopted, was conscious of a feeling of relief. It had not occurred to her that Sir Patrick would bring Neil with him. 'Where are they?'

'In the drawing-room, with Lady Kenmare. There are a lot of others in the study, doctors and such like, but they're no concern of ours.' At the top of the stairs Anna drew back, as if to let Helen precede her. But as Helen passed she grasped her by the arm. 'Mrs Kenmare.'

'Yes.'

'Be careful what you say, Mrs Kenmare. Follow Lady Kenmare's lead. Every word may matter. Do you understand?'

Helen, surprised, was not sure if this was meant as advice or threat. She tried to release her arm, but found it impossible without undue force. She stared down at Anna's broad, peasant face, the eyes like brown buttons, red-rimmed – had Anna wept for John? – the iron-grey hair parted in the middle in a kind of parody of her mistress' style, the dour hostile expression. And Helen remembered that it was Anna who had held the gun purposefully in her hand.

'I understand,' she said.

But the grip on her arm didn't relax. Instead, the fingers dug deeper, hit a nerve. Helen winced – the pain was acute – and no longer caring for civilities she tore her arm free.

'Mrs Kenmare, John can't be sacrificed for nothing. I warn you.'

It was a threat, Helen thought as she ran down the stairs. She had only half caught the words, but the menacing tone had been sufficient. Helen shivered. As soon as it was decently possible she would leave this house, and never return. She could still feel the ominous pressure of Anna's fingers on her arm.

As she entered the drawing-room Sir Patrick Cordar and Neil Tarrent got to their feet. Sir Patrick said, 'Mrs Kenmare, may we offer you our most sincere condolences. A most dreadful thing, most dreadful.'

'Thank you.' Helen stood irresolute, wondering what was expected of her, wishing she was any place else.

'Get yourself some coffee, my dear, and come and sit down,' Clara said. 'A frightful shock,' she added to Sir Patrick.

'Yes. Yes, of course. For you all. Quite understandable.'

But Neil Tarrent had already moved to the side table, and was pouring coffee into a large breakfast cup. Helen went to join him and, turning to smile at her, he knocked against her arm. He heard her sharp intake of breath, and simultaneously saw the livid marks on her skin below the short sleeve of her dress. Their eyes met.

'Milk? Sugar?'

'Neither, thanks.'

Taking the cup he held out to her, she went to sit opposite Clara. She sipped her coffee, which was hot and strong; as usual, Anna had been efficient. She realized that Sir Patrick was watching her, waiting.

'Mrs Kenmare, I've no wish to distress you, but there are some questions I must ask. I'll keep them as short as possible.'

'I'll tell you all I can, Sir Patrick.'

'You were the last person to see your husband alive?'

Helen bowed her head. 'As far as I know.' Anticipating the next question, she said, 'He was late home and I was worried about him. When he came in he was soaked – he'd got caught in that big storm we had. But after I was in bed he came to say good night, and seemed fine again. He said he had work to do, and not to stay awake for him.'

'He seemed normal – just as usual?'

Purposely she misunderstood the question. 'Sure. He was fine, as I say. The rain had been warm, and even if he was going to get a chill he wouldn't have noticed it yet.'

'Do you know where he'd been earlier in the evening – how he came to get caught in the rain?'

'No.' Helen glanced at Clara.

Clara said, 'I've no idea either, Patrick. I think we assumed he'd had trouble finding a cab.'

Sir Patrick turned back to Helen. 'And did you hear any odd noises during the night or early this morning, Mrs Kenmare?'

Helen shook her head. She had decided she would tell no outright lies, whatever Anna and Clara might say, but Sir Patrick was leading her, making things easy. The questions continued, but they were all sympathetic rather than probing. Sir Patrick clearly didn't want to dig too deeply. Helen responded to the questions she was asked, but volunteered nothing. She let Clara do most of the talking.

By noon it was all over. Unlisted phone numbers had been called, strings pulled and arrangements made. Two Special Branch Officers, one of them very senior, had arrived, accompanied by CID men from the local station. Together they were interviewed by Sir Patrick, while an SIS doctor examined the body. All that was left of John Kenmare had by now been removed to the police mortuary, and plans were being made for a coroner to sit alone as soon as possible, bring in a verdict of accidental death and release the body for burial. The legal requirements of sudden death were apparently being complied with, but in fact all the interested authorities had agreed upon the vital need for a cover-up, just as Clara had forecast.

Outside the Kenmares' house the doctor was having a final word with Sir Patrick. Neil Tarrent stood by. He was concerned for Helen Kenmare. Admittedly the circumstances were tragic and shocking, but surely they didn't altogether account for her withdrawn behaviour, the obvious lack of her usual frankness. Then there were those bruises on her arm. They were new, very recent. Not John Kenmare, if she hadn't seen him since last night. So, who? Tarrent shook himself. He was concerned about Helen. Concerned? What a bloody stupid word. Who was he kidding? He was hellish worried about her, and determined to talk to her alone, ensure she was all right. But when and how?

The doctor was saying, '. . . sure, with all the big guns we can bring to bear on him, the coroner'll play along. But he'll know as well as I do that it definitely wasn't an accident. Not unless the bugger was playing Russian roulette with himself.' The doctor was a robust character, and the joke he had inadvertently made delighted him. He roared with laughter. 'No one shoots himself in the temple by accident.'

'Suicide, then?' Sir Patrick saw no humour in the situation.

'Presumably. A good deal of it would fit. The powder burns . . .' The doctor pondered, humming to himself. 'There is one oddity,' he added.

'What?' Sir Patrick was immediately attentive. The doctor might have a warped sense of humour, but he was an astute man and knew his job. 'Something troubled you?'

'Not exactly. But I'd have thought, you know – someone like Kenmare, a professional—'

'What are you trying to say?'

'Just this. I'd have expected him to put the damn gun in his mouth. He must have known that was the way to make certain. This business of pointing the thing at one's forehead, it's always dodgy. He could easily have done himself a lot of damage without finishing himself off. Yet he took the risk.'

'Yes, I see. But it's difficult to understand how a man's mind works when he's in that sort of state.' Sir Patrick climbed into his car. 'Let me have a copy of what you report to the police.' He sketched a farewell salute.

Tarrent got in beside him and the car moved off. Glancing up, Tarrent thought he caught a glimpse of Helen's face at the drawing-room window, but there was nothing he could

210

do about her at the moment.

'An accident,' Sir Patrick said. 'He heard a noise, got up to investigate, took his gun – he had a licence for it, of course – perhaps tripped over something, and shot himself. Scared off the would-be thief. Great tragedy. Brilliant man. Memorial service soon. Write me a couple of paragraphs on those lines, Neil. I'll clear it with the right people, and we'll get the Office to spread it round the press.'

'Yes, sir.' Tarrent hesitated. 'Do you think we'll get away with it?'

'I sincerely hope so, at least as far as the public's concerned. There'll be talk in official circles, naturally. Bound to be. After all, the damage assessment on Kenmare will involve a lot of people and mean a lot of questions. It won't be so easy now we can't interrogate him. But we've still got Bonalov. It seems he was right about Kenmare. Maybe we can have more faith in whatever else he's got to say.'

'Sir, what about Kenmare's family?'

Momentarily Sir Patrick looked blank. 'What about them?'

'I know you managed to avoid police interviews this morning, sir, but they'll have to be questioned sometime, won't they? I mean, properly – about John's past, his contacts – all that sort of thing.'

'Yes, of course. But not by me, thank God. Poor Clara! It'll be a matter for the security boys how much of the truth they tell her, or whether they let her go on thinking it was an accident. I hope they spare her. I'd like to think John hoped so too. Perhaps that's why he didn't leave any sort of suicide note. Maybe he guessed the line we'd want to take.'

'Yes, sir,' said Tarrent doubtfully. 'But there's Helen Kenmare, too. With your permission, I'd like to have another talk to her myself.'

'You? Why?'

'Well, sir, it seemed to me she knew more than she said this morning. She was very – very reticent, I thought.' Tarrent picked his words carefully; he might as well cover himself if he could. 'After all, John was her husband. It's possible he confided in her at the end, told her some of his troubles. And she might say more to me in an informal chat

211

than under interrogation by a security chap.'

'Yes, it's possible.' Sir Patrick's thoughts had turned to other matters, his next interview with the Prime Minister, cooperation with the security service, what Bonalov might have to say about Kenmare's death. 'All right, Neil. But use some judgement. Remember what a shock all this must have been. Better leave it a day or two.'

'Thank you, sir,' Tarrent said. He had no intention of leaving his approach to Helen a moment longer than he could help.

It was early evening before Neil Tarrent was able to collect Amanda's car and drive to the Kenmares' house. He rang the bell for the second time that day, and for the second time Anna opened the door. He asked boldly for Mrs Kenmare.

'No. You can't see her. She's resting.'

'I'm sorry to disturb her. But please tell her I'm here and it's important.'

'I will tell Lady Kenmare.' Reluctantly Anna opened the door wider and allowed Tarrent into the hall. 'Wait here, please.'

Tarrent didn't wait. He followed Anna up the stairs and into the drawing-room. Considering the day's events, he was confronted with a scene of incredible domesticity. Lady Kenmare and Helen were sitting in armchairs, sipping sherry and sharing the evening paper in apparent equanimity. For a moment he thought his earlier misgivings had been imaginary. Then Helen looked up and caught his eye, and he knew he had not been wrong.

'I must apologize for bothering you again so soon, Lady Kenmare. It's really Mrs Kenmare I want, or rather Sir Patrick wants.' Tarrent smiled encouragingly at Helen. 'If you wouldn't mind coming along to the office, Mrs Kenmare, I've a car outside, and it won't take long.'

'Whatever for?' Lady Kenmare took charge, and was not friendly. 'Why on earth should Sir Patrick want Helen to go to your office at this time of the evening? Honestly, Mr Tarrent, this is an imposition. It's been a devastating day for all of us. We're trying to recover a little. And you burst in with this extraordinary request. It must wait till tomorrow.'

'I'm afraid it can't, Lady Kenmare.' Tarrent looked at Helen, willing her to cooperate with him. 'A large envelope has been found in John's office safe. It's marked "Personal and Private", and our lawyers tell us it's got to be opened in the presence of his next of kin – his wife. Otherwise . . .'

'Of course I'll come. I don't mind.' Helen put down her glass.

'No, my dear.' Lady Kenmare turned back to Tarrent. 'If this envelope is marked "Personal and Private", why didn't you bring it with you? We could have opened it here. Surely that would have been more sensible.'

'We've no idea what's in the envelope, Lady Kenmare,' said Tarrent blandly. 'Given the nature of John's work, it could be – anything. That's why it must be opened in the office, in front of official witnesses – and as soon as possible.'

There was the merest flicker in Lady Kenmare's eyes, but it was enough. She knows, Tarrent thought. Her precious son must have told her last night, though she'll never admit it. Christ, it must have been a blow! Perhaps that's why she shows so little sign of grief. And Helen? Had Kenmare told his wife too?

'I still say your request is absurd, Mr Tarrent. I'll telephone Sir Patrick at once and tell him so. Mrs Kenmare's in no fit state . . .'

'Clara, I'm fine.' Helen intervened firmly. 'I'll be happy to go with Mr Tarrent if it'll help in any way. Please don't make a fuss about it.'

'Very well. Do as you wish, my dear.' Clara didn't like being thwarted, but she knew when she was beaten. 'Goodbye, Mr Tarrent.'

'Good night, Lady Kenmare.'

Anna showed them out and watched them get into the car. She stared after it as it drove away, her heavy face set in grim lines. It was a mistake, she thought, a bad mistake. John should never have married the American girl. You couldn't trust her. Heaven alone knew what she might say to that man Tarrent.

TWENTY

'You mean it was all lies, all that stuff about the envelope in John's safe?'

'All lies, I'm afraid.' Neil Tarrent drove north through Hyde Park, adjusting automatically to the early evening traffic, his mind on the girl beside him. 'I'm sorry Helen, but I couldn't think of any other way of talking to you alone.'

'About John?'

'About John – yes. And you. Those bruise marks on your arm, for instance.'

'That wasn't John,' Helen said quickly.

'No. I know. It couldn't have been. Anna, I suppose?' He didn't wait for her reply. 'Why, Helen? What had you done? Or what did she think you might do?'

Helen didn't answer. Her eyes blurred with tears. She had been glad of a chance to get out of the house, to get away from the charged atmosphere, to be free of constant observation by Anna and Clara. But she was not yet sure she was prepared to discuss her husband with a relative stranger – and a stranger with unknown official affiliations, at that.

Tarrent prompted her gently. 'Helen, try to trust me. John told you about himself, didn't he? About his – his real work, I mean.'

For a moment Helen stared out of the car window. At last she said reluctantly, 'He told me he worked for the Russians, yes. But you knew that already.'

'We were pretty sure.'

Helen was silent again, but Tarrent guessed that now she had begun to talk, she would continue. He looked for somewhere to park. He couldn't give her his full attention while he was driving. They had just crossed the bridge over the Serpentine, and he made a sharp right turn and stopped beside the lake.

214

'Shall we stay in the car? The grass is still wet after yesterday's rain.'

As if he'd not spoken, Helen said, 'John wanted me, and his mother, and Anna, to go to Russia with him – to Moscow. It was all laid on – a boat on the coast, a false passport for him. I don't remember the details. I scarcely listened.'

The words came softly, in a rush. Tarrent didn't interrupt. He let her talk, confirming what he knew or suspected.

'. . . his mother had refused to go with him. But I didn't actually turn him down, and when he left me last night he was still—' Helen sought for the right words. '—still full of purpose. I was sure he meant to go – by himself, if he had to.' Helen paused. 'Anyway, that's why I was so surprised as well as horrified, when – when—'

'—when he shot himself,' finished Tarrent bluntly.

Impulsively Helen turned to him. She had to tell someone, to talk out her doubts. 'Neil I'm scared. I've been thinking all day. And I believe – maybe – he was murdered.'

'But who? Why? Tarrent was less startled than he sounded. He hesitated, then decided to put his hunch into words. 'It's Anna, isn't it? You think Anna killed him.'

'Perhaps. Yes. No. Oh, I don't know. I don't know what to think. But John was all set to go to Moscow. Why should he change his mind so suddenly? It wasn't because of me. And if he did change his mind, why didn't he leave a note, some kind of – of message – if not for me, for his mother. They were awfully close.'

'Perhaps he did, and Lady Kenmare destroyed it, or kept it for herself.'

Helen sighed. 'That's possible. Anna called Clara first, naturally. She had plenty of time to do anything. They both had.'

Plenty of time? Was that true? Helen tried to remember. There had been the shot. That was what had woken her; she was sure of it now. Then she had got up, put on gown and slippers, looked out of the window. How long before she went downstairs? If Anna had been in the kitchen when the shot was fired, it would have taken her minutes to find John, get Clara out of bed and take her wheelchair to the study. Yet Anna and Clara had been there arguing over the gun –

clearly well over the first shock of John's death – when she had interrupted them.

'. . . and there's the question of motive,' Neil Tarrent was saying. 'It's hard to believe Anna killed John merely because he'd done dirt on everything the Kenmares stood for, but I can't think of any other reason.'

'For Clara's sake, to avoid a scandal?'

'Possibly. Though Lady Kenmare strikes me as tough enough to face anything. After what you've all been through in the last twenty-four hours, I'd have expected her to be in bed under sedation. But from what you say, she seems less upset than you are.' Tarrent looked anxiously at Helen.

'I'm okay.' Helen managed a grin. 'Better for having talked about it. I suppose the truth is I've never liked Anna much, and seeing her with the gun in her hand – I – I must try to forget it.'

'You don't have to go back to the house, you know. Or I could come with you to collect some things. I've been lent a flat in London. And there are always hotels—'

Helen sensed his hesitation. 'No. No, thanks,' she said quickly. 'I guess I've just been stupid.'

'Don't think that.' Tarrent hurriedly tore a page from his notebook and scribbled on it. 'This is the phone number and address of the flat. And this is my office number. I'll come running if you need me, Helen. I promise.'

'Thanks.' Helen folded the paper and put it in the pocket of her dress.

She didn't really trust him, Tarrent thought. Why should she? He'd been no real help, probably just made things more difficult for her with Clara. But her doubts about the suicide, her suspicions of Anna, were interesting, to say the least. He was certain she had more to tell, but—

'I must go.' Helen abruptly interrupted his train of thought.

'Yes. Yes, of course, if you must.' He was reluctant.

'What am I to tell them? About the envelope, remember? Clara'll want to know.'

'Tell them the envelope wasn't personal at all. It was nothing to do with you – or them. You could say we seemed excited about its contents – copies of secret papers of some kind, you thought.' Tarrent grinned. 'That should hold her.'

'Sure,' said Helen, suddenly bitter at the prevarication and intrigue surrounding her. 'Truth or lies? What does it matter? With you so-called intelligence people it makes no goddamn difference, does it?'

Tarrent swallowed an angry retort. He resented her implied comparison with John Kenmare. But he started the engine, and said mildly, 'All right, Helen, I'll take you back, then.'

It was like an inquisition, Helen thought, and she objected to it. Questions from Clara were one thing – and perhaps not to be resented, however probing. But Anna was another matter. She was behaving as if she were in charge, as if both the others were in some way answerable to her.

'I've told you,' Helen repeated angrily. 'No one questioned me. I didn't see Sir Patrick. Only Neil Tarrent and this man who—'

'What did you say his name was?'

Helen, who had been trying to address herself solely to Clara, swung round to Anna. 'It's none of your damn business,' she said.

Unperturbed, Anna regarded her grimly. 'If it's Lady Kenmare's business, it's also mine.'

'Rubbish! What the hell does that mean?'

'Helen, my dear, you're getting hysterical,' Clara intervened. 'Do please try to be calm. Perhaps it would be best if you went to lie down. Go to bed now, and Anna will bring you some supper later.'

Helen stood up. She looked from one elderly woman to the other. Different faces, but the same implacable gaze. In her mind she saw again the scene in the study that morning, and instantly she was sure, beyond a shadow of doubt, that Anna had killed John – and that Clara had connived at her son's death. She felt hollow with fear.

'I expect you're right,' she said. 'I am tired. I'll go up. Good night.'

Once in her room Helen acted swiftly. She knew what she must do. Pack a few things, take what money she had, and her passport, and get out of the Kenmares' house. Not tomorrow. At once. Her only regret was that she hadn't decided earlier, when Neil Tarrent had suggested it. Now she was alone, and afraid.

She found a small suitcase and put it on the bed. She tried to be methodical. Enough things for a weekend. Nothing that John had given her. But it wasn't easy to pick and choose. In spite of herself she wasted time, becoming a little frantic.

There was a sharp rap at the bedroom door. 'Wait!' she shouted, her mouth dry. She pulled the suitcase onto the floor and pushed it under the bed, thrusting unpacked clothes after it. The door was already opening.

Anna came in, carrying a tray. 'You're not undressed,' she said reproachfully. Her gaze travelled over the room – a coat thrown over the back of a chair, a pair of tights lying on the floor, the flounce at the base of the bed rucked up to reveal the corner of a suitcase. 'You've been packing, Mrs Kenmare. Why is that? You're not going anywhere. You're going to eat the supper I've brought you, and then you're going to bed for a nice long sleep.'

'Put the tray on the table. I'm not hungry. I'll eat later.'

'No. The soup will get cold. Eat now!'

'I don't want it.'

'Mrs Kenmare, you will eat.' It was an order. Helen's impression had been right. Anna was no longer subservient; she was in command.

'How are you going to make me?'

Anna shrugged. 'I can't force you to eat. But remember the first Mrs Kenmare. They said she jumped from a window.' Anna looked at the drawn curtains. 'It's a long drop from here to the basement. What would they say this time? Suicide while grieving for her husband?'

Helen stared at her in horror. 'You killed John's first wife? But why? You must be mad!'

'No, Mrs Kenmare, I'm not mad. I disposed of Rhoda because she'd learnt too much. She'd become a danger to John's real work – our work.'

'Our work – your work?' It seemed to Helen that her mind wasn't functioning. She heard herself say weakly, 'You mean – you're part of it. You're a traitor too.'

'*Nyet*. I am not a traitor. I am a Russian. I'm a Muscovite, though it's many years since I've lived there.' Anna permitted herself a proud smile. 'But I've served my country well.'

'But why kill John?'

As Anna had come further into the room, Helen had retreated. The edge of the bed caught the back of her knees, and she sat down. Anna set the tray across her lap.

'Eat,' she repeated. 'Yes, I shot John. It was an order. He was determined to go to Russia, and the Soviet Government couldn't refuse him. It would have been bad for the morale of others like him if it became known that there was no sanctuary for them in the Soviet Union. But he was of no use any more, and if he went the name of Kenmare would be useless too. So he had to be sacrificed.'

'The name of Kenmare? Why should that matter.?'

Helen wasn't interested in the reply, but she was determined to keep Anna talking. Involuntarily she had sipped at a spoonful of soup. Maybe it was her imagination, but the seemingly slightly bitter taste had brought reality home to her. Drugged sleep – death – were close unless she took action.

Sitting as she was, she had lost the advantages of height and mobility, all she possessed. Anna wasn't young, but she was very strong; she lifted Clara about with ease. Helen knew that if it came to a physical struggle she wouldn't stand much chance against the older woman. She thought of the window a few yards away and shivered.

'Eat up!' Anna said.

'It's too hot.'

'Rubbish! Stir it, and stop wasting time, Mrs Kenmare.'

Putting down the spoon, Helen clasped the bowl of soup in her hands. It was hot, very hot. She bent her head and gave a sob. Anna reacted automatically by taking a step towards her. Without hesitation Helen threw the contents of the soup bowl straight into Anna's face.

As Anna staggered back, scalded and temporarily blinded, Helen pushed the tray from her lap, and ran. Money, passport, clothes, all her careful preparations forgotten, she tore open the door and started down the stairs. Losing a shoe, she kicked off the other. She had one purpose, to get out

219

of the house, to relative safety. Anna, she knew, was a hard, tough woman; she wouldn't be delayed for long.

Indeed Anna, still barely able to see, was close behind her. She had reached the landing and was shouting down the stairs. 'Stop her! Clara! Clara! Stop her!'

Clara Kenmare heard the cries. Swinging her wheelchair round in a tight circle, she propelled herself out of the drawing-room at high speed. She took in the situation at a glance – Helen running downstairs and Anna leaning over the banisters above – and she realized it was up to her to block Helen's path. Her momentum took her across the landing and she slammed into the corner of the wall at the head of the stairs fractionally ahead of the fleeing girl.

For a split second Clara was triumphant. Helen couldn't pass. Then the chair tilted sideways, a wheel slipped over the first stair. As she felt herself begin to fall, Clara Kenmare screamed piercingly.

Anna echoed her scream, but was helpless on the floor above. There was nothing Helen could do either. Together, they watched the heavy wheelchair bounce down the stairs, turning over and over, throwing Clara out and then crashing on top of her.

There was a long moment of silence. It was broken by a snarling cry from Anna, more animal than human. Reminded of her danger, Helen flung herself at the stairs again. She averted her gaze from Clara's body in the hall, dragged open the front door and was free in the square.

She continued to run, terrified that Anna would follow her, until her breath came in short gasps. She leant against a wall in the shadow of a house. Her legs were weak and she was shaking, but at least there was no sign of Anna.

What on earth was she to do? Where should she go? She thought at once of Neil Tarrent. She could have wept with relief when she felt in the pocket of her dress and found the paper he had given her. But she still had to get to him.

A passing couple peered at her curiously and, when they had gone by, the woman's high English voice carried back. Helen caught the words, 'drunk – disgusting'. They made her aware of her appearance. Her dress was too thin for the evening chill and she had no jacket. Worse, no shoes. And no money.

She began to walk, following the couple. She was afraid of being alone on this quiet street. When the couple entered a building she stopped again. She had no idea where she was. She could have been moving in a circle.

Then a taxi turned the corner ahead of her. She waved, prayed that it would stop. She gave the driver Tarrent's address. To her surprise they were there in minutes.

'I'm sorry,' she said as they pulled up in front of a block of flats. 'I haven't any money. If you'll wait—'

'Now look, lady, I've been had like that before. You go in the front and out the back and I'm left with the meter running.'

'No. Please.' Helen pulled off her wedding-ring and held it out to him. 'Take this. It's worth more than the fare.'

The man hesitated. Then something of Helen's desperation communicated itself to him. He shook his head. 'Keep it, love. Maybe I'm a bloody fool but I'll trust you.'

'Thanks.'

She didn't wait for the elevator – the stairs would be quicker – and she arrived breathless at the door of the apartment. If Neil wasn't there . . .

'Oh thank God,' she said as Tarrent opened the door. 'Thank God!'

Lady Cordar had dinner guests that evening and was not pleased at Tarrent's phone call for Sir Patrick, but one look at her husband's face as he came out of his study was enought to keep her silent.

From now on events moved rapidly. The Security Service, the Special Branch and the local police arrived at the Kenmares' house almost simultaneously, closely followed by Tarrent and Sir Patrick. The front door was not locked and it was easy to enter. Lady Kenmare's body lay in the hall, beneath her wheelchair. Her neck had been broken in the fall.

There was no sign of Anna. A safe in Clara's bedroom was open and empty. No jewellery, no money, no incriminating papers were to be found. Anna had been very efficient, and very thorough.

'I've a watch on your man's flat and a woman officer with Mrs Kenmare,' said the Special Branch Superintendent. 'But they're not really necessary,' he added glumly. 'This woman Anna'll be on her way out of the country. And I doubt if we'll catch her, though we're doing our best.'

Sir Patrick grunted. He was far from sure he wanted Anna caught, and he suspected his opinion would be shared by the Prime Minister. Another whitewash job was inevitable.

'Personally, I'm going to see my Russian,' he said. 'Colonel Bonalov knows a good deal more about this set-up than he's told us. It's time to put some pressure on. Where's Tarrent?'

'Here, sir. I've packed a bag for Mrs Kenmare, and arranged for it to be sent to the flat.'

'Right. Then come on. We've a long drive ahead. I only hope that Bonalov's in bed when we get to the safe house. It'll give me great pleasure to root him out of it.'

In the event, though it was almost midnight when they arrived, Bonalov was still up – but not happy to see them. 'Am I to have no peace?' he complained bitterly. 'Sir Patrick, I've been interrogated for something like eight hours today.'

'Eight hours? Tomorrow it'll be twenty-four, Colonel. With drugs, strobe lights and all the rest, if necessary. We're not as soft as we seem, you know. We may not be up to the refinements of the Lubyanka, but we can try hard.'

Bonalov's eyes narrowed. In his dealings with Sir Patrick the Director had often been curt and acid, but he had never before felt the force of the man, the anger that was just below the surface. Something had touched Sir Patrick on the raw.

'What has happened, Sir Patrick?' Bonalov said.

'Tell me about John Kenmare – from the beginning. Who recruited him? Contacts? Everything. This time I want it all, and I want the truth. If I catch you deceiving us, Colonel Bonalov, I swear we'll wring you dry, then send you back to Moscow. And we'll make sure the Kremlin knows how much you've told us. Do you understand?'

'Yes.'

222

'Right. Then start with his recruitment. Who did the talent-spotting? Who turned him over?'

Alexei Bonalov drew a deep breath. It was clear to him that the chips were down. This was his last chance to persuade the British to accept him, his last hope of a comfortable life in the West. But it meant burning his boats. He would never see Moscow again, never watch the women clearing the snow in Red Square, never pick mushrooms in the woods, never again taste the moist rich earthiness of Russian bread.

At last he said, 'Clara Kenmare recruited him.'

'Go on.' Sir Patrick's voice was tight.

'Bonalov shrugged. 'Clara had spent two years in Russia on a ballet scholarship before the war, and she'd shown herself – what shall I say? – sympathetic to us. Then her career was ruined by that unnecessary crippling accident in the United States. Not unnaturally, she blamed the Americans for it. She was very bitter, and it was thought she was ripe for an approach. Indeed she was. She turned out to be one of our most successful agents.'

'As a talent-spotter? A recruiter?'

'Mainly. She married Sir Peter Kenmare under instructions. He was a great admirer. He'd already proposed several times, but she'd turned him down. Now things were different. What could she hope for alone? Sir Peter offered her a great deal materially – and a chance to get back at the Americans. She accepted him, and she got an ideal background, a perfect cover, opportunities to meet anyone she wanted. She was a beautiful woman, tragic in her wheelchair. There weren't very many who resisted her hospitality, her friendship, and often they talked to her more freely than they should.

Sir Peter was twenty-five years older than she was. He died in 1955, a long time ago.'

'True, but by then her circle of friends was wide – as you yourself know,' Bonalov said pointedly. 'After all, she was still Lady Kenmare. She was able to continue her work.'

'What about Anna?' Tarrent asked quickly, afraid that Sir Patrick's ill-contained anger would explode.

'Anna. Yes. Her real name was Anna Smerinova. We put her in as Clara's controller, and together they brought up young John. You might say he never had a chance. When the time came he was given his own control. He did good work, too.'

'The people Lady Kenmare recruited, do you know them?'

'I know of some, and I could make some guesses.'

And Bonalov named a dozen. Two of the men had been dead some years, though they had been distinguished in their time. But the others were all eminent and influential here and now – in the Cabinet and the Shadow Cabinet, the senior civil service, the armed forces, the unions, the media, the arts.

Sir Patrick's anger had given way to a kind of resignation. 'It's an appalling situation,' he said as he and Tarrent drove back to London in the fading daylight. 'God knows how far-reaching the effects will be. If it's true. If Bonalov's to be trusted.'

Tarrent was listening, though half his mind was on Helen Kenmare. Absently he replied, 'As you say, sir – that's what we still don't know. Of course we'll go through all the routines, but maybe in the end we'll never be sure whether Bonalov was planted on us or not.'

Sir Patrick shrugged, and Tarrent said no more. Once we set up these ploys, once we play these games, he ruminated, the doubts inevitably follow. He had never liked the aftermath of operations, especially messy ones – the mopping-up, the interviews, the delicate judgements, the ultimate decisions. He thought back over the Bonalov defection – the parts played by the Dronskys, by Kerensky, Kenmare, Clara and Anna – and above all by Simon and Betty Mont. Whatever happened to the men named by Bonalov, whatever the results for Sir Patrick, for the Government, for the nation, personally he'd deserve some leave. And he wondered if he could persuade Helen to come away with him, to forget in some place free of shadows.

Then he wondered, for people like me, are there such places?